THE
FAMILY
TRIP

BOOKS BY DANIEL HURST

The Holiday Home
The Couple's Revenge

THE DOCTOR'S WIFE SERIES
The Doctor's Wife
The Doctor's Widow
The Doctor's Mistress
The Doctor's Child

THE
FAMILY
TRIP

DANIEL HURST

bookouture

Published by Bookouture in 2024

An imprint of Storyfire Ltd.
Carmelite House
50 Victoria Embankment
London EC4Y 0DZ

www.bookouture.com

ISBN: 978-1-83525-607-7
eBook ISBN: 978-1-83525-606-0

PROLOGUE

'What do you think happened to the missing family?'

'I don't know, but it's shocking, isn't it? A mother, father and little boy just disappearing?'

I continue walking past the two gossiping strangers and don't dare to glance in their direction, well aware of what they are talking about and my connection to it.

Everybody in Ireland is looking for the Conways, the wealthy American family who seem to have vanished a few days after they came here on holiday.

But I know where they are.

I'm on my way back from the supermarket, passing rows of houses, lively shops and bars in this bustling part of the city not far from the River Liffey. To my left and right, I see patrons of pubs sitting at outdoor tables, sipping pints of Guinness in the sunshine, some with shopping bags by their feet, no doubt full of items purchased on nearby Grafton Street. As for me, I have a bag in one hand filled with sugary snacks meant to perk me up and a clear blue sky above my head; but being out of my house is lowering my mood, not lifting it. That's because, out here, I'm getting more of a sense of just how many people have joined the hunt for the family from Boston who were reported missing during their stay on the Emerald Isle.

I've seen all the news reports on the television, the ones that talk about the pilot of their private plane saying that they failed to show up for their flight back to the east coast of America. I've also heard all the scaremongers in the media who have speculated about the family's whereabouts, even though, as of yet, there has been no trace of the three missing souls. Right now, I'm looking at a discarded newspaper on the ground as its front pages flutter open in the breeze. As they do, I see a photo of the youngest member of the Conway family who is missing – a smiling boy with brown hair – the photo provided by someone back in America who knew him and gave this image to the media to help with the search. I wonder how many of these newspapers will be purchased today. There's no doubt this story is huge, so the print profits must be soaring.

A husband, a wife and their young son, all here in Ireland on holiday and all vanishing, seemingly without a trace. It's little wonder this story is making headlines, not just here but on both sides of the Atlantic, particularly when the family in question have a net worth of over fifty million dollars, and the husband and wife have been pictured dining with ex-presidents and other people of power. Everybody wants to know where this perfect family is, which is why there are so many news crews filling the streets of the Irish capital as I try to avoid them on my way home.

I see several recognisable US media brands emblazoned on the side of bulky vans – Fox News, CNN, MSNBC – mixed in with Irish and British stations like RTÉ, BBC and Sky, and inside the vans are camera operators, sound engineers and journalists with microphones in their hands. Some journalists are already talking to the camera, and I hear a New York accent as I pass a blonde reporter who is presumably live on air right now in America. I also hear a snippet of what she's telling the viewers back in her homeland.

'There have still been no sightings of the Conway family, despite the relatives of the missing couple offering a five-million-dollar reward for any information that might lead to discovering their whereabouts.'

I keep walking on, dodging the media crews and members of public who are standing around and gawking, all of whom must wish they had some knowledge about the missing family; then they might be able to get their hands on that huge financial reward currently being offered. But none of them can, because none of them know where they are.

Only I do.

But there's no chance of me coming forward with that information. If I do, I will never get to receive and enjoy any of that reward money. I'll just be arrested and made to spend the rest of my life in prison, while my photo is shown on the news and I become infamous in several countries at once.

I'll just keep my head down and get back home, and because this short trip to the supermarket has been so stressful for me, I don't think I'll go out again for a while.

I'll just stay inside and hope all of this blows over.

But my paranoid mind tells me that will never happen.

Everybody wants to know what happened to that family.

I'm seconds away from my front door when I see the police cars. They're parked outside my home and there are several officers getting out of them, moving with intent, possibly about to give all the journalists in this city something to spice up their next reports.

No, this can't be happening. How have they found me? How do they know about my involvement with that family?

I stop walking as it dawns on me in horrifying detail that I can't go home now, or I'll be arrested. But what can I do? Turn around and walk the other way? That might not be an option either. Not with the secrets I'm hiding.

I have to stop the police getting closer. I can't let them enter my home. If they do, they'll know what I've done. But I can't stop them. They'll just detain me and go inside anyway.

I'm screwed and have no choice.

I have to run.

But how can I?

I'm grappling with that when I feel a strong hand on my shoulder, and I know it's already too late. I get confirmation when I hear the voice of a man standing right behind me.

'Tell us where they are, Shannon. Or else this isn't going to end well for you...'

TWO WEEKS EARLIER

ONE

SHANNON

The wind whips around the towering walls of Dublin Castle, and the grey clouds I can see on the horizon threaten to make a mockery of this summer's day, but I hope the weather won't turn too quickly and ruin this scenic setting. This famous castle doesn't need fading light or a flash of lightning to look more atmospheric – it manages that all on its own as it stands proudly on one of the highest points in this famous city.

'So why did you become a tour guide?'

I smile politely at the question as I fasten an extra button on my jacket, as if it's not something I've been asked before and I'm therefore pleased and impressed with the originality of it. But the truth is, of the dozens of tourists I deal with each week, several of them ask me the same thing at some point during their guided trip.

Do doctors, bakers or taxi drivers get asked why they went into their line of work? I'm not sure, but for some reason a lot of people seem genuinely intrigued as to why I chose to be a tour guide over any other job I could have. All I can do is answer it in the same way as I always do, which is with honesty.

'I love this country and get a thrill out of showing it to

people who are seeing it for the first time,' I reply, genuinely meaning what I have just said, as I tuck a strand of my dark hair behind my left ear, a strand that had become displaced by the strengthening wind.

'Well, it's certainly a beautiful place,' Paul, the sixty-seven-year-old Englishman, replies as he walks alongside me and his wife, Geneve, around the external walls of the castle.

'It sure is,' I say.

Paul asks me if I'd be kind enough to take a photo of him and his partner in front of the historic building, and I oblige. Technically, all photos taken on this tour should be captured by me and be made billable to the customers at the end of the trip. That's what my employer expects anyway. But I sometimes like to bend or simply break the rules, depending on the nature of the people I'm showing around. This couple are lovely, the pair of them here in Ireland to celebrate their recent retirements, so I don't want to try and squeeze them for as much cash as possible, despite my boss wishing I would do that very thing. These two certainly do have some money, each retiring after a lifetime working in banking jobs in London – clearly affluent, if their expensive sunglasses, mobile phones and watches are anything to go by. But I'm not going to take advantage, and there wouldn't be much point in doing so, anyway. It's not as if I'd see any of the extra profits that I might get from selling them photos. That would all go to my boss, and I'd just be left with my daily rate of pay, which is pitiful considering I live in Dublin, one of the most expensive cities in Europe.

'There you go. I took a few, so I hope there's one there that you like,' I say as I hand Paul's phone back to him, and the couple eagerly check the images I captured before seeming happy enough with them. The three of us walk away from the castle then and return to the 'company car' I drive, which is actually just a small van painted emerald green and emblazoned with the name of the tour company I work for, and the pithy slogan my boss came up with to accompany it.

Let real Irish people show you the real beauty of Ireland.

That's it. That's the slogan. My boss is a lot of things, but a wordsmith he is not.

What riles me the most about the feeble slogan is that it's only partially true. Okay, so he does only employ Irish people, like myself, to give the tours, but we hardly get to show people the real beauty of Ireland. All we do is tick off the most generic places that tourists could easily find for themselves if they weren't lazy or rich enough to pay somebody else to find them. Most of the trips I make are in and around Dublin, which is a fantastic city, but there's so much more to this country than the Guinness factory, a castle and several densely packed streets full of crowded pubs and restaurants. There's the countryside, rugged landscapes filled with beaches and caves and mountains, fields where the earth just seems to stretch out before you like a green carpet, and pretty villages and towns where the sheep population easily outnumbers the human one. That's the real Ireland, yet the only time I get to see that reality is on my days off, when I escape Dublin for a short while and get closer to nature before returning to the city and getting back to work. I wish I could show people that side of Ireland, certainly people like Paul and Geneve, who have paid hundreds of euros to come here and stay in a hotel and see the sights, yet will probably leave without really seeing the things that would have made this trip truly unforgettable.

'I know you said you're only here for a couple of days, but you really should think about extending your trip. You'd love County Cork, or how about Killarney National Park? I could give you a list of places to visit, no extra charge, of course.'

'Thank you, but we have to be getting back home,' Geneve

replies from the seat behind me as I steer the brightly painted van back into the centre of Dublin. 'We just wanted to tick off Ireland from our bucket list, and the next stop is Egypt to see the pyramids.'

I decide not to say anything about how simply coming here for two days surely does not qualify as ticking Ireland off their bucket list; they've barely seen five per cent of what this country has to offer. I also don't mention how them going to Egypt and probably only seeing the pyramids isn't quite going to give them a full taste of Egyptian culture. Instead, I just make polite small talk until we arrive back at the office from where the tours start.

'Thank you for choosing us to be your tour guides,' I say as we disembark. 'I hope you had a great time and wish you a safe onward journey.'

I'm thanked before the happily married couple wander away, with Paul telling Geneve he wants one last Guinness before they go to the airport. I head inside and smile at a couple of my colleagues as I make my way to my desk. We're a team of five here, four tour guides and Patrick, our manager, who basically reaps the rewards of all the work his employees do for him. He's never the one outside in all weather, going through the same motions, giving the same touristy spiel. He can be found either in here, at his desk, telling us all to work harder, or next door at Mickey's, the cheapest pub in this part of Dublin. The fact he isn't at his desk as I take a seat at mine suggests he's enjoying some liquid refreshment nearby, but at least I don't have to deal with him now.

'Good day?' asks Oonagh, my colleague at the desk opposite.

'Meh,' I reply with just enough enthusiasm for her to know that yes, I am still bored, to go along with the fact that I'm still worried about money and the past problems it has caused me, and, overall, generally unsure if I'm wasting my life and would be better doing something else instead.

Oonagh is such a good friend that my uttering of one very short, monosyllabic word is enough for her to get all of that, and she knows that the best thing for me now would be a cup of tea and a biscuit. That's why she goes to the kitchen while I log on and check my digital diary. As I thought, I have no more tours booked in for today, but that could change if any tourists wander into the office and ask for a last-minute trip. Hopefully not, because rain is probably on the way, despite it being the middle of summer here, although the seasons tend to have little bearing on the weather in Ireland – it can rain at any point in the year.

With my diary clear, I go into my emails, mostly to check if any future tourists have sent an enquiry about a potential trip, but also to check if Patrick has sent us yet another health and safety module that we have to complete to satisfy the ever-changing compliance rules in our industry. Sure enough, he has. If it wasn't for the fact that Oonagh returns promptly with my tea and biscuit, I'd be in danger of falling asleep at my desk due to how dreary my daily, ordinary life is.

'Cheer up. Only another thirty-five years or so to work before we get to retire,' my colleague says with gallows humour, trying to make me laugh; we're in our early thirties, retirement age is a long way off for the both of us.

'Wonderful,' I reply before taking a bite of my biscuit and pushing from my mind the worrying thought that I haven't paid a single penny into a pension of any kind yet, mainly because I never have any spare money to do so once my monthly debts are accounted for.

'I've told you before and I'll tell you again,' Oonagh starts, preparing to reference something that we've wistfully discussed in the past, 'we need to set up our own tour guide agency. Oonagh and Shannon's Express Tours.'

'You mean Shannon and Oonagh's Express Tours,' I correct her, jokingly wanting my name to go first.

'We can sort the finer details out later,' she replies with a chuckle. 'But we should do it. Why should Patrick keep eighty per cent of the takings from each trip that we organise, when we could get the whole one hundred per cent for ourselves?'

'You know why,' I say mournfully, half reading the health and safety module. 'Because it costs money to start a business. *A lot of money*. There are so many overheads. We'd need an office as well as a vehicle or two to do the tours in. Then there's all the admin, the accounts, the rules we have to follow and the fines we'd get if we didn't. Just look at these health and safety guidelines that we're supposed to memorise. It's a logistical nightmare, trust me.'

My colleague has heard me say all this before, because I actually attempted to start my own tour guide agency once. It was nine years ago now, when I was twenty-four and filled with a desperation, as well as a youthful naïveté, to improve my circumstances and escape my life of part-poverty. I say part-poverty because I wasn't homeless and starving, so it wasn't that bad, but I was financially crippled by having a low-income job in a place that was becoming more expensive the more tourists came here. It was those tourists who seemed to give me a glimmer of a way out, so I took out a bank loan and eagerly went about trying to run my own business showing some of them around Ireland. But while I had customers, the costs of getting them around the island spiralled, and it quickly became obvious that I was going to end up in a worse financial situation than the one I was in before. That's why, rather than let my debts build any higher, I closed the business, although not before what little money I had left was stolen by my boyfriend at the time. Crazily enough though, that's not the only reason I had to leave him.

With nothing to my name, and no parents to borrow money from as they had both passed when I was a teen, I got a job here, where I have dutifully spent the last several years slowly paying back the bank loan I foolishly took out when I was young, when I thought I had what it took to be an entrepreneur. It was also when I believed in the concept of love, but my ex soon put paid to that.

Patrick, my lazy employer, doesn't have one tenth of the passion I have for Ireland and the sights to be seen here, but he did have the startup capital required to open this tour agency and keep it running. Now he's the one enjoying the fruits of it while I'm worrying about my next electricity bill when it arrives in the post.

While Oonagh chatters on about how we could be rich one day if we could only figure out a way to make it all work, I open another email and the contents of it quickly has me zoning out my friend's voice. The message is from a woman called Rosalind and, unsurprisingly, she is inquiring about a guided tour. But what is surprising is what comes next.

She doesn't want a typical tour. She wants something unique.

More than that, she is willing to pay a lot of money for it.

And I mean a lot of money.

The kind of money that could be the answer to all my problems...

TWO

ROSALIND

The laptop sitting in front of me on my mahogany desk has just been put to very good use, as I've just pressed send on one of the most important emails of my life. But after checking my inbox, there's no reply yet, so I'm forced to wait impatiently for the next move of a woman who is almost three thousand miles away in Ireland. While Shannon O'Shea is in Dublin, I'm in Boston, Massachusetts, in the affluent suburb of Wellesley, to be more specific.

This is my home and what a stunning home it is.

Gazing out of the window, I see the house across the street, the one that has just sold for $3.5million. I've yet to meet the new owners, but the previous occupants have already moved out, eager to get on their way because they had new jobs to start in San Francisco. That couple both worked in tech, so I suppose the West Coast is the place to be – that's where all the new money is. But I prefer the east, where the old money is, and this is where my family, and my husband's family, made their fortunes many years ago.

I know I was privileged to have inherited $10million on my twenty-first birthday, but I've made sure to earn my own way in life too, working at various Boston financial institutions throughout my twenties before I met my husband and he suggested it was time I took things a little easier. I'm forty-five now, and life certainly is easy, at least for the most part, but how hard can it be when you not only have a nanny, but a personal chef, trainer and housemaid too?

The man I married, Donovan Conway, comes from an even wealthier family than I do. After falling in love, it made sense to join our two families together and ensure even more success and wealth for us all in the future. He still works, not because he has to but because he's good at what he does; but I have my own set of skills too, even if I'm currently lounging around at home absent-mindedly staring out of a window.

I am going to be the one who reels in Shannon, the woman who is the one threat to our perfect lives, and for that my husband will be eternally grateful.

Hello Shannon,

I have been researching tour guides in Ireland and your name has come up a couple of times in reviews, which is promising. I am writing because my husband and I are hoping to visit Ireland very soon, traveling over from America, and we would like to employ the services of a tour guide to assist and enhance our trip.

We both used to live in your country, several years ago now. We moved there for work as my husband's ancestors hail from your part of the world, but his job was very demanding while there, and we didn't get to do much traveling then, meaning we left without seeing the very best that Ireland has to offer. We hope to correct that this time.

I notice on your employer's website that you offer day trips around Dublin as well as the odd trip a little further afield, but nothing much out of the ordinary. I was wondering if you offer more bespoke, private tours, ones in which you take your clients to see much rarer sights? My husband and I do not wish to be shown the same things as everybody else, we want to see the real Ireland, off the beaten track, because I'm sure that will lend itself to a much more memorable experience for us both.

Can you assist with this? The bio on your employer's website says that you grew up in Ireland and have extensive knowledge of all areas, so I presume you can. I understand this may be a slight departure from the services your employer usually provides, which is why I suggest you might consider keeping this to yourself and running the tour independently in this case. I appreciate this is likely asking a little more of you than usual, so taking that into account, we are willing to pay far more than the prices your website advertises.

Would $10,000 be enough to take us on a personalized five-day tour? We would cover all expenses along the way too, of course, including hotels and meals.

I look forward to your response,

Regards,

Rosalind Conway

I sit back in my office chair and finish re-reading the email I sent ten minutes ago. It says everything I need it to say and not a single thing more, but of course it does; I'm a perfectionist and I spent a while composing it. Now all I have to do is wait for Shannon's response, but I shouldn't imagine it will take her too long to reply, considering the sum I've just quoted her.

To kill a few more minutes while I wait, I go back to the

website through which I found Shannon's contact details and peruse her details once more.

Shannon O'Shea joined the tour group in 2016 and has become a valued member of the team ever since. After growing up in Kilkenny and spending her childhood enjoying the great Irish outdoors, Shannon moved to Dublin. Her knowledge of the local area, combined with her passion for Irish culture and history, makes her the perfect person to enhance your trip.

Book a tour with Shannon today!

The biography is short and simple, accompanied by an image of Shannon. She's an attractive young woman with stunning red hair and dazzling green eyes, and I'm sure there are plenty of males who are tempted to book a tour with her just off the strength of her photo alone. But I wasn't tempted to reach out to her based on her good looks, or even what sounds like her qualifications to be an exceptional tour guide. I have made contact with her deliberately, because she is the person my husband and I need to get alone, preferably in as quiet and isolated a spot as possible.

'Sorry, Mrs Conway. I didn't realise you were in here.'

I turn to look at the door and see our diminutive nanny, Philippa, standing in the doorway, all mousey hair and oversized cardigan, and she looks nervous to have interrupted me, as she should do.

'What is it?' I ask, irritated. I don't want any distractions while I'm waiting for the response to my email.

'I was just looking for Barnaby's bear and thought it might be in here.'

'Why would it be in here? He doesn't play in here,' I snap, before taking a deep breath and reminding myself to calm down when dealing with irritations like this. 'I've told you already. He doesn't need that bear anymore. He's too old for it.'

'But he's asking for it.'

Another deep breath.

'Tell him to play with one of his other toys. Lord knows he has enough of them.'

'But Mrs Conway, he—'

'Will you leave me alone, for heaven's sake!' I cry, exasperated at having to emphasise my point even more, feeling a headache that's been lurking all morning growing stronger by the second.

'Sorry, Mrs Conway,' comes the meek response before Philippa does as I wish and leaves, presumably returning to the playroom where she is looking after my son. I pay her to make my life easier, not harder, but she doesn't always remember that, which is frustrating. Maybe I'll replace her soon; there must be lots of other nannies out there who would relish the chance to work here and be paid what I can offer them. Then again, she is good at her job, so maybe I'll keep her around for a little longer yet. She's worked for me for almost five years now, so she's almost part of the furniture around here, albeit a pretty piece of furniture as she's not even thirty yet, although I like to think I look better than her even if I'm older. It helps that I wear designer clothes every day while Philippa dresses in dowdy, oversized attire more suited to running around after a little boy all day.

I check my inbox again but there's still no response from Shannon, so I get up and pace around in this large room that houses a desk, two bookcases and an enormous flatscreen TV that neither me nor my husband ever actually turn on. I find myself by the window again, looking out on the street, and I notice that the trash collectors are here. The bulky van full of waste is making its way down the street and it'll be collecting my trash soon. I'm glad about that because, once it's removed, Barnaby's bear will be gone for good.

My son's teddy, the one the nanny was just trying to find for him, is stuffed inside one of the black bags in the trash can. I put it there myself last night while Barnaby was sleeping, and I did so because I believe I am right. At eight, he is too old for it now in my view, and it's time he grew up a little bit and found something else to play with. I'm worried that having comforters like that won't give him the toughness he is going to need if he is to thrive when he's older, and while it might seem harsh, I am only thinking of what may be best for him in the long-term. I'm sure he'll kick up a fuss over the next few days because he can't find his bear, but he'll move on from it eventually and I'm hoping our upcoming trip will expedite that process.

Barnaby will be accompanying my husband and I when we fly to Ireland, just as soon as Shannon has accepted my request, although I made sure to leave out any mention of our child in my email, mainly because that will hopefully make her accept my request quicker. At this stage, the main thing is that she accepts us, so she can learn about Barnaby at a later date.

I just need her to reply and say yes.

And then I hear a ding from my computer.

I have a new email.

Rushing back to my computer, I sit back down and quickly check the new arrival in my inbox, and I smile when I see that it's a reply from Shannon. Opening it, I quickly read.

Thank you for your email and it's wonderful that you are choosing to make Ireland your next trip. I have no doubts that you are going to love it here and I certainly agree with your desire to see less touristy places and try to discover the real essence of Ireland. I would like nothing more than to be able to help you with this, but unfortunately, the tours we offer here are set and fairly limited. Private, bespoke tours like the one you are requesting are not really something we can offer, as much as I wish we could. I would love to accept, but I must follow the rules set by my employer. I hope you understand and if you wish to book one of the tours offered on our website, it will be a pleasure to help you. I have attached a pdf of these tours to this email, as well as a few of my own personal suggestions of things you should see while here.

I wish you all the best with your trip, enjoy your time in Ireland and if you do wish to book an official tour, please let me know!

Shannon

After reading the email, I immediately begin composing a reply, wanting to catch Shannon again before she turns her attention to other messages from other potential clients. While she might think her response to me was professional and satisfactory, I am not going to leave it there. Anyone who knows me will be well aware that I am stubborn and never stop until I get my own way, and I have a feeling that when Shannon reads my next message, she's going to think twice about her next response. That's because I'm going to offer a new financial incentive for her – that is the beauty of being rich. Money is no object and, when that's the case, it becomes very, very easy to get what you want.

As I finish typing my next email and prepare to press send, I have a feeling I'm going to get what I want very soon.

There's no way Shannon can say no to what I have just offered her...

THREE

SHANNON

$20,000!

I keep staring at the number on my screen, blinking several times, as if it is a mirage that will vanish any second now, but it doesn't appear to be doing so. *It's very real.* That's actually the figure that this American woman has just offered me to give her and her husband a private tour around Ireland.

A quick use of a currency convertor tool to get the figure into more understandable terms for me tells me what it is in euros, and it is an incredible amount of money. Every cell in my body is screaming at me to accept this offer, if it is actually genuine, which it may not be. This could just be a prank, some random person playing a game with me, though I have no idea why they would target me. Whoever this is could think it's funny to make up something like this and get me all excited before disappointing me when it turns out to be false. Maybe I should just assume it's a joke and ignore it. If they are serious then they'll get back in touch with one of my colleagues in future to try and book again.

But what if it's real and this money ends up going to them and not me?

I glance across at Oonagh and see her typing away on her keyboard, wondering what she would do in my situation. She'd probably tell me about the email she just received and get my opinion on it. Or would she really do that? Would she actually keep it to herself because that would be the best way of ensuring she got the $20,000 and nobody else?

The door to the office opens and Patrick walks in, full of a cocky swagger that is no doubt enhanced by the two or three drinks he's had at the pub this afternoon while his employees were doing all the work for him. I watch as my boss strolls towards me and wonder if he's going to stop and mention that he's received an email from this Rosalind character too. He might have done so, and it could be the reason for his seemingly good mood. It sure would be a bumper pay day for his business if he could make $20,000 from one tour. I bet he'd actually do some work then and offer to conduct the tour himself, just so he could keep one hundred per cent of the money. But he doesn't mention any email at all. He just winks at me and tells me to keep up the good work before sitting down at his desk and letting out a satisfied sigh.

I probably should tell him about my proposition now because, as my employer, he has a right to know, but if this is real then I'd be stupid to do that. Rosalind specifically asked me to do the tour, not Patrick or anybody else in this office, and it seems she did so based on my good reputation, so why should I give this up? The first thing Patrick would say is that we don't do private tours; and even if I told him about the money that was at stake, he'd just automatically come up with a way to ensure he got most of it himself.

I decide to keep this quiet for the time being, and give it some more thought. I work on replying to a few other emails while I play Rosalind's particular message over and over in my mind. If it is genuine, it really has the capacity to change my life: $20,000 for just showing an American couple around my home country for a few days? Not only would it be easy work for me, but it would be a pleasure. I could get out of Dublin and go and visit all the places that truly make this country beautiful and unique. I'd be free to set the tour to my personal tastes and not have to blindly follow the arbitrary rules my boss has made up for me. Once the tour is over, I would have a huge chunk of money that I could do so much with. I could pay off the remainder of the loan I still owe to the bank after my failed business attempt. What's left over could be used as a deposit on a house, so I can finally end my endless cycle of expensive renting, and I could continue to try and recover from my ex-boyfriend's theft that almost left me homeless. Barring that, it would just be nice to actually have some savings in my bank account for a change instead of living pay cheque to pay cheque each month. There's also the possibility of using it to have another go at starting my own tour guide company. I could do things safer and smaller this time. I was overexcited the first time and spent too much money, but I could build it slowly and steadily. Maybe I'd get Oonagh on board like we've talked about before. This could be the beginning of a booming business for the pair of us. I'd certainly do a lot more with the money than Patrick would. He'd probably just upgrade his sports car and buy himself another couple of suits, or worse, fritter it all away over the next few months by drinking in Mickey's. The money wouldn't change his life at all, but it would certainly change mine.

I'm so unsure what to do that we reach the end of the working day and I still haven't gone back to Rosalind again. I hope she isn't emailing any other tour guides in the city about her proposal; they might have already accepted and then I'll be too late. I will have missed my opportunity. But as Oonagh logs off her computer and tells me how happy she is that it's time to go home, I have a feeling Rosalind will still be waiting for my reply, so I make up my mind to get back to her promptly.

I decide to wait until everyone else has left the office, particularly Patrick; but my boss never stays late, and he doesn't disappoint me tonight.

'Working overtime, are we?' Patrick asks with a wry smile as he notices me still sitting at my desk. He pulls on his suit jacket and heads for the door. 'You know you don't get paid for that.'

There's no need for him to remind me of that grim fact, and certainly no need for him to take some sort of morbid pleasure in it, but I just smile and tell him I'm almost finished.

'Don't forget to put the alarm on,' he says to me as he leaves, and I assure him I won't. Now I'm left in the office all alone.

I quickly reopen Rosalind's last email and read it again before starting to type out my reply. It's one in which I reiterate how I'd love to accept and explain how it goes against all the rules of my employment and I fear I'd lose my job if I did so. It's a safe, boring response, but I have to look after myself. If this does turn out to be a prank and I accept it, I could be fired, and then I really would be screwed.

With my next email ready, I press send and sit back in my chair, hearing it creak, and the noise is quite loud in this otherwise silent office. It's creepy being here by myself and I miss Oonagh's chatter, but I won't linger for long. I'll just give it ten minutes or so to see if Rosalind replies, and then I'll go home. I have to wait here to monitor my emails because I won't have access to them outside of this office, and I'd rather not spend all night pondering what may or may not be waiting for me in my work inbox until tomorrow morning. But I don't have to wait, because Rosalind replies quickly again. I open her email, wondering just who this woman is and why she is seemingly so keen to correspond with me.

You seem very worried about following the rules, Shannon.
But you know what they say. Rules are meant to be broken.

That's it. That's the email. Talk about short and sweet. I guess Rosalind really doesn't care for the rules, but maybe it's easy for her to say that because she's not the one who is risking losing her job. Then again, I assume she's rich if she is offering so much money, so there's probably not much she has to worry about these days. But I'd be lying if I said her email hadn't got me excited a little. What if Rosalind is right? What if rules are meant to be broken? I'm hampered working here under Patrick's strict regime. Imagine if I could be unshackled and free to take my own clients and run my own tours. The potential could be limitless, starting right here with this $20,000. Maybe I should take a risk. Live a little. Rosalind certainly seems to think so.

I will email her back with my definite answer, and I'll do it shortly. I just won't do it on my company email account. I don't want Patrick to see my email one day and use it against me in any disciplinary action. That's why I write down Rosalind's email address on a piece of paper and stuff it into my pocket before deleting the emails so far, logging off and leaving my desk. I set the security alarm and then leave the office, heading out onto the busy streets of Dublin to make my way home. The cafes, bars and restaurants seem full, plenty of Dubliners out enjoying the light evenings of summer before the dark nights of winter return again in a few months. They all look like they've had a good day; it's usually a rarity for me to be in the same position, but with what just happened, have any of them had as good a day as me?

Being offered $20,000 from a total stranger to do something that comes naturally to me?

This might just have been one of the best days of my life.

FOUR

ROSALIND

My husband will be home from work shortly, which is why I check on our chef's progress to make sure dinner is going to be ready just as soon as he walks through the door.

'Your evening meal *sera bientôt servi*,' says François, the French chef who has cooked for me and my family for the past three years, and I smile as I understand the partial use of his native language, pleased that dinner will be served shortly. He's never given me any reason to doubt him before, so I leave him to it, taking a glass of wine with me out of the kitchen. I plan on relaxing on a sofa until Donovan gets home, but those plans are spoilt somewhat by the noise coming from my lounge. When I walk in, I see my son and the nanny chasing each other around what is now a very untidy room.

'Look at this mess! What is going on?' I cry as I take in the sight of all the cushions on the floor, not to mention the toys. This room is usually my sanctuary, but right now it looks like a toy store.

'We're playing!' Barnaby cries as the little whirlwind jumps over all the discarded items; but Philippa has clearly noted the look of disgust on my face, because she has stopped running around now and is quickly starting to tidy up.

'Let's pick up some of these toys now, Barnaby,' she says to my son as she puts the cushions back on the sofa, but does he listen to her? Of course he doesn't, and that's because he's clearly far too wound up and excited to stop now.

'Why have you let him get so worked up?' I ask Philippa as Barnaby rushes past me and bumps into my legs, almost causing me to spill my wine.

'We were just playing a game,' Philippa tries as she continues to tidy up.

'I'm paying you to look after my son, not turn him into a feral animal,' I say scornfully before turning and walking out of the room, going in search of somewhere quieter to wait for Donovan to get home.

As the noise continues in the lounge, I take a seat at the dining table. I'm just about through with my wine when I hear the sound of an engine outside the house. That'll be my husband's car, the one he spent six figures on and the one he commutes in. The other cars he has in the garage are his toys for the weekend, and they're far more expensive toys than the ones our son currently plays with.

'What's going on?' Donovan asks when he finds me sitting at the dining table with an empty glass in front of me and the sounds of screeching still coming from the lounge.

'Ask the nanny,' I say with a shake of my head. 'The nanny you hired.'

Donovan tells me he will sort it out and leaves to go and do just that. A moment later, the house falls quiet. It's irritating that my husband is able to quieten Barnaby quicker than me, but he has a presence that I lack. When Donovan enters a room, everybody knows it. That is down to his imposing stature. At six foot six, he has the height to capture attention, and with an athletic build honed from years of gym work with a personal trainer, he has the physique to command it too. He tells me his appearance helps him in business, but it also helps in his home life; Barnaby knows better than to defy his dad, the little boy always falling quickly into line whenever his father is around.

I sometimes wonder what it must be like to be such an intimidating presence. I'm barely five foot five and slender, so people are hardly wary of me like they are with Donovan. But then again, as my husband likes to remind me, I am capable of getting attention and intimidating people in other, more subtle ways, like with a single look or simply a flick of my head. Donovan calls me the silent assassin, but then laughs and says it's without the silent part, which usually makes me laugh too. That's because we both know that what I lack in stature, I more than make up for with my cutting tongue.

'Dinner is served,' our chef says as he enters the dining room carrying two plates. Upon each a succulent piece of salmon sits on a bed of fresh salad.

'This looks exquisite, thank you,' I say as the two meals are set down on the table; as Francois offers to get me another glass of wine, Donovan reappears.

'Make that two glasses, my good man!' my husband says triumphantly as he takes his own seat at the table, licking his lips at the tasty seafood waiting for him to tuck into.

As the chef leaves us momentarily, the quiet house and the smug look on Donovan's face suggests he got Barnaby to calm down and allowed Philippa to regain control of the situation in the lounge.

'Thank you,' I say. 'He's been wild today, and she hasn't been much help.'

'He'll be back at school after our trip,' Donovan replies as he unfolds a white napkin onto his lap. 'How are our vacation plans going, by the way? Any progress today?'

'Yes, I emailed Shannon and we've been corresponding,' I reply as the chef returns with a glass of wine for each of us.

We thank him before he leaves, then Donovan raises his glass to mine. 'Excellent news. Did she accept the first offer?'

'She's still showing some reluctance, so I upped it to twenty thousand dollars.'

'A small price to pay to get her where we want her.'

I raise my glass too, and we clink them together before taking a sip.

'I agree,' I say as we begin eating. 'I think she'll accept the offer any time now. She's just expressing a few concerns about her boss.'

'I'm sure she'll figure out a way to do it,' Donovan says confidently as he cuts into his perfectly cooked salmon. 'A woman like her can't afford to turn down money like that.'

'That's true,' I reply. Our lives are worlds apart, but they're about to collide spectacularly over the coming days.

'How soon do you think we can take the jet?' I ask Donovan as he adds a little pepper to his meal. It's not that François hasn't seasoned it correctly, it's just my husband really loves pepper.

'My pilot is on standby. We can go as soon as Shannon agrees to meet us. I'll just switch a few things around at work. As we've already taken Barnaby out of school early, we're ready to go as soon as she says the word.'

'Perfect.'

The thought of a long journey from America to Ireland is tempered somewhat by the knowledge that we'll be making it aboard a private plane. We like to travel in style, although that's not the only reason we won't be entering Ireland on board a commercial jet alongside a few hundred other passengers. Flying privately will allow us to use smaller airports and speed up the whole process of getting in and out of the country, as well as making the whole trip more discreet overall. Discretion is certainly what we are after and, if we play this right, we can be in and out of Ireland and back home in Boston with only a very small number of people knowing we were ever there at all. Even those aware of our family trip won't have any clue about what we're planning to do, which is the most important thing.

That's how my husband and I will stay out of prison, after all.

'Daddy, have you seen my bear?'

Donovan and I turn to see Barnaby in the doorway and, unsurprisingly, he's still looking for his bear, that damn teddy I threw away earlier. But the toy will already be on a pile of trash at the waste recycling unit by now.

'We're eating,' he reminds our son, and Barnaby knows better than to keep pestering us during our evening meal.

'Sorry,' Philippa says as she ushers Barnaby away from the door, and I'm beginning to wonder if 'sorry' should be our nanny's middle name. It's all she seems to say to me these days.

Once we're alone again, we're free to continue our meal in peace.

'So what happened with the bear?' Donovan asks me with a knowing smile. 'I'm guessing you might have the answer to that one.'

'Let's just say I have taken care of the problem,' I reply with a wink. 'You agree he is too old for such a thing now?'

'I do. But—'

'What?'

I sigh as I put down my cutlery, because I know what's coming. My husband is going to suggest that I go a little easier on our son. He sometimes raises this idea every now and again. I guess throwing his bear away has prompted this one.

'As long as he's happy,' Donovan says. 'I mean, the bear kept him quiet. Isn't that better than taking it away completely? He'll probably be a nightmare going to bed tonight without it.'

'We were both in agreement. It was time for it to go. Don't second guess the joint decision we made.'

'Sure,' Donovan says, wisely avoiding an argument, and he goes back to his meal.

I do the same, trying not to get annoyed. Donovan has always been a little softer with Barnaby, as he was with our other child when she was growing up. That's our teenage daughter, Esme, who is currently fifteen miles away from home, staying in a private boarding school for girls. He can be strict, but he can be soft with them too, leaving me to be the main disciplinarian most times. Some could say I treat our children harshly, but I'm not raising them any differently to how I was brought up, and I turned out fine. I know my parents don't complain when they get to sit at the yacht club and boast about me and my husband and the beautiful grandchildren we've given them. It's a hard job being a mother and I am doing it the best way I can. My children will realise that when they're older and successful like their parents are. They will see that my way is the best way.

I hear a bleep from my phone and quickly pick it up off the table. I'm hoping it is what I think it is – *an email from Shannon.*

'It's her,' I say, and Donovan stops chewing as he waits to see what I have to say.

I open the new email to check it, while also wondering what time it is in Dublin as they are a few hours ahead of us. It must be quite late over there now, so if Shannon is messaging me at this hour, she must still be seriously thinking about my offer.

And she is.

I'm going to need a deposit if I do this. I'll be taking a risk with my job and not telling my boss about it, so I need some insurance, just in case he finds out: $5,000 deposit and the rest payable just before your trip to Ireland begins. Is that okay?

'She wants a deposit,' I tell Donovan, 'five grand.'

'Do it,' he replies without skipping a beat; I quickly reply to Shannon to tell her that will not be a problem and for her to send me her bank details. Almost as quickly, Shannon replies with the account that she would like the money sent to, and I easily access my banking app and transfer the funds as absent-mindedly as if I had just found a hundred-dollar bill on the street and put it into my pocket.

'Done,' I say, and Donovan nods before he raises his glass again.

'I guess we're going to Ireland then,' he says with a smirk. 'Time to fuel up the jet.'

FIVE

SHANNON

My bank balance has never looked so healthy. The addition of nearly €5,000 to my languishing account has given it a much-needed boost, and suddenly my fortunes have turned. I can't believe my request for a deposit was actually accepted.

I guess this means it isn't a prank.

This is real.

If this is the case, then there is still another $15,000 for me to make upon completion of my task. I get to work on ensuring that can happen, and the first thing I need to do is request time off from my boss so that I'm free to show this American couple around Ireland.

Hi Patrick! I was wondering if I could take next week off work? Sorry for the short notice. I just haven't had a holiday for a while. Is that okay?

I hit send on my text message and wait to see what my employer's response will be, praying that he will approve my annual leave. I never know with him, because he can change from being a good boss or a bad boss in the blink of an eye. I'm praying for the good version as I pace around my humble flat in Darndale, an area to the north of Dublin where crime rates tend to be higher than other parts of the city. I briefly look outside through the window and see a couple of shady-looking characters hanging around on the street corner, as well as hearing a police siren in the distance, but there's nothing new there.

Reminding Patrick that I haven't had a holiday for a while wasn't just a tactic on my part to garner sympathy from him; it's simply a fact. I actually can't remember the last time I was off work, it was so long ago. It must have been Kelly's wedding. That'll be it. One of my school friends got married last September and I was present for the event, not that I enjoyed it much because all the guests brought their children and, as the only one without a little one of my own, it wasn't much fun to stand by the bar drinking by myself while all the families hit the dancefloor.

Wow, that's a long time ago now. I'm certainly overdue a break. Except it's not really going to be a break, is it? I will be working, possibly harder than I've ever worked before – *it's just that my boss will have no idea about it.*

I know I'm taking a risk by keeping this secret from Patrick, but what are the odds of him finding out about this unofficial tour? I'll be taking this couple to such far-flung, remote places that he'll never know. All his tour guides will be in the centre of Dublin, but I'll be far away from this city.

Finally, I thought you were never going to take some time off. Sure. Holiday approved. Where are you going?

Patrick's response is a green light to go ahead with Rosalind, but I just have to field his question, so I spin him a lie, replying to say that I'm not sure yet and might go over to England to see a few friends. If he thinks I'm out of the country then he really won't suspect me of giving a tour here instead.

With my time off granted, I know there is nothing standing in the way of giving this American couple what they want, so I send a message to Rosalind, giving her the dates when I am available. I presume she will have a calendar to check and a few personal or professional engagements to rearrange on account of the short notice, but that is not the case. She replies quickly to say she will send me her flight details shortly so I can meet them at the airport when they get here.

Wow, this is moving really fast. Should I be worried? The sight of the extra money in my account helps set my mind at ease. By the time my week 'off work' is over, I'll be looking at even higher numbers in there. I might as well milk this cash cow for all I can, so I'm not going to back out now.

What I am going to do is start planning.

I go over to the small bookcase in the corner of my living area and pull out a couple of travel guides before opening them and laying them out on my messy coffee table. There are a couple of old cups of tea here, as well as a plate from breakfast and some bills that need paying, but tidying up has never been my speciality. Now I have a more important job to do. I need to start prepping for the trip next week if I'm going to give this couple $20,000 worth of sightseeing.

I could feel pressure at such a challenge, afraid that I might leave the Americans feeling let down and short-changed if I fail to deliver, but I don't. I actually feel invigorated; I'm finally getting the chance to show what I can do in this space, and I know it's what I could have done if only I hadn't run into financial difficulties earlier in my career.

One incredible, unforgettable tour of Ireland coming right up.

As I turn the pages of the travel guides and jot down logistical details on a notepad, my brain is firing out ideas that my pen is struggling to keep up with. The countryside and clifftops. The caves and the coves. The quaintest pubs and the finest restaurants. The villages and the friendly villagers within them. So many astounding Irish sights to see and people to meet and all of them available to be explored.

As I quickly fill one sheet in my notepad and turn the page to start writing on another, I cannot wait for this trip to begin. I almost feel bad for getting paid so much money to be leading it, because it won't just be the paying couple who reap the benefits. I'll get to enjoy it as well; I'll be right there alongside them every step of the way. That's one of the benefits of being a tour guide, I get to be on tour too. But I do need this kind of cash if I'm to ever get myself out of the perpetual cycle of money worries, and this could be just the thing I need to ensure that I'm never on the verge of homelessness again. Living with such money worries, to the point where you fear for a roof over your head, is not something I'd wish on my worst enemy, and I'll do whatever it takes to ensure I never experience that again.

With any nerves I had about failing this couple dissipating in a swarm of ideas, I realise that, before I start making any actual bookings anywhere, I need to consult Rosalind about some of the finer details, like hotel reservations for example. Do I make them, or will she want to do that? I'm happy to do it, but there's the small matter of paying for them. Like Rosalind said in her original email, she'll cover expenses, so what's best? Do I send her a list of hotels and she picks her favourites and sends me the money to book them? Or do I have free rein to reserve whatever I think would work and then just send her the bill for them afterwards?

I realise then that there is a lot of work to be done before they even get here, and it seems like too much work to manage going back and forth via email. That's why I decide to send her a message, proposing that we iron out the details of this impending trip in another way – via video call.

The email I send to Rosalind suggesting a virtual meeting leads to the longest delay in her responding to me. She usually replies straight away, but she hasn't got back to me yet, and as the minutes tick by I wonder if I've annoyed her with my request for a video call. I just thought that it might be easier for me to ask my questions that way rather than bombarding her with a long list in an email. I also thought it would be nice to actually see each other's faces, even if only on camera, so we can build up a more personable relationship before we're thrust together at the airport in a few days' time. It would also give me a much better understanding of the person I am dealing with here, because there's only so much you can get from this imper-sonal form of communication. But what if Rosalind doesn't want that? What if she's camera shy or just too busy to take such a call? Maybe she likes email because she can correspond that way while on the go, living whatever hectic lifestyle she has. Have I just conveyed to her that I'm not as busy myself and might even be a little needy? No, surely not. This is just me trying to be professional and ensure I do the best job I possibly can.

So why isn't she replying to me?

My anxiety builds the more I stare at my phone and wait for an email to appear on it, so I decide to busy myself by doing the tidying up that I should have done before I went to work this morning. I leave my phone alone, telling myself Rosalind will reply when she has a spare minute, and move the dirty plate and cups to the sink in my small kitchen while I wait. This one-bedroom flat doesn't look like much, but it certainly costs enough. Damn the rental prices in Dublin. It's a joke that, for all the money I pay, I can't even have a kitchen larger than a medium-sized airing cupboard. The bathroom is just as tiny, just big enough to squeeze a toilet, sink and shower in, while my bedroom is dominated by the bed, which leaves little room around the sides for me to actually walk. Most of the time, I just fall forward on to the mattress rather than getting in from the side because there simply isn't the space, especially not once my claustrophobia-inducing cupboards full of clothes are added in. While I'm more than happy to give people a tour of Ireland, I'd be less comfortable giving them a tour of my home, because I'm not exactly proud of it. It's not much to show for a woman of my age, and on most days it looks like a student lives here, or worse, a child, such is the mess. It's not much at all, but it's all I have and I'd rather this than the alternative, which would be losing this place when the bills become too difficult to pay. But I know I'll move on to bigger and better things one day, and with the money Rosalind and her partner are paying me it could come much sooner than I had thought.

I kill some more time by making my surroundings a little more presentable, dusting the furniture and some of my decorative ornaments, which include my large Celtic spear that hangs on the wall above my sofa. It was a gift from a client who told me all about how it looks just like the ones used by our Irish ancestors in battle, and it does look cool, even if it is more of a dust collector these days. By the time I have put my feather duster away, I see that Rosalind has replied to me. I snatch up the phone – are we going to have a video call? And am I finally going to be able to properly speak to this mystery woman?

No need for a video call. Just book the specifics of the tour as you see fit in terms of restaurant reservations, day trips etc. and I can send over any extra funds required for you to do this. Regarding accommodation, I will sort that for us all. Just email the areas of Ireland we will be in each day, although don't give too much away. We want to be surprised during this tour! As for our arrival into Ireland, we will be landing at a private airstrip on the south coast. I will forward on the address of this shortly along with our landing time. Please meet us there so we can commence the trip. Regards. Rosalind.

So there's no video call, but that's hardly what has my attention the most in this email. A private airstrip? Does that mean they're coming over from America on a private plane? Oh my gosh, who are these people? I knew they were wealthy, but it's one thing to send a few thousand pounds via bank transfer. It's quite another to fly across an entire ocean with the whole plane to themselves.

I'm nervous, but I'm just as excited; it's obvious that this is going to be about much more than making some serious money. It's about having a memory that will last me a lifetime.

Something tells me that I'll never forget my time with the Conways.

SIX

ROSALIND

There's a clear blue sky over Boston today, which makes me feel better about the fact that we'll be flying very soon. It's not that I have a fear of flying, but I do get a little anxious before take-off, aware that my fate and the fate of my family is solely in the hands of the person in the cockpit. It's funny, but even with all the money in the world, I wouldn't be able to buy my way out of danger if something catastrophic happened while thousands of feet up in the air.

Let's hope our flight to Ireland goes smoothly then.

As our driver steers us onto the runway, where our private plane sits on the tarmac, this trip has certainly got off to a solid start. I'm sitting in this Rolls-Royce with my husband, son and nanny, and all our luggage is behind us, ready to be carried on board as soon as we stop. Donovan has our passports ready to show to the owner of the private airstrip shortly, and it's just a matter of minutes now until we will be swapping our seats in this car for seats on the jet. Then the engines will start up and we'll be on our way to the Emerald Isle, flying in style and hurtling towards a meeting with our Irish tour guide, who has no inkling of what we're really employing her for.

'Barnaby? Are you okay?' I hear Philippa ask my son, and I turn to look at our boy to see what the matter is. When I do, I see that his eyelids are heavy and he looks like he is struggling to stay awake, which is obviously what has made our nanny so concerned. But I'm not worried, not at all, and that's because Barnaby looks exactly how I would have expected him to look at this stage of our trip.

He's sleepy and of course he is. *Because I crushed just over half a sleeping tablet into his pre-flight meal.*

'He's fine,' I say to Philippa as the car comes to a stop and our driver wishes us a good trip.

'Are you sure?' the nanny replies annoyingly, making me wonder if bringing her with us was a good idea after all.

'You're coming on this trip to help, not hinder,' I reply smartly. 'Barnaby is absolutely fine. He just needs some sleep, and he has a long flight now in which to get it. Let's go. Unless you'd like to stay here, but remember, if you do, you won't be getting paid again until we get back.'

'You're right. He's fine,' Philippa quickly agrees. I knew she would when I put it like that.

I follow Donovan out of the vehicle, satisfied that I won't get questioned about Barnaby again, and soon he'll be fast asleep and no trouble to any of us for the duration of this flight. Donovan and I have employed the sleeping pill tactic before when flying with our son for more than a few hours, aware that our son gets nervous ahead of flying, so this gives him a chance to rest during our time in the air rather than nervously clutching the armrests of his seat and asking us what happens if we crash. By extension, it's easier for all of us to relax in the cabin with our child restful. It always works too, barring that one time we got the dose wrong and Barnaby didn't sleep at all, but we haven't made that mistake again. He certainly looks ready to slip into slumber now, shuffling his feet on the tarmac as we make our way to the plane.

'Good morning,' Donovan says as he hands our passports to the owner of this airstrip and, while they're being checked, I turn back to make sure our luggage is being carried on as planned. It sure is and, once Donovan has our passports back, the four of us are free to board.

As we climb the stairs to the aircraft, I consider how my husband and I briefly thought about making this a purely family trip, just the three of us, and leaving Philippa at home. But we have a lot to do in Ireland and it'll be much easier to achieve if we have childcare, so Philippa made the cut. Although I made it clear to her before, just like I did a moment ago, that she is here to aid us, and that means not just keeping Barnaby quiet, but keeping quiet herself too. If she can manage that, she'll get another one of the bonuses that I have been known to give her on occasion since she's been working for us.

'Welcome aboard,' says a smiling Juliette, our regular cabin crew attendant, who looks pretty as she always does in her buttoned uniform. She greets Donovan and me with equal warmth, nodding politely at Barnaby and Philippa before showing us all to our seats.

I strap myself in opposite Donovan on one side of the cabin, while Philippa gets Barnaby in his seat before taking her own across from us. As I'd hoped and expected, Barnaby's eyes close before the engines have even started, and by the time they are fully firing up he is definitely asleep.

'Bless him, doesn't he look sweet when he's sleeping?' I remark to Philippa to allay any suspicions about what might have really caused my son's drowsiness, and she doesn't say anything to that. But I didn't think she would anyway. This is her first long-haul flight with us, so she doesn't really know what Barnaby is like on these.

'Would you like anything to drink before take-off?' Juliette asks us, and Donovan quickly orders a whiskey, which causes me to frown.

'I thought you weren't going to drink on this trip,' I say, reminding him of what he told me himself while we were packing yesterday.

'Just one or two. It's a vacation, after all,' Donovan replies as Juliette scurries away to fetch it for him.

Knowing my husband as well as I do, I realise he's nervous, but not because of the fact we're moments away from leaving the ground. It's because of what we're on our way to do. With the plane beginning to taxi down the runway, this suddenly seems very real, and now I feel like I might need a drink too.

I call out to Juliette to make me a drink as well, and after she has handed our glasses to us, she straps herself in at the front of the plane as the jet picks up speed.

I notice Philippa grip her armrests as we hurtle down the runway, before looking at the restful Barnaby opposite her. Then I glance at Donovan and see he has his glass to his lips while staring out of the window beside him. I know he's in a pensive mood, which isn't like him at all, so I decide I should say a few words to set his mind at ease over these next seven hours while we're in the air. First, I allow the pilot to get us off the ground safely and, as we climb into the sky, I feel a brief sense of weightlessness as my stomach lurches slightly and the jet's engines grapple with gravity while the aircraft rises.

Once we're at a stable height and the plane has levelled out, we can remove our seatbelts. I waste no time telling Philippa to give me and my husband a moment of privacy. She unbuckles the seatbelt that was fastened across her cardigan and hurries away to the back of the cabin, where Juliette begins chatting with her, while I lean into Donovan, who has already finished his first whiskey.

'You know we need to do this,' I say to my husband. 'For us. For our marriage.'

'I know.'

'Things will be better when it's done. We'll both be happier.

Less to worry about. More time to focus on us again, rather than other people.'

'I still think we should have just paid somebody else to do this. Take care of Shannon, I mean.'

'You know it's better if we do it. We'll regret it if we don't. This is our chance to say what we have to. And it means no one else will ever know.'

Donovan doesn't look so sure, so I reach out and take the hand that isn't still clutching the empty glass.

'We're a team and we win. That's what we do,' I remind him. 'Life hasn't been easy for us, and we've had to fight for everything we've got. Our money. Our relationship. Our children.'

Donovan glances across at Barnaby, who is snoring softly in his seat.

'If we don't do this then our family is at risk,' I say. 'So settle those nerves and stay focused. Our marriage depends on it.'

I sit back in my seat, my warning administered, and it looks like Donovan has got the message because he doesn't seem in a rush to order himself another strong drink. Instead, he simply smiles at me.

'You're right. I'll just feel better when we're on the plane home.'

'So will I,' I reply over the sound of Barnaby's latest snore. 'And it won't be long.'

I stop talking now, because Philippa returns to her seat, but that's fine – she's missed everything we have to say and still has no clue that this journey is anything but a family trip.

Even more importantly, neither does the person we are flying to meet – she still has no idea what our real intentions are.

Now we're on our way, and very soon, Shannon will be wishing that she never met us...

SEVEN

SHANNON

I stare at the entrance to the building and frown – even though this is apparently the right place, it's not what I was expecting.

'Are you sure this is it?' I ask my taxi driver.

'Yeah, this is Lanargan Airport,' he replies with a chuckle. 'What's the matter? Expecting somewhere bigger?'

'Well, yeah, kind of,' I say as I keep staring out of the window. 'I wouldn't exactly call this an airport. It's tiny.'

'Me neither, to be fair. An airport is a place full of planes, screaming kids and duty free shops. This is just somewhere rich people come and go without having to deal with any of that. I won't be flying from here anytime soon, that's for sure.'

My driver's grumble about the inequality of life makes me think I should pay him quickly so he at least has a little more money in his pocket than he had before, so I do that, handing him his fare, and then get out. He stuffs the cash in his jeans before getting out to help me take my suitcase from the back of the vehicle.

'You must be doing well for yourself,' he says as he lowers my case to the ground.

'Excuse me?'

'If you're flying from here. This is where the rich catch their flights.'

'Oh no, I'm meeting people flying in, actually,' I correct him, almost embarrassed that he might think I would be so flashy as to use private airports in my day-to-day life.

'A rich boyfriend?' the taxi driver says with a wink. 'How wonderful. Well, enjoy your time, whatever you end up doing. And spare a thought for us mere peasants while you're having fun.'

He chuckles as he gets back behind the wheel, but by pointing out how exclusive this place is he makes me feel very out of my depth. I'll also be very alone if he leaves me here. That's why I consider asking the driver if he could wait with me until the flight arrives, but before I can do that he gives me a wave and drives off.

Looking all around me, I see green fields surrounding the stretch of tarmac, which pass as a car park, and other than the building behind me and the strip of tarmac beyond that, there is nothing else here. I feel like I'm the only person at this tiny airport in the middle of nowhere. This really is private, so much so that I start to worry again that I'm in the wrong place. I pick up my suitcase and hurry inside, hoping to find somebody in here to set my mind at ease. I really hope I haven't got lost; if I have, there's no chance of me getting to the right place in time to meet the American couple, and then I might lose out on the rest of the money they plan to pay me for the tour. I'd hate for that to happen, not just because I need that extra cash, but also because it's taken me a long time just to get here.

I left Dublin four hours ago and had to take a train and a taxi, but I remind myself that Rosalind promised me in one of her emails that my expenses will be covered this week. I'm praying I'm right as I walk through the sliding entrance doors to the airport and look around.

There's not much to see in here, just marble flooring and a

white desk, but no people... Now I'm really worried. This can't be right. If this is an airport, where are all the other passengers? Never mind them, where are all the workers? The baggage handlers, the security guards, the pilots, the cabin crew, the cleaners – everybody that adds to the bustling nature of a place where planes take off and land every day.

'Good afternoon, madam. May I be of assistance?'

I spin around at the sound of the voice behind me to find a man in a smart suit staring at me.

'Erm, I'm here to meet somebody. Two people, actually. A couple, flying in from America. They should be landing in ten minutes or so. I think they're on a private plane. I'm not sure if—'

The man raises his hand, and I instinctively know to stop talking.

'That's fine. I know who you are referring to and, yes, their flight is due to land shortly. You can take a seat over here until then. Would you like a drink while you wait?'

I just stare back at the man, almost in a daze, because this weird place just gets even weirder. I'm used to chaos and crowds at airports, not handsome men in suits offering me a drink as soon as I've walked inside.

'Erm, a glass of water if that's okay?' I ask, and the man nods before walking away and disappearing into a side room.

While he's gone, I take a seat on a bank of cushioned chairs and stare out of the floor-to-ceiling windows that overlook what I guess is the runway. It's clear out there, but I start to see signs of activity. A buggy drives past, driven by a man in hi-vis clothing, and a woman in a smart uniform emerges from a side door before taking her place at the white desk opposite me. She smiles at me before tapping away on the laptop in front of her, and I'm wondering if she is 'passport control' here. The man returns with my water. He briefly chats with the woman and checks his watch. I check mine too and see that the flight is due to land any moment now. The man and woman go to the window to look out, and I decide to join them. As I do, I see a small dot approaching in the sky. The dot grows larger until I realise it's a plane coming right towards us, and it gets lower and lower until it lands in front of me on the other side of the glass.

I watch as the private plane slows down before taxiing to its final parking spot. The buggy speeds towards it once it's stopped. The man and woman beside me quickly spring back into action, and I'm told to return to my seat on the other side of the desk, so I do that, not wanting to get in the way of whatever slick operation is in motion all around me.

As I retake my seat and nervously sip my water, I think about the makeshift sign I made before coming here, the one I put together last night before coming to this airport. I wrote *The Conways* in bright blue ink on a white piece of paper and planned to hold it up at the arrivals gate so they would know I was the person who had come to meet them. I don't think I'll bother getting that out of my suitcase now, not just because I clearly won't need it, but because it will be embarrassing. The couple on that plane that's just landed have an entire airport to themselves, where the staff here have clearly been waiting solely for their arrival. My cheap sign is nowhere near as sophisticated as the things they are used to, so I'll leave it in my suitcase along with my inexpensive clothing and low-priced make-up accessories. But one thing I can't leave is the anxiety I have; these people I'm meeting are going to be unimpressed with me when they see me. I may be judged, and without really knowing what they're thinking until I spend time with them, I'm fearing they aren't going to be amazed by the person they've paid to meet.

I can't see the plane from my seat now so I miss out on watching the couple disembark, but I can tell they are on their way because the woman at the desk stands up, brushes down the front of her uniform and plasters a big grin on her face. She must do this same routine for all the rich people who pass through here. I suppose it's not the worst job in the world. I don't see a wedding ring on her finger, so I wonder if she is hoping to snare herself one of the wealthy men who use these private planes, and one day she might be able to leave that desk behind and actually jet away herself. If so, I can't blame her for trying.

The door behind her opens and I see the man in the hi-vis clothing pushing a trolley full of luggage towards me. He is followed by a man and woman, so I guess this is them.

Rosalind and Donovan Conway.

I gulp nervously as I take in their appearance.

She is wearing designer clothing, and her jet-black hair is immaculate, like the kind you see in the adverts where those female celebrities flick their luscious locks back and smile for the camera, while being paid millions of dollars to do it. Her make-up also looks like something straight out of an advertise-ment, and if it was, there would be a queue of women lining up to buy whatever lipstick, eyeshadow and concealer Rosalind is currently wearing. I'd ask her about it myself if only I knew her better.

Effortlessly, she very quickly puts the woman at the desk in the shade in terms of who looks better. She does that to me too, but I can't feel too bad because I doubt there are many women in the world who look as good as Rosalind does right now. Speaking of looking good, the man she is with is eye-catching in his own way. Tall, toned, dark and handsome, wearing a smart sweater, tight jeans and crisp-white trainers, he has a youthful style and the confidence to carry it off. There's a calm swagger to him, I guess caused by the noncha-lance of wealth; but most endearingly, he has manners. I see that when he thanks the baggage handler who is working in front of them, and also turns to hold open the door for the woman behind him. Wait, there's another woman? I take in the sight of the female arriving with them and have no idea who she is. She looks to be a similar age to me, isn't dressed as well as the couple and looks decidedly less happy than they do too, but that's not important. What's important is that I was expecting two people, not three.

Then, suddenly, there are four.

The sight of the young boy bringing up the rear is even more shocking. Rosalind definitely did not mention any children to me, so who is this? I must be getting confused. Surely I'm still just showing a couple around. This other woman and the boy must be going elsewhere. Maybe they're not even connected to the couple; they might have just shared the flight or come in on another plane that I haven't seen land. But then, after the woman at the desk has received four passports and checked them all, the four arrivals are free to move past her and towards me. As I get up from my seat, I'm confused – it does look like they're all together.

'Rosalind?' I say tentatively, and the woman in the expensive clothing eyes me up and down as she stops in front of me.

'You must be Shannon.'

'Yes, that's right. It's a pleasure to meet you,' I say, sticking out my hand for her to shake and trying to be as friendly and welcoming as an Irish person can be. But Rosalind doesn't take my hand or reciprocate the warm greeting. She just walks right past me, following the baggage handler out of the airport.

I'm not sure what to do about her snub, fearing I'm already off to a terrible start, but I'm quickly reassured.

'Sorry. She's not usually like that. She's just tired from the flight.'

I turn to Donovan Conway and see him smiling at me, which results in the feeling of butterflies in my stomach. Instead of being nervous, I now feel a little giddy.

'Oh, it's okay. I understand. You've come a long way,' I say quickly. 'How was your flight?'

'Perfect, thank you,' Donovan replies. 'But we are tired, so it would be great if we could get going.'

'Of course,' I say, but there are a couple of issues with that. One is that I was told that a vehicle would be supplied for me to drive around in and conduct this trip, but I didn't see one outside when I got here. But two, and more urgently right now, I was only expecting a couple on this trip, not four people – and the plans I've made didn't factor in a child.

'The car is here now,' Donovan says after checking his phone, and it's as if he read my thoughts. It feels even more like that when he turns to the two people standing beside him.

'Shannon, this is my son, Barnaby, and this is our nanny, Philippa. Don't worry, the car will be big enough for all of us. So, how about we get going?'

Donovan strides past me, closely followed by Philippa, who ushers Barnaby out along with them, and I'm left standing open-mouthed beside my suitcase as the airport is once again empty.

What is going on?

Why would Rosalind lie to me?

How has this suddenly turned from a couple's trip to a family one?

I don't know, but I guess I better follow them all outside if I still want to get paid.

EIGHT

SHANNON

Hurrying out of the airport, I see the four passengers ahead of me. But I also see something else that wasn't here when I originally arrived in my taxi.

It's a luxurious, black 4x4 parked right in front of the doors. *This must be the car that Rosalind has hired for us.*

My first thought is that it's a beautiful vehicle. My second thought is that there is no way I can possibly drive it. It's huge, far bigger than anything I've driven before, and not only that but it's clearly ludicrously expensive. What if I was to bump it or scratch it? Would I get in trouble? Would I have to pay for the damage? How much does the insurance cost on a car like this? I am overwhelmed with questions, all of them on top of the ones I already had, but before I can say anything, Rosalind turns to me and has a question of her own.

'Where are we staying tonight?'

I frown because I'm not sure I heard her right.

'Excuse me?'

'I asked you where are we staying tonight? Is it far to drive? It's been a long flight and I'm tired, so I'm looking forward to going to bed soon. So how far away is our hotel?'

I stare at the American woman and try to fathom a response, but it's tough – there's only really one thing I can say in the circumstances. Unfortunately, it's very awkward, but I don't have much choice but to just come out with it.

'I haven't booked a hotel. You said in your email that you were going to arrange the accommodation.'

Rosalind's face drops, and I realise she seems to dispute the truth I have just told her.

'Please tell me you're joking,' she says, and I notice Donovan turn around to look too. He had been watching the baggage handler put his luggage into the back of the 4x4, but he's clearly heard there might be a problem here. And there is a problem, at least there is for me if I can't convince Rosalind that she is mistaken.

The obvious way for me to prove that I am right and she is wrong is to find the email she sent me on my phone and show it to her. That will clear this up easily, or at least prove that I'm not lying or being incompetent. But I don't want to resort to that just yet, because I don't want it to seem like I'm trying to defeat her or get one over on her. I want to keep things friendly and light between us as we've only just met. The problem is, it doesn't seem like 'friendly' and 'light' are words in Rosalind's vocabulary, if the look on her face is anything to go by.

'Okay, maybe there has been a bit of confusion, but not to worry. I can sort a hotel out quickly and we can be on our way,' I say, hoping to just resolve this hiccup without an argument.

'Confusion? There is no confusion. As our tour guide, and a very well-paid tour guide at that, you didn't think your customers might need somewhere to stay while they were here?'

I can see that Rosalind is not going to drop this and is keen on making out like this is my fault, so maybe I am going to have to show her the email, to prove I've done nothing wrong. But before I can get my phone out, Donovan steps in and defuses the situation.

'Rosalind, go and join Barnaby and Philippa in the car,' he says, and he points to the 4x4 where the child and nanny are already getting onto the spacious back seat.

'But—' his wife begins, and he cuts her off.

'Come on. We're all sleep-deprived, so let's not let that cloud our thoughts,' Donovan says. I note how calm and composed he is, which seems in direct contrast to the woman he chose to marry. They do say opposites attract but, so far, I'm really not seeing what attracted this man to this woman, beyond her good looks anyway. But then again, it wouldn't be the first time rich people made stupid decisions. Maybe Donovan could have picked a better life partner if he hadn't been so dazzled by Rosalind's beauty.

Much to my relief, and after one more scowl from the American woman, Rosalind gets in the car, leaving me with Donovan and the baggage handler. Before he turns to me, Donovan thanks the man who carried their luggage out and hands him what looks like a sizeable tip. The baggage handler is thrilled by what he's just got and thanks Donovan before leaving us. But unless I can turn this situation around quickly, I'd say there's little chance of receiving a tip like that at the end of this trip.

'Look, I don't know what's happened, but I don't care,' Donovan says decisively. 'The facts are that we need a hotel to stay in tonight because, as you can see, my wife needs some rest, as does my son. So, if I give you ten minutes, can you come up with something nearby?'

It's a challenge, but he has asked nicely, plus he's smiling at me again and I feel funny when he does that, so I smile too.

'I'll do my best,' I promise, and Donovan seems happy enough with that.

'That's all I can ask,' he says, and then notices that I still have my suitcase with me. 'Oops, looks like we missed one. Let me take that for you.'

He effortlessly picks up my heavy case, and though I try to tell him that I can manage it on my own, he puts it into the back of the car for me. Then he reminds me he'd like to get on the road in the next ten minutes, so I quickly take out my phone. But before I can get to work I still have one very big issue to raise.

'Sorry, Donovan. Erm, can I just have a word?'

'Sure. What is it?'

'It's just that in the emails with your wife, I was told it would just be the two of you travelling here. There was no mention of your son or your nanny.'

'Oh, I see. Well, our plans changed a little bit, as you can see. Is that a problem?'

Donovan smiles at me as he waits for my response.

'Well, no. I mean, I can try and work around it. It's just I've done quite a bit of planning for this trip, but it was all on the basis of it being for two people, not four. More romantic things, if you get what I mean.'

'I see.'

'I hadn't really planned any activities for a child. How old is he?'

'Barnaby is seven and he's a good kid. He'll be happy to join in with whatever we do. And with Philippa here, she can easily handle him. She can also look after him while we enjoy some of these romantic trips you have planned. Sound good?'

'Erm, okay,' I say, surprised Donovan seems so casual about this. But if he's not worried then maybe I shouldn't be, and I guess he will take all of this into account when judging my performance at the end of the trip.

'Anything else?' he asks me breezily.

'The hotels I'm supposed to find now. Is there a budget for these?'

'No budget,' Donovan replies, effortlessly saying two words that reveal just how wealthy he is, almost as much as the fact he came here on a private plane. 'And here's my travel card. Just book anything you need to on here.'

He takes out his bulky leather wallet and hands me a card, which I presume he preloaded with travel money before he set off from America.

'Any more questions?' he asks me casually, as if he will easily be able to handle them if there are.

'No. I mean, not unless there are any other surprises in store for me,' I say as I look down at the card. 'As you might be able to tell, I'm not really a surprises kind of girl.'

I laugh then and it's a relief to hear Donovan laugh too.

'Surprises? No, nothing else I can think of. What you see is what you get now,' he replies with a chuckle. Then he checks his expensive-looking watch. 'Wow, we left home nearly ten hours ago. We really could do with getting to our hotel soon.'

'I'm on it,' I say, taking the very big hint that I need to get to work.

I need a hotel and quick.

If we were in Dublin, or even anywhere near there, I would know of several hotels that could potentially accommodate us all. But we're not near the city, we're out in the sticks, so this is going to prove trickier. What makes it even harder is that I literally can't just find anywhere around here that might have a vacancy. These people are millionaires, so they will expect a certain level of accommodation.

Are there any five-star hotels nearby?

I wrack my brains before thinking of one I read about in a travel guide a couple of months ago. What was it called again? I use Google to try and narrow it down and, when I find it, I waste no time calling the property and praying they can fit us in. I know rooms there are pricey, but Donovan said there was no budget. Rosalind also said in her email that expenses were taken care of, or at least she did at one point, although anything that woman said in the past seems to be in dispute at the moment.

'Good afternoon. How may I help you?'

'Oh, yes, hello. My name is Shannon, and I was wondering if you had any rooms available at your hotel. We'd need two or three. Actually, maybe four.' The presence of the nanny has thrown me off. 'The best rooms you have, ideally. And we're looking to check in today if possible. Can you help?'

'Today? No, my dear. I'm sorry. We're fully booked.'

Oh no.

Thinking on my feet, I ask the receptionist about any hotels of a similar calibre in the area, but am told this hotel is the best and the only other one nearby is a three-star residence. *Three stars.* Surely that won't do for the Conways. I guess I'll have to look further afield, but that means a longer drive and, after a long flight already, I doubt Rosalind will have the patience for that.

Beggars can't be choosers, so after getting the name of the other hotel, I quickly call there and repeat my same desperate line about needing rooms today.

'Yes, we do have rooms available today,' comes the reply, which is both good and bad. Good because it solves my problem, but bad because why isn't this place fully booked? Is it because it's not very highly rated? I don't have time to worry about that, so I tell the receptionist that we are on our way and will be checking in on arrival. Now all I need to do is use this big car to get us there.

Tentatively getting in behind the wheel, I see that Donovan is beside me in the passenger seat while everyone else is behind us.

'Is the hotel sorted?' he asks me, and I confirm that it is.

I look at the huge steering wheel, gearstick and fancy mod-cons that come with this car.

'Sorry, just give me a moment. I've never driven one of these before,' I admit, trying to buy myself a few seconds, but it doesn't seem to work.

'Can we get going now?' Rosalind asks from the back seat with a huff.

'Hit that button to start the engine and we'll take it easy from here,' Donovan says quietly, and I smile to thank him for his help as I attempt to get us going.

I press the button he just told me to press and the engine fires up. No sooner have I tapped lightly on the accelerator pedal than I get a sense of the power that this car possesses. We lurch forward and I quickly slam on the brakes and then stall.

Barnaby laughs, but Rosalind quickly tells him that it's not funny.

'Sorry,' I say as I go to try again, restarting the engine and shifting gears. As I do that, my hand accidentally brushes Donovan's right leg beside me.

'I'm sorry!' I cry, afraid that he might think I did it on purpose, but he didn't even flinch.

'No worries,' he says. 'Just take it nice and slow. Like I've said to my pilot many times over the years, I'd rather it take longer and we get there in one piece than rush things and have an accident.'

If it wasn't for Donovan and his nice ways, I might have considered giving up already, but he encourages me to not write off this trip as a disaster just yet. As I start again my driving is a little more controlled this time.

We're on the move, all five of us, and as we leave the airport the next stop is the hotel. Sure, it's nowhere near the start to the trip that I thought it would be, but at least it's begun and surely things can only get better from here.

Right?

NINE

SHANNON

I think I'm getting to grips with driving this car. I haven't crashed it yet, so I guess that's a positive. Then again, I am going a little under the speed limit, so I'm playing it safe, though the occasional tutting from the back seat is my reminder that I should perhaps put my foot down a little bit more. The tutting is coming from Rosalind – who else? – but like her husband told me, it's better to get to your destination in one piece than not at all, so I won't be rushed. While I might be getting more comfortable with the vehicle, I'm still far from comfortable with the passengers inside it. I'm still very much in the process of trying to get to know them.

'Are we nearly there yet?' Barnaby asks me from the back seat, and while that might usually be an annoying question for a driver to hear, I'm actually grateful for it because it has broken the latest awkward silence.

'We're about ten minutes away,' I reply cheerily. 'So not long now. Are you excited to be on holiday?'

'Yeah, we don't go away much.'

I'm surprised by Barnaby's response. I would have presumed having rich parents and access to a private plane would have meant holidays were one thing that were common. It seems not, though Donovan tries to correct what his son just said.

'We do take vacations,' he says to me quietly, but Barnaby hears.

'No, we don't. I usually get left at home with Philippa.'

I glance in the rear-view mirror and see the nanny sitting in between Barnaby and Rosalind, and think about how she hasn't said a word since I met her. Is she generally quiet, or scared to speak in front of her employers? Someone who is not afraid to speak up is the woman sitting beside her.

'Barnaby, be quiet. Shannon needs to concentrate on driving,' Rosalind says.

'No, it's okay. It's nice to talk,' I reply breezily, not wanting Barnaby to feel bad. 'My dad used to talk a lot while he drove. Said it helped break up boring journeys. Sometimes we would play I spy. Would you like to play that, Barnaby?'

'Yeah!' comes the excited reply from the back seat, but just before I can pick the first letter to start the game with, the fun is cut short.

'Calm down!' Rosalind snaps at her son before I notice her glaring at Philippa. 'It would be nice if you helped.'

'I'm sorry,' Philippa says. She turns to Barnaby, whispering something to him, which seems to get Barnaby to be quiet. I don't know what was said, all I know is that this doesn't seem like a very nice way to treat the youngster.

The awkwardness has returned to the car now, and I'm not sure what to do about it. I'm hoping Donovan might offer something, but he's mostly been using his phone since we started driving, replying to messages or emails or whatever things a busy man like him has to do after a long flight. I see Barnaby looking forlornly out of his window as the sun sets over the passing countryside, and wish I could say something to make him smile, but I'm nervous to engage with him now. Rosalind clearly prefers it when her son is quiet.

What is that old saying that people of a certain generation used to say about kids?

Children should be seen and not heard.

Rosalind clearly subscribes to that.

It's funny because I'd have thought a child like Barnaby, born to rich parents and all the luxury that comes with that, would be considered lucky. But seeing the way his mother speaks to him and how downbeat he generally looks, I'm not so sure he's any happier than a kid born into very little. I never had much growing up, but I did have the love of my parents, may they rest in peace, and that's all I needed. But does Barnaby have that? If so, his mother certainly has a funny way of showing it.

'So, I believe you've lived in Ireland before,' I say to both Donovan and Rosalind as I recall a detail she mentioned in her original email to me, and I'm hopeful that one of them will engage with me further. 'Does it feel good to be back?'

'Yeah, it's been too long since we were here,' Donovan replies, finally putting his phone away.

'How long has it been since you left?' I ask, eager to learn more about this family.

'We must be nearly there by now, surely,' Rosalind interrupts. 'Where is this hotel?'

'Five minutes away,' I answer, but that interruption has nipped the conversation in the bud and now Donovan is back on his phone again, so I leave it.

This is going to be a very long trip if nobody is willing to engage with me, but as I get to within two minutes of the hotel, my thoughts move away from the silence in the car and more onto whether or not this accommodation is going to be deemed acceptable. I'm really hoping Rosalind doesn't hate the hotel I've booked for tonight, because after a rough start I need a win.

'Here we are,' I say optimistically as I turn off the main road and steer us up a long gravel driveway. For a moment, I'm hopeful this three-star place is actually going to be nicer than I would expect. Then I see the property and my hopes fade; it's not grand or luxurious or even charming. It's very basic, and I almost feel a bit ridiculous approaching this hotel in such a flash car.

'Is this it?' Donovan asks me as he looks up from his phone, and I detect a hint of disappointment in his voice, which bothers me a lot more than when Rosalind seems irritated with me. With her, I've already made my mind up that she is a bit of a cow, so I expect it. But Donovan is nice and polite, not to mention very attractive, so it feels worse if I let him down.

'Yes. This was the only hotel in the area that had vacancies,' I explain.

'I can see why,' Rosalind chips in.

'If it hadn't been for the confusion over the hotel bookings then I could have—' I start, but Donovan quickly interrupts me.

'This will do. We all just need a good night's rest and then we're ready to begin the trip tomorrow.'

I bring the car to a stop, and Donovan quickly gets out, going around to the back to make a start on the bags. I look hopefully through the windscreen at the front door of the hotel in case a member of the staff is coming out to help us, but there is no sign of anybody, so I get out of the car to lend Donovan a hand. Barnaby is already out and running around, chased by Philippa who is trying to get him to stand still, while Rosalind simply stares at the hotel with a look on her face that says she hasn't ever stayed somewhere this basic since she was born.

The inside of the hotel is only marginally better than the outside. I can see a very old wooden staircase surrounded by a garish floral pattern carpet. As we reach the reception desk, I am almost grimacing at what the bedrooms here must be like. I'm aware this is also Rosalind's fault, and as I look at her frowning as she surveys the hotel around her, I feel like reminding her of that one more time. Probably for the best, the appearance of the receptionist interrupts me, and I quickly go about getting us all checked in. It seems I make yet another faux pas when I mention needing a family room, on the assumption that Donovan, Rosalind and Barnaby will all be sleeping together. But it seems I'm wrong again.

'Oh no, Barnaby will be in with the nanny,' Rosalind quickly corrects me. 'My husband and I will have a double room to ourselves, so no need for a family room.'

I don't want to second guess the sleeping habits of this family, or irritate Rosalind anymore, so I allow the receptionist to take the details and it's not long until we have the room keys in our hands.

'Do you serve any food here?' I ask optimistically before we leave the desk, aware that I'm going to be hungry in a few hours' time and that there didn't seem to be many places to get something to eat on the drive here.

'No, the chef has gone home for the day. He'll be back at breakfast time tomorrow.'

'Oh, okay,' I say as Rosalind sighs, but Donovan tells me that they had a couple of big meals on the flight over, so they will be fine.

At least they're okay then, and it's just me who will starve this evening.

'It's just for one night,' I hear Rosalind mutter to herself as we all head for the staircase ten minutes later to find our rooms. I ignore that and, as we reach the first floor, I'm definitely ready to have a break from her. But if I'm feeling like this already, how am I going to get through this entire trip with her? I glance at Philippa and wonder how she could possibly put up with Rosalind twenty-four seven, but the nanny seems to be very stoically going about her business, looking after Barnaby and barely showing any emotion at all. Maybe she's just as strange as Rosalind in her own way. I guess I'll find out more about her during the course of this trip.

'Room 107. This is us,' Donovan says, before putting the key into the lock and giving it a turn.

I am in Room 110, while Barnaby and the nanny are in Room 108, but I linger to make sure the Conways are happy enough with their room before going to mine. As Donovan opens the door, I get a glimpse of a carpet even more colourful than the one in the reception area, as well as a very basic TV on a dressing table and a double bed that barely looks like it could fit two people.

'Hmm,' Rosalind says judgingly as she enters the room, clearly happy to leave the rest of us to get settled elsewhere.

'Sorry. I just want to confirm what time you'd like to leave tomorrow morning,' I say tentatively, figuring it's best to make a plan now.

'You tell us. You're the tour guide,' Rosalind snaps as she looks back, and I've just about had enough of the way she's speaking to me. I pride myself on being able to get along with anyone, but Rosalind is proving to be the exception to the rule. Clearly pre-empting my frustration, Donovan says eight a.m. will be fine.

'Looking forward to what you have planned for our first full day together,' he says heartily, and that helps ease my anger.

'Just up your game on the accommodation front,' I hear Rosalind say before she disappears into her bathroom, but I leave it at that and tell Donovan I will see him in the morning.

'Sleep well,' he tells me. Except, before sleep, I have a lot of work to do. Now I have to go and book the rest of the hotels for this trip, or at least I assume I do.

As I head for my room, I see Philippa unlocking her door and Barnaby standing beside her, so I take the opportunity to have a conversation without Rosalind around.

'Hey, we haven't had much of a chance to talk yet. Are you

okay?' I ask the nanny with a smile on my face. She seems nervous, even with her employers no longer watching over her.

'I'm fine, thank you,' she says before turning to Barnaby. 'Come on. Let's go inside. You need to have a bath and then it's straight to bed.'

'But I'm hungry,' Barnaby moans, and I can't blame him. I'm ravenous too.

'You had lots of food on the plane, now come on, go inside,' Philippa tries again, but Barnaby is still reluctant.

'I want to go and see Daddy,' he says, which sounds like a perfectly reasonable request to me.

'No, Mommy and Daddy are resting now. Go inside, Barnaby. I don't want to have to ask you again.'

Barnaby huffs and puffs before eventually entering the room, but he's not happy about it and, not for the first time, I feel sorry for him. This does not seem like a happy child.

'Goodnight,' Philippa says to me before she enters the room.

'Wait, I—'

The door closes before I have a chance to say anything else.

Left out in the corridor with only my suitcase for company, I find my own room and go inside. It's bare and basic, but it has a bed and that's all I need. I slump down on to it and think about what I'm doing here. Do I really need the money this much? I could just quit now and go back to Dublin.

No, I can't. Not only do I not have my own transport to get out of here, but I accepted the $5,000 deposit from the Conways, which I presume I'd have to refund if I left. I'd also feel bad ditching them, plus there's the not so small matter of the extra $15,000 I still stand to earn. I just need to toughen up and get through this trip, and I know I can do it because this is my profession and I'm damn good at it. It'll be over before I know it and I'll be richer than I've ever been before. The prospect of making my life infinitely easier than it has been for years will keep me going through whatever tough times come over the next few days.

But as I lay my head down on my pillow and feel my stomach rumbling, I worry that the money is not worth this. There's something 'off' about this family. The nanny too.

What is it?

If I want to stick around long enough to get paid, I guess I'm going to find out.

TEN

ROSALIND

This is easily the smallest bathroom I've been inside in my entire life. The shower was probably the worst as well, the water a mere dribble rather than a flowing jet like the one in my luxurious bathroom at home. The bedroom is no better, with space at a premium and a strange, musty smell that makes me wonder when it was last properly cleaned. But at least I have a little more space because our son is staying in another room with the nanny and my husband has just gone out for a run. So I have some peace and privacy, for a short while, anyway. I intend to make good use of that, and as I flop down onto the bed wearing my dressing gown, with my wet hair wrapped in a towel, I think about the woman who drove us to this hotel.

Of course, Shannon was right and I was wrong. I did tell her in one of my emails that I would sort out the accommodation during this trip. I lied and pretended like it was all her fault that we didn't have anywhere booked for this evening. I only did that to mess with her. The game playing has begun. If she thinks that's bad, she should wait and see what else I have in store for her. But I can't be totally mean to her or she'll hate me, if she doesn't already, and I don't want to risk her leaving us before we've finished what we came here to do. That's why I'll try and go a little easier on her tomorrow, which should help her relax a little, but it will merely be a tactic designed to confuse her even more, just like the tactic of having Donovan be so very nice to her.

I know she likes him. I noticed the way her eyes lit up when she first saw him at the airport, and I know his politeness has only endeared him to her more. He's merely been acting, as have I, and this is all just a ploy to get Shannon right where we want her.

I wonder what our tour guide is doing right now. Frantically trying to book hotel rooms for the rest of this trip, no doubt. I bet she's looking for five-star accommodation, and I bet she'll feel pleased with herself if she is able to successfully secure it for us. She's also probably got a great plan for tomorrow, our first day on her tour, and I bet she's thinking she can quickly redeem herself after getting off to a slow start today. I'll let her think that, for a little while at least, but whatever she does next her fate is already sealed.

She's doomed.

She just doesn't know it yet.

The hotel room door opens and a sweaty Donovan walks in. He quickly peels off his T-shirt and then stands before me at the foot of the bed in nothing but his shorts and sneakers. He has his hands on his hips, a chiselled abdomen, and he's breathless from his run. I am feeling a little frisky and invite him onto the bed to join me. It doesn't take long for the pair of us to lose what we are wearing and, after a passionate encounter, we are lying intertwined beneath the sheets.

'Wow, it's been a while since we did that,' Donovan muses.

'I told you this trip was what we needed.'

'You were right about that.'

'Just imagine how good life will be when we've done what we came here to do.'

'That plane ride home should be fun,' Donovan says with a wink. 'We might have to renew our membership for the Mile High Club.'

I like my husband's thinking, but temper his excitement with a dose of reality.

'Keep your focus,' I tell him. 'We have Shannon right where we want her, but this is far from over yet.'

'I know. But we're so close now.'

'Yes, we are,' I say with a satisfied smile, enjoying the company of the gorgeous man beside me while thinking of Shannon in her room down the corridor, all alone.

'I'm going to take a shower,' Donovan says, before giving me a kiss and getting out of bed.

As he goes to get clean, I stay snuggled under the warm duvet, though I'm not simply being idle. I take the opportunity to have a look at Shannon's social media accounts, curious to see if she has updated anything on there since she has been with us. There have been no updates and I guess that makes sense, because I know she told her boss that she is taking a week's holiday, so she can hardly be telling the world what she is really doing.

I have a quick scroll through some of Shannon's older photos next, not that I haven't already done this before. The sight of her in all these images, smiling for the camera as she enjoys nights out with friends, city breaks in Europe and even a few gym sessions proves to me, and anybody else who checks her life out online, that she is a woman with few responsibilities. She might be judging me for hiring a nanny to look after my child, but she can't possibly have any idea how much work it takes to raise a little one. I can tell that from all the photos of her dancing, drinking and generally enjoying herself. She might not have much money, certainly not anywhere near as much as I have, but she does have something myself, Donovan and many other parents don't have.

Time.

As I have many times before, I feel a strong sense of hatred towards this woman. She needs to be punished. And she will be very, very soon.

'What are you looking at?' Donovan asks me as he re-emerges from the bathroom, steam entering the bedroom behind him as I look up, his naked form wandering over towards his suitcase in search of clothes.

'Just snooping on Shannon,' I reply honestly.

'Why not go and knock on her door and see her in person?' Donovan replies as he pulls on a T-shirt.

'You go and see her if you like.'

'Would you like me to do that?'

I stare at Donovan and think about how we could easily play another game with Shannon.

'Maybe. But not tonight. Let's get some sleep.'

Donovan agrees and, as he slides into bed beside me, I turn off the lights and enjoy the peace and serenity of sleeping in a quiet room.

'I hope Barnaby's being good for Philippa,' Donovan says, and I agree.

'I'm sure he is. He's tired, even after we knocked him out with those pills. It's been a long day.'

'Tomorrow might be even longer, depending on what Shannon has planned for us.'

'I bet she's working on it right now,' I predict.

'Yeah, probably. She does seem like the conscientious type. I felt a little sorry for her when you played the trick about the hotel bookings.'

'You felt sorry for that woman? Really?'

'Only a tiny bit. Don't get me wrong, I still hate her.'

We relax a little more into our pillows as our eyes adjust to the dark.

'It's weird being back here,' I say as I stare at the flimsy

curtains hanging from the grotty pole over the window. 'In
Ireland, I mean. Don't you think? Like a glimpse of our old lives
when we used to live here.'

'Yeah, it is. Only seems like yesterday when we were
leaving here and flying back to America. Have you missed it?'

'I don't know. But I'm glad we came back.'

'Me too.'

A silence falls between us both now. I am thinking back on
the time when we lived here. Donovan and I were already
happily married when we came here, as well as parents, but it
felt like an adventure, a break from the norm, and we were still
young enough to not let things worry us quite as much as they
do today. We enjoyed our time here. Though, like we have
already told Shannon, we didn't get to see much because
Donovan was working, and I was a busy mom. But this country
left an indelible mark on us both.

I could leave it there and go to sleep, if my jet lag will allow
it, but just before I do, I have one more question for my
husband.

'Do you really think we'll get away with this?'

He takes a moment to answer, but I don't mind because I
prefer it when my husband considers things.

'Yeah. We got away with it before. Why can't we do it
again?'

That is true and helps put my mind at ease, though that
doesn't mean what comes next doesn't carry just as much risk as
our previous actions.

'We could have got caught,' I remind him cautiously.

'But we didn't, and we won't get caught this time either.
We're too smart, too many steps ahead and too rich to mess this
up. We'll be fine, trust me.'

I do trust Donovan so, with that, I close my eyes and wait
for sleep to take me. When it does, I don't dream of rolling
green hills, picturesque villages and sandy beaches, like some

people who have just got to Ireland might do. I don't even think of stereotypical things like leprechauns and pots of gold or the tricolour flag fluttering in the breeze.

I dream of one thing only.

Swift and brutal action resulting in the only thing that my husband and I want to see now.

Shannon's lifeless eyes staring up at us as we stand over her dead body, smiling.

ELEVEN

SHANNON

I check my watch and see that it is quarter to eight in the morning. That means I should be seeing Donovan and the rest of the group in just over fifteen minutes, or at least I will if he is keeping to the time he gave me last night before we went to our rooms. I have timed this meal so as to avoid seeing them until I've finished, and that gives me a few more minutes to finish the meagre breakfast I have in front of me, the best thing I could order from the 'chef' who works here.

I opted for scrambled eggs on toast, but what came to my table from the kitchen was a poor imitation of that. The eggs are dry, the bread is barely toasted and my meal is cold after only a couple of mouthfuls. I don't bother to complain or send the food back because, like everything else about this hotel, it's cheap and basic and I can't really expect any more.

Fortunately, once we check out of here shortly, the rest of the hotels during this trip will be much better. At least I hope they will be for the price I've paid to make reservations. Once I was aware that Rosalind had a habit for backtracking on things she had said, and that the accommodation had fallen onto me to sort, I went to work, staying up late last night making bookings on my phone. I have secured us rooms at some of the finest hotels in Ireland, all within reasonable driving distance of the various tourist destinations I plan on showing my paying customers, and I'm sure they will be up to their lofty standards. I'd be lying if I said I wasn't savouring the thought of earning Rosalind's respect and having her give me admiring nods when she sees the itinerary I have planned for us, rather than all the tutting and head shaking she was doing in my direction yesterday.

Despite going to sleep last night with worries about the family, I woke up with a renewed sense of optimism, hopeful that things would work out just fine with them. Although after a fairly mediocre breakfast, not to mention the rain falling outside and threatening to put a bit of a dampener on the day ahead, I'm starting to feel nervous about being around Rosalind again. I wonder if she will be in a better mood with me after a night's sleep. The beds here aren't the comfiest, and I was tossing and turning for a while myself, but that probably had less to do with the lumpy mattress and more to do with wondering why this family has me feeling a little uneasy. I'm currently waiting for them to show up, and as the one waitress here takes away my plate of leftover food and I finish my glass of orange juice, I wonder if they will be on time.

'Are you ready? We've been waiting outside for ten minutes.'

I turn around and see Donovan standing behind me.

'Oh, I'm sorry. I thought we said eight o'clock,' I say, checking my watch and seeing that there's still ten minutes to go until that pre-arranged time.

'We were all up early. Jet lag,' Donovan mumbles. 'We had our breakfast over an hour ago and checked out not long after. If you don't mind, we'd rather make a move now.'

'Oh, yes, of course,' I say, getting up from my seat quickly and feeling bad that they have all been waiting for me for so long. I possibly should have pre-empted the jet lag, but what can I do? At least it's Donovan who has come to find me and not his wife. I bet she wouldn't have been quite as civil with me, though he seems a little grumpy, which is not good – he's the nicer one of the pair.

I quickly check out and carry my suitcase outside to the car, where I see Rosalind standing with her arms folded while Philippa tries to get Barnaby to stop pulling petals off a rose bush. A light drizzle is falling, but it's lessening, so hopefully that bodes well and summer will return to these shores almost as quickly as it left.

'Where are we going then?' Rosalind asks me impatiently as I unlock the car.

'There's a waterfall about twenty minutes' drive from here,' I say. 'It's one of the natural wonders of Ireland. How does that sound?'

'A waterfall?' Barnaby repeats excitedly, and I smile at him.

'Yeah. Cool, right?'

'How big is it?'

'Huge. And loud. You can hear the water crashing off the rocks below. And if you get close enough, you can feel the water on your face.'

'Can we swim in it?'

People do swim there, but I look to his parents because they'll have to be the ones who make the final decision on that.

'Let's just go and then we'll see about that,' Donovan says, scratching the stubble on his sculptured chin before telling everyone to get in the car. He might be a little grumpy and bossy, but I quite like how he tells us what to do, not that I let anyone else know that. The last thing I need is Rosalind realising that I'm starting to develop a bit of a crush on her man, though I would never dream of doing anything about it.

I get us out onto the road, spending far less time worrying about the car now I have a little experience driving it, and as we head for the waterfall, the clouds continue to clear and a bit of blue sky starts to show. That will be good for the photos, I think to myself, planning to take lots of pictures of the group so they have some nice memories to look back on at the end of this trip.

Philippa is still just as quiet as she was yesterday, while Barnaby says a few things that Rosalind mostly ignores. But Donovan is chatty, and he makes a few comments about how this is the part of Ireland he saw least when he was here before, so he's glad I've chosen to explore this area with them. That sounds as close to a compliment as I've had from this family so far, so I gratefully take it and use the confidence boost to try and endear myself a little more to Rosalind.

'I have to say, I love your outfit today,' I say as I look at Rosalind's reflection in my rear-view mirror, complimenting her on the smart coat, trousers and hiking boots she is sporting.

'Thank you,' she replies rather unexpectedly, not dismissing me like I feared she might.

It's not much but it's progress, I suppose, so then I have a go at dazzling Donovan too.

'I did a bit of research last night into the ancestry of your surname,' I say. 'Did you know that your descendants hailed from the southern part of the island, near Cork?'

'I didn't know that,' Donovan replies, looking impressed.

'Your surname is very common in the south. It's quite common all over Ireland, actually. I went to school with someone with the same surname. It's a good, strong Irish name.'

'O'Shea isn't too bad either,' Donovan replies. 'There's a fair few O'Sheas in Boston.'

'I'd love to visit there one day,' I say, before pushing my luck slightly with a cheeky joke. 'Maybe you guys can return the favour and show me around when I do?'

I laugh to let them know that I am joking and, amazingly, both Donovan and Rosalind laugh too.

Wow, look at me, making this awkward situation work.

That extra $15,000 is as good as mine.

After a surprisingly pleasant drive, I park near the waterfall and then lead the way to the natural wonder, striding ahead while my four followers come behind me along the snaking path that cuts through the forest. It looks like there's nothing but trees until we eventually come to a large clearing. When we do, we all see the water pouring down the cliff face ahead of us and landing in the lake loudly, but not annoyingly so. The cascading water is a tranquil sight and the noise it produces is calming, akin to what some people who struggle for sleep might listen to through their headphones at bedtime for its soothing properties.

'Wow!' Barnaby cries, which I guess means he likes it. I feel proud at causing such a reaction in the young boy.

'Spectacular,' Donovan adds, before I look to Rosalind for her opinion.

'Not bad,' she says, and I laugh. Getting feedback like that from a woman like her is some achievement.

'What do you think, Philippa?' I ask the quiet nanny as I notice her watching Barnaby frolicking by the water's edge.

'It's beautiful,' she says genuinely. 'Thank you for bringing us here. Barnaby loves it.'

'He's too close to the water,' Rosalind interrupts.

I expect Philippa to go rushing to pull him away, not that Barnaby seems in imminent danger as he's at a safe distance from the water. But Philippa doesn't do that.

'He's fine,' she replies, but she must regret it judging by the look Rosalind gives her. If ever there was a stare that could turn a woman to ice then it would be the one Philippa is receiving right now.

'Barnaby, come a little further back,' Philippa says now as Rosalind's withering look fades away, but it was a hint, as if any of us needed it, that this is a woman who you do not want to get on the wrong side of.

'Can I swim?' Barnaby asks.

'No, we don't have time to unpack and find your swim clothes,' Rosalind says, but Donovan peels off his jacket and T-shirt and looks ready to get in himself.

'I think we can take a dip,' he says. 'It does look very inviting.'

Suddenly stripping down to his boxer shorts, I admire the physique of the man who steps towards the water. Then, without wasting any time or even dipping so much as a toe in to acclimatise to the cold water, he jumps in off a couple of rocks.

Barnaby squeals in delight as his daddy emerges from the water, pulling off his clothes too and looking to join in the fun.

'Fine, you can get him dry again,' Rosalind says to her husband as he invites her in too.

'No chance,' she replies, and then she tells Philippa to get in the water as Barnaby is in there.

'I don't mind going in and helping out with him,' I say, not wanting the nanny to feel like she has to get undressed and get into the water if she doesn't want to; she looks like she appreciates the offer. 'I'm used to the cold water here,' I say as I take off my sweater and get to work on removing my jeans. Before I can, Rosalind steps towards me.

'I don't think it's very appropriate for you to undress in front of my son,' she tells me. 'Or my husband, for that matter.'

'Oh, erm. Sorry, I was just going to swim.'

'This is our holiday, not yours,' Rosalind says scathingly, and I guess she is right, though she could have put it a nicer way. Then she steps in closer to me and speaks again, ensuring only I can hear what she says next.

'And if you think one waterfall is going to cut it then think again. For what we're paying you, you'll need to do better than this.'

I'm crestfallen as I realise Rosalind does not think this waterfall is worthy of featuring in the trip I have planned for them. Even with her husband and son having a fun time splashing about in the water, it seems she is unhappy with me.

As Rosalind steps away and goes to stand near the water's edge, I think about rushing up behind her and pushing her in. It would be so satisfying to see her disappear beneath that water then pop back up with her expensive clothes soaking wet and her make-up all smudged. I bet Barnaby would find it funny, Philippa too. Even Donovan might stifle a giggle before going to his wife's aid. But I don't do that, standing back solemnly and watching as Rosalind tells Philippa to take a few photos of her family, as if she can't even be bothered to do that herself.

Then a very strange feeling comes over me.

I've never before felt like I could hurt somebody, not in a vicious, nasty way, anyway.

But I feel like I could hurt Rosalind.

More bizarrely, I almost feel like I will have to at some point during this trip.

I try to brush that very unsettling feeling off as I watch Donovan and Barnaby swimming, and by the time they've got out, I've mostly managed to return my focus to the rest of the trip. But as we're making our way back to the car, Barnaby asks if we can play a game of hide and seek.

'I'm not sure we have time for that,' Donovan says, looking at me and very politely seeming to be considering whatever itinerary I have planned. But there is room in it for a little playtime, so I smile and stop walking.

'Let's do it. Shall I count to ten and you go and hide?' I ask Barnaby, and the little boy looks thrilled before he dashes off into the trees on the hunt for a good hiding spot.

'Don't go too far!' Rosalind calls after him, though it's unlikely Barnaby is paying attention to her. He quickly vanishes from sight as I start counting out loud.

'Donovan, go and get him. This is silly,' I hear Rosalind say to her husband in between my numbers, but he tells her that it's just a bit of fun – and of course it is.

'Nine... ten! Ready or not, here I come!' I cry before heading for the treeline where Barnaby slipped through.

The foliage is denser than I thought as I tread over it, hearing twigs snapping beneath my feet and momentarily getting my ankle caught in a vine. I free myself before pausing and looking around. When I do, I see nothing but more greenery in all directions. Maybe it's going to be harder to find the little boy than I thought.

'I'll find you!' I call out as I start moving again, wondering if Barnaby will hear me and make some kind of sound that gives away his position. It could be a giggle, or it could be a nervous breath, but I don't hear anything.

I look up, wondering if he might have climbed a tree and be sitting on a branch staring down at me, but I don't see him there either. Then I check behind a couple of the larger tree trunks, presuming he's crouching behind one of those, but no luck there either.

'Where is he?' I hear Rosalind ask me. I turn around to see that she has joined me, closely followed by Donovan and Philippa.

'I haven't found him yet. He's picked a good hiding place, that's for sure,' I say breezily, to show that it's only a matter of time before I locate her son. But as I keep searching, I still can't find him. Rosalind starts to panic and call out to him, and I worry this game is taking a turn for the worse.

I'm hoping Barnaby is just going to come out of his hiding place and ease the tension that's building, but there's still no sign of him, and now Rosalind is getting really distressed.

'I told you this was a bad idea! What if he's fallen and twisted his ankle?' she says to Donovan. 'How the hell are we going to find him out here if he can't get back to us?'

'I'm sure he's fine,' I say.

'Oh, you're sure, are you? Well, that just fills me with confidence, thank you very much,' Rosalind snaps back and, for a brief second, I fantasise about grabbing one of these vines and wrapping it around her neck to strangle her. But Barnaby is the priority here. As Donovan and Philippa begin calling out for him, I realise the game is over and this is getting serious.

Where are you, Barnaby?

I'm worried for you now, though I'm worried for myself too.

What will Rosalind do to me if something bad has happened to her child?

TWELVE

SHANNON

'Barnaby!'

It's become a very familiar cry as the four of us desperately seek out the hiding child. But is he still hiding, or has he come to harm? I fear it may be the latter – if he was okay then he surely would have given up his hiding place by now.

So what has happened to him?

I dare not make eye contact with Rosalind as we keep hunting, traipsing over bushes and tree stumps as we look for any sign of Barnaby, for fear of her cutting me down with a withering look. But I eventually concede and glance at her and, when I do, I see nothing but concern etched on her face, making me feel terrible that I have contributed to her pain.

Why did I offer to play this game with Barnaby? We could have been back in the car by now and on the way to the next destination. Instead, what if something awful has happened?

Donovan is striding ahead of us, forging a path through the foliage and calling out louder than any of us, and I guess he's worried too, given how quickly he's moving. Philippa looks very troubled also, alternating between calling out and checking behind trees, a nervous energy about her that makes me feel even more of an outsider.

This is a close-knit unit, and I just might have messed it up.

And then we hear a voice returning our calls.

'Losers! I'm up here!'

We all stop and look up, following the sound of the call, and when we do, we see Barnaby sitting on a branch, his legs swinging below it as he grins widely.

'I win!' he says, clearly pleased with himself, and I'm pleased now too because I'm not going to be in trouble – at least not as much trouble anyway.

'Get down from there immediately!' Rosalind instructs him, and he quickly does so, dropping to the ground before rolling and leaping back up to show he is perfectly fine.

I breathe a massive sigh of relief as Rosalind checks her son and sees that he is fine. As we turn back to find our way to the car, I make a mental note to not enter into any more silly games during the rest of this trip.

Better to play it safe than have Rosalind hate me even more.

If I'm not careful, she'll end up strangling me with one of these vines rather than the other way around.

I am able to put aside all fantasies about hurting Rosalind and forge on with the next part of the trip, which features a visit to a country castle. Barnaby again thinks the experience is 'cool', clearly his buzz word, and both Donovan and Philippa seemed interested enough to wander around the castle walls for an hour and take a few photos. But once again, and very predictably at this stage, Rosalind seems bored, disinterested and occasionally rude, so much so that I am frustrated enough to want to do something about it. I am planning to have a word with her husband about his wife's behaviour towards me as soon as we get a moment alone, to see if there is anything I'm doing wrong or anything I might be able to change about my approach that could improve Rosalind's experience. I'd rather try that first before snapping at Rosalind if it continues, and I'm hoping that moment is going to come now as we go for a late lunch. The setting is a traditional Irish pub that all the online reviews say serves the best food in the country, as well as the best Guinness too, which is quite a bold claim in this part of the world.

'Wow, the food here looks great,' Donovan says as he hungrily eyes up what the diners at an adjacent table are tucking into.

'There's so much on the menu,' Philippa adds, speaking up for the first time in a while, but she is progressively becoming chattier, and I guess that means she is having a good time. But she is also having a busy time, because Barnaby is proving to be a bit of a handful. A moment later he drops the salt and pepper shakers he was just playing with on the floor, creating a loud noise that has everyone in the pub looking in our direction.

'What are you doing?' Rosalind snaps, but she's talking to her nanny, not her son.

'Sorry,' Philippa says before picking up the shakers from the floor, then telling Barnaby that he isn't to play with them anymore. Barnaby huffs, but I have an idea of how to keep him occupied until our food arrives.

'There's a play area in the back garden here,' I say. 'It's got swings and a slide. Do you want to go and see it?'

'Yeah!' Barnaby cries with his childish enthusiasm as he gets up from the table.

'I'm happy to take him while you all relax,' I suggest.

'No, Philippa can take him,' Rosalind says, and the nanny gets to work like the diligent, albeit downtrodden employee that she is.

As they leave the table, I bury my head in the menu rather than look at Rosalind, but then I have an idea. A woman as highly strung as Rosalind could do with something to relax her a little, and there is something I haven't tried yet.

'You guys have to have a pint of Guinness while you're here,' I exclaim. 'Shall I order?'

'Sounds good to me,' Donovan replies.

'Perfect. Rosalind?'

But she doesn't look as keen as her husband.

'It wouldn't be very sensible for both parents in charge of a child to be under the influence of alcohol, now would it?' she says to me.

'Oh, sorry. I just thought Philippa was looking after Barnaby so—'

'So what? I can just get drunk and not give a care in the world?' Rosalind snaps back. 'Sorry to tell you this, Shannon, but it doesn't work like that. Just because we have a nanny, it doesn't mean we can do whatever we want. Kids take up a lot of time and work. You'd know that if you were a mother yourself.'

That last sentence cuts me almost as much as if Rosalind had picked up one of the knives from the table and jabbed it through my skin. I have to bite my tongue to avoid going back at her with something that might be just as hurtful, like telling her she is a terrible mother, perhaps.

'I'm going to go to the toilet,' Rosalind says, getting up before I can retort. 'Just order me the salad when the waitress comes around, whenever that might be.'

Rosalind walks away, but my eyes are burning into the back of her the whole way until she disappears from view, and Donovan must see that because he tries to get my attention.

'Hey. I'm sorry about that. I really am. She doesn't mean it. She's not usually like this.'

'Not usually like this? She's been nothing but awful to me since I met her. I haven't seen one positive personality trait since I've been around her. She's just plain mean and I've had enough of it.'

I shake my head to show how exasperated I am.

'Woah, wait, calm down,' Donovan says, clearly upset at my distress. 'I'm sorry. I apologise on her behalf and I'm sure she'll apologise too if I ask her to. She's just—'

'What? Rude?'

I surprise myself that I just said that – it was very blunt of me – and I fear I've overstepped the mark. But Donovan doesn't seem surprised by my words at all, or offended, for that matter.

'No. She's just stressed.'

'Stressed? About what?' I ask. Growing in confidence in this interaction, I forge on, continuing to walk a very thin line between being honest and being offensive. 'She sits there and does nothing while her nanny runs around after her child for her. What does she have to be stressed about?'

'It's not easy looking after a troublesome little boy.'

I frown because that doesn't sound right to me.

'Barnaby's not troublesome,' I say. 'He's a little angel. But she treats him like he's a terror.'

Donovan can see how worked up I am about this and gives me a second to calm down.

'It's complicated,' he says, surprising me.

'What's complicated?'

'My wife's relationship with our child. My relationship with him is too.'

'What are you talking about?'

Donovan hesitates to answer before eventually doing so.

'Our son is adopted,' he confesses.

'Oh,' I say, pushed back on my heels a little because I genuinely didn't know.

'Yeah, so we have a bit of a difficult dynamic,' Donovan goes on. 'Or at least a different one.'

'When did you adopt him?' I ask.

'When he was very small. A baby. Newborn.'

'Oh, wow. Does he know?'

'That he's adopted? No, he doesn't. We'll tell him one day, but we haven't done it yet. Rosalind would prefer to wait for him to be a little bit older, so it'll hopefully be easier for him to understand.'

'Don't you think he might understand now? He seems quite grown up for his age. He's very smart.'

'Maybe. I don't know. As you might be able to imagine, it's quite worrying for me and my wife to think about doing it. I mean, how will he react? Will he still love us, or will he want to find his real parents?'

'Of course he'll still love you. You're all he has ever known.'

'I know.'

Donovan is in agreement but is still reluctant.

'I'm sure he won't love you any less,' I say, on account of how worried Donovan looks about this. 'But it is the right thing to do, to tell him.'

'Yeah,' Donovan says with a sigh. 'But that's the reason why my wife is so on edge. She knows that day is getting closer, and she's terrified of it. She's been terrified for years.'

I feel bad now; all this time I just thought Rosalind was nasty. I didn't know she had something serious on her mind, like telling her son that she's not his birthmother. That must be daunting. She doesn't have to take that out on me – it's not my fault – but it does explain her tetchiness.

'I'm sorry. I feel bad now,' I admit.

'It's not your fault. It's our issue, not yours. Just one of the consequences of the decision we made when we became adoptive parents.'

I have some questions and wonder if I should ask them or keep them to myself, but with everyone else still away from the table, I might never get another chance, so I go for it.

'Why did you adopt?' I ask, though the answer may be obvious.

'My wife can't have children,' Donovan replies swiftly. 'We

tried for years and nothing, so then we had all the tests done. Rosalind was devastated, to put it mildly. I thought we were going to break up. She actually told me to leave her, but I said that would never happen. Then we considered adoption. We actually adopted before Barnaby. We have a daughter, Esme. She's at a boarding school in Boston.'

'Oh, wow,' I say, surprised to learn they have another child who hasn't accompanied them on this trip, but I'm also feeling terrible because of how I've been thinking of Rosalind. It sounds like she's been through a lot, dealing with infertility and worrying about having a family, yet I didn't stop to consider that she had a past. I just judged her off the first twenty-four hours that I met her.

'I'm sorry,' I say, which feels like the only thing I can say. 'I feel terrible now.'

'It's okay. You weren't to know. I just thought I'd mention it, but it also doesn't give my wife an excuse to talk down to you. You're right, she has been a bit rude, so I'll have a word with her and ask her to be nicer.'

'Oh, God, no, don't do that! There's no need!' I say, terrified that Rosalind will know that I said something.

'It's fine. I'll do it in a way where she won't know you spoke to me about it.'

Donovan smiles to reassure me. But then I think of somebody else Rosalind has been rude to.

'What's the deal with the nanny?' I blurt out, unable to stop myself. 'I mean, she doesn't seem particularly happy, and Rosalind can be a bit harsh with her too.'

'Philippa's great,' Donovan says, batting the air. 'She's quiet, but we like that about her. She just gets on with the job. Again, my wife can be a little short with her, but even with a nanny it's still tricky having a young child around. Tempers can flare. I guess I'm just a little bit better at keeping mine under control than my wife. But she's not a bad person. Honestly.'

'Oh, I'm sure she's not,' I say, still feeling guilty about what I said. Before anyone else comes back to this table, I take the chance to ask a question I am curious about.

'With adoption, how did it work? I mean, did they match-make you with your children, or...?'

'It was quite a long and complicated process, and it was a long time ago,' he tells me as I see Rosalind re-emerging from the bathroom on the other side of the pub. 'But it was worth it.'

'Forgive me for saying this, but I have to point it out,' I say nervously. 'Your wife doesn't seem like the motherly type. I mean, if anything, it seems like Barnaby's presence annoys her more than it makes her happy.'

'She loves her children,' Donovan snaps back quickly. I go to apologise, but Donovan leans in towards me. 'Like I said, I'll have a word with my wife about how she's been with you. But there is something you can do to ensure she is happier around you going forward. You're doing a good job so far, but I think you can do better. My wife really wants to see remote, obscure parts of Ireland, and what we've seen so far hasn't quite fit the bill, hence why she might have been a little abrasive with you. We're paying a lot of money for this trip, as you know, so we want to get everything we hoped for and more.'

I hear Donovan's message loud and clear, both about his wife's past and the rest of this trip, just before Rosalind reaches us. I leave it at that, not just because we have company again but because it seems I have overstepped the mark a little by raising my doubts. I feel like I need to make up for this, so I get the attention of one of the bar staff and place an order for drinks, organising Donovan his Guinness and a soft drink for Rosalind. Then I decide to give this pair some privacy.

'How about I leave you to have a bit of peace?' I say, getting up. 'I'll go and find Philippa and Barnaby in the play area.'

I leave the couple and wonder if Donovan is going to take this opportunity to speak to his wife about her behaviour towards me. Possibly, but even if he doesn't, and even if nothing changes, I'll be a little more understanding of Rosalind in future, now that I'm aware she's had a few problems in the past and has reason to get stressed sometimes.

As I find Barnaby outside, playing in a ball pit with another child while Philippa stands nearby watching him, I wonder if the nanny knows the situation with the adoption. It doesn't really matter how this family unit was formed, all that does matter is that they love each other. It's funny, but as I watch Barnaby playing, I think about how his parents have all the money in the world and yet life has still presented them with obstacles.

I suppose that makes me feel a little better about my own life.

But only a little.

THIRTEEN

SHANNON

Taking on board what Donovan said about the need to really make our future tourist stops as obscure and remote as possible, I have frantically sent a few emails and changed a few plans. I did it all while the rest of the group were inside enjoying a hearty meal at the traditional Irish pub. I told them I wasn't particularly hungry and would leave them to enjoy some private time but, really, I was standing in the pub car park making new bookings. I'm hoping that what I've come up with now is really going to impress them all, especially Rosalind.

As we drive north to Donegal, the place I've decided to take us next, I am already seeing a difference in the American woman. She hasn't snapped at me once since lunch, nor has she ignored anything I've said either. She's been much more receptive to my attempts at conversation, and as I've chatted about various things a tour guide might muse on, from tales of Irish folklore to more modern points of interest – like where some of the most famous Irish celebrities have their mansions – she has even laughed a few times with me. I guess Donovan did speak to her, and he must have done it in a delicate way like he assured me he would, because there have been no problems since.

Donovan himself has been in good form too during this long car journey up the island, though I put that down to the fact that he indulged in three pints of Guinness at lunch, and the strong black ale has clearly gone to his head a little. It's nice because his extra energy and exuberance only helps lift the mood in the car more. Barnaby is his usual playful self, and he isn't being told to be quiet as often, while Philippa has even asked me a few questions about places we are travelling through, showing a keen interest in this part of the trip. All in all, things are going well and I'm confident they'll only get better, because when they see what I have in store for them next, it'll be impossible for them not to be blown away.

I have planned a trip to a secluded island where, as a group, we can take part in various activities in private, giving Rosalind and her husband exactly what they asked for when they employed my services.

Something different to what everybody else gets.

Before that, there is another hotel to check in to, and I'm just as excited for them to see this because it's much more to their tastes. I have been able to reserve some incredible rooms at a five-star hotel and, after a long drive, it's a relief when the luxurious accommodation comes into view.

Our car's tyres crunch over the gravel driveway as I look for a parking spot beside several other classy vehicles, and I spot a few residents of this hotel wandering around in the luscious green grounds, enjoying the sunny end to the day.

'This is beautiful,' Rosalind says from the back seat, and I smile to myself as I bring the car to a stop.

We all get out and, very quickly, there is a man in a uniform on hand to take our bags for us. It's a far cry from the last place we stayed at and, as Barnaby runs across one of the lawns in the direction of a water fountain, Donovan surveys the scene before saying two words that fill me with pride.

'Good job.'

The three of us head inside to check in at the grand reception, which is flanked by two large paintings of Irish royalty, while Philippa keeps watch over Barnaby, who is still playing outside. After we have got our rooms, ones that look incredible in the photos online, Rosalind turns to me.

'What do you plan to do now?' she asks me.

'I have a lot planned for tomorrow, so I'd recommend a relatively early night. But there is a wonderful restaurant here that you might wish to eat in. I've already reserved you all a table, but I can cancel it if you don't wish to use the reservation and would rather have room service. It's no problem.'

'Oh no, a restaurant sounds perfect,' Rosalind says. 'But what will you do?'

'I'll just relax in my room,' I say, very much looking forward to having some 'me time'.

'How would you feel about watching Barnaby for a little while?' Rosalind asks, surprising me.

'Me? Watch your son?'

'Yes, just for a couple of hours or so while my husband and I dine in the restaurant this evening. Would that be okay?'

I don't have any experience of looking after children, and am surprised she's asked me, but Rosalind seems serious.

'What about Philippa?' I ask, not wanting to make it too obvious that it's her job to watch Barnaby, but mentioning her because might she be a little offended if somebody else is tasked with the job she is paid to do. It would almost be like this couple suddenly hiring somebody else to be their tour guide while I'm still with them.

'We were thinking about giving Philippa a few hours off,' Donovan says. 'She deserves it with the amount of running around Barnaby has had her doing so far on this trip.'

'Oh, I see. Erm...' I stall, thinking it through. I am nervous about the thought of being left as a babysitter, even if it's only for a few hours, and even if the parents are still in the same building as us. But I also don't want to say no – it sounds like it might be the only opportunity the nanny gets to have a break herself.

'Of course,' I say, forcing a smile on my face to cover my lack of confidence.

'Great!' Rosalind cries. 'You won't have to do much. Barnaby is still a little jet-lagged, so I imagine he'll fall asleep pretty early. It's more just sitting nearby and watching over him until we get back.'

'No problem,' I say, hoping that it really won't be. 'I'll just speak to the receptionist and have them amend the booking for dinner to just two people. Seven o'clock okay?'

'Perfect,' Rosalind says and, after we make the arrangements for later, she suggests to her husband that they go and find their room.

I go to find mine too, and as I walk in and drop my luggage by the bed, I can hardly believe I'm staying in a place as glamorous as this. The huge bed has a thick duvet that I am already looking forward to crawling under, while the bathroom is sparkling, the porcelain gleaming and almost making me feel sorry to have to go in there and shower because I'll disturb it. Plush velvet curtains hang beside a window that offers a view of a courtyard beside sprawling lawns, and there is a huge flatscreen TV opposite the bed, just above an oak desk and a large armchair. If it wasn't for the fact that it was being paid for by somebody else, I'd never be able to afford it but, as it is, I'm a guest here along with all the wealthy people in the neighbouring rooms.

As I check out the expansive bathroom and eye up the large shower, I hear Barnaby out in the corridor, giggling and running past my room. Philippa tells him to slow down. He is a little whirlwind and soon I'll be the one responsible for looking after him. Was it wise of me to agree to babysit him? Surely it'll be fine. Like Rosalind says, he'll probably just sleep. If not, we can watch TV and chat. How hard can it be?

I hear two knocks on my hotel room door but already know who it will be as I go to answer it.

'Are you ready?'

I smile at Donovan before following him out into the corridor and closing my room door behind me.

'I think so,' I say, admiring the smart attire of the American man who is clearly dressed for dinner. I've freshened up myself by having a shower, and have just put some casual clothes on, items more suited to babysitting than dining in a fancy restaurant.

'You look nice,' I say to Donovan without thinking as I follow him down the corridor. I immediately feel embarrassed at dishing out such a compliment – it gives away too much of how I feel about him.

'Thank you,' he replies before I can apologise or add anything else, and then he tells me that Barnaby is in his room tonight so Philippa can have a quiet night alone in hers.

He opens a door and I enter a very loud and chaotic suite. Barnaby is not asleep, as Rosalind said he probably would be, and is jumping on the bed instead, a bed that is surrounded by piles of clothes and toys. The youngster has clearly made his mark on the room, and as Rosalind emerges from the bathroom, fiddling with a diamond earring and looking spectacular in a sparkly dress, I can see that she is ready to get out of here and go somewhere quieter.

'Calm down,' Donovan tells Barnaby, who does stop jumping on the bed, though it's clear he's still a long way off being calm enough to settle down to sleep. This might be more challenging than I thought, but there's no time to say anything as the couple rush for the door.

'Have fun! We'll just be downstairs if you need us, but I'm sure you'll manage,' Rosalind calls optimistically. Before I can reply, Rosalind and her husband are gone.

The hotel room falls silent and I look to Barnaby, who is lying on his parents' bed and looking back at me, almost as if he is intrigued as to what I plan to do now to keep him entertained.

'How about a movie?' I suggest.

'Yay!' Barnaby cries, clearly liking that idea, which I'm grateful for because I don't have any other ones. But I should have guessed I couldn't go wrong with TV.

I grab the remote and turn the television on, before taking a seat on the chair beside the bed. Barnaby is sprawled out, looking very comfortable.

I'm not sure what types of movies are suitable for a boy his age but, as I'm flicking through the channels, we find some kind of superhero action film, and Barnaby says, 'That one!' I stop scrolling and select the option he wants.

We sit quietly for a few moments while watching the action on screen, and I'm just thinking about how this is easy after all when Barnaby suddenly speaks.

'I don't want to go home,' he says quietly.

'Excuse me?'

'I like it here.'

'You mean in Ireland?'

'I mean away from our house.'

I frown. I'm not sure what he means by that. 'Your house? Don't you like it there?'

Barnaby shakes his head.

'Why not?' I ask, feeling a little confused. I'm imagining his parents own a huge home that is full of everything a child could ever wish for.

'I never get to see Mom and Dad,' Barnaby admits. 'Dad

works all the time, and Mom leaves me with Philippa. She's nice, but I like it here because I get to spend time with them too.'

What Barnaby has just said breaks my heart and I'm not sure how to respond to it. I'm definitely not qualified for this.

'I like you,' Barnaby says. 'You're really nice too.'

'Thank you,' I reply with a tear in my eye, because this really is the sweetest little boy in the world. But he's clearly unhappy about his life back home and, even though he's gone back to watching TV, I can still see that he's upset. Then he speaks again, and suddenly I'm troubled too.

'Be careful around Mom and Dad,' he tells me quietly, avoiding eye contact with me, which only makes what he has said more unsettling, as if he is genuinely nervous to look at me as he gives me the warning.

'What do you mean?'

'They're dangerous,' he goes on, still looking away.

'I'm sorry, I don't understand.' I laugh nervously. Barnaby must be joking. I'm guessing this is a prank; maybe he's not so sweet after all.

'It doesn't matter,' he says, but he doesn't laugh or do anything that would indicate it was a joke after all. So was he actually being serious?

'Sorry, what did you mean about your parents being danger-ous?' I ask again.

'I shouldn't have said anything,' Barnaby quickly replies. 'I might go to bed now.'

Barnaby gets up and walks away from the action movie to get into the small bed beside his parents' larger one. I guess I should make it quiet for him in here, so I turn the TV off and dim the lights, but just before he closes his eyes I try one more time.

'Barnaby, is everything okay?'

He takes a moment to think about it before shaking his head.

'What's wrong?' I ask.

'I'm worried.'

'About what?'

Barnaby shrugs.

'You're only seven. You're far too young to have any worries,' I say, trying to reassure him. I'm assuming he's got himself all worked up about something that is utterly inconsequential in reality. But then he frowns.

'I'm not seven, I'm eight,' he says, clearly correcting me.

It's my turn to frown now. Donovan told me his son's age at the airport, and it differs from what Barnaby is telling me.

'Are you sure?' I ask him, wondering if he's just playing a game.

'Yes. I was eight on the twenty-third of April, and I will be nine on my next birthday.'

Barnaby says it so matter-of-factly that he can't be lying, and then he says goodnight before closing his eyes. But I just keep staring at him as he falls asleep, the whole time wondering about two things.

Why would his parents lie to me about his age?

And why would their son warn me that they are dangerous?

FOURTEEN

ROSALIND

'This is just what we needed,' I say to my husband as I hold out my glass towards his.

'I'll drink to that,' Donovan replies as we clink glasses before both taking a sip of our red wines. By the time we put them back down again a waiter appears to take our order.

'I'll have the lobster,' I say, and Donovan makes one last check on the extensive menu and orders the fillet steak.

'Excellent choices,' the waiter says before scurrying away to put the chefs to work.

As I watch him go, I feel like we could be in any one of the trendy restaurants where we regularly dine in Boston rather than halfway across the world. The excellent food choices, the ambient atmosphere and the exquisite wine are all similar. If it wasn't for the strong accents of the staff here, I'd never know we were outside of America at all.

'So what do you think? Shannon has done well, right?' Donovan says as he sits back in his seat, his crisp shirt crinkling a little around his toned waist.

'Very impressive,' I say. 'I'm sure she's feeling very pleased with herself.'

'I wonder how she's getting on with Barnaby.'

'Hopefully he's not being too difficult for her,' I reply, though not caring too much if he is. She could have always said no to babysitting him this evening. Then again, I had a feeling she wouldn't do that. That's because she's subservient to us; it's pretty easy to get her to go along with anything we want her to, because we're paying her, which reminds me...

'I'll mention the beach tomorrow,' I say, as Donovan eagerly eyes up the steak that is being delivered to the plump man at the table next to us. 'I assume she'll arrange it for the day after. That will be the location where we carry out our plan.'

'Sounds perfect,' Donovan says, his eyes still on the juicy piece of meat that oozes a little blood when the man cuts into it. I wonder if my husband is purely watching that because of his hunger and anticipation of his own steak, or because the sight of a sharp knife slicing through red flesh is making him think about what he might do to Shannon very soon.

I let him have his little moment of fantasy or pleasure or whatever it is – he deserves it – and I'm happy for him to possibly be visualising killing our tour guide. I'd rather him than me. I want her dead as much as my husband does, but he can do the killing. Like everything in life, I like to delegate, and murder is no different. Besides, it's not as if he doesn't have experience, although in this case experience doesn't always make things easier.

'Are you having any second thoughts?' I ask him, and he turns away from watching the diner devouring the steak and looks back to me.

'None whatsoever,' he answers confidently. 'You?'

I shake my head. 'It's just that, after what we did before, you expressed a few regrets. I was wondering if you were thinking the same again.'

'That was different,' Donovan tells me, sensible enough to keep his voice low so that none of the other diners can hear what we're discussing. 'It was all new to us then. I was more nervous, more afraid of getting caught. Plus, I wasn't entirely sure we were doing the right thing by getting rid of those other people. But now enough time has passed, I see that it was the best thing we could have done, and once Shannon is dead, it's over. I'll never have to kill again.'

'That's right,' I say. 'We'll have nothing to worry about once this is over.'

I watch a few of the people around us eating and drinking before I speak again.

'Do you think it makes it easier, knowing we've done something like this before?' I ask.

'Rosalind, this isn't the time or the place,' Donovan replies, looking at our fellow diners.

'Which one has been your favourite so far?' I ask, which is a slightly bold question. I'd accept it if Donovan didn't feel like answering it. But the smirk on his face suggests he might like reminiscing over our past.

'Stop it,' he says, looking like he very much means it.

'Come on. Indulge me,' I say, continuing to probe, but my husband really isn't on the same wavelength as me.

'I think we should change the subject.'

'But what else could possibly be as fun to talk about?'

'We're not in the privacy of our room now.'

'No, we're not. We're in a lovely restaurant in Ireland, and we're only several hours away from doing what we've wished to do for a long time. So let's enjoy it.'

'I am enjoying it,' Donovan says, but he could do with telling his face that.

'I'm just trying to say that we make an excellent team, and there's so much more to come,' I add as the waiter returns to our table.

'More wine?' he asks.

'Yes, I think so,' Donovan replies before finishing his first glass with a hearty glug.

'Are you celebrating anything this evening?' the waiter wants to know.

'As a matter of fact, we are,' I reply. 'We're celebrating the fact that very soon, a dark cloud that has hung over us for a long time will be removed, and we won't have anything to worry about when it's gone.'

'I see,' the waiter replies, though there's no way he can possibly have any idea what I am really referring to. 'Is this a business deal or—'

'Oh no, it's very personal,' I reply, correcting him, happy to do so because it's okay for him to know that this is far bigger than just some work thing.

'I see. Well, let me go and fetch you that wine,' he says, hurrying away so he doesn't keep us any longer.

'Careful,' Donovan warns me. 'Let's not get too carried away and say something we might regret.'

'Oh, he's just the waiter. He doesn't understand what we're talking about,' I say, very confident of that. He's more likely to be worried about keeping his job than what other people are chatting about.

'I suppose.'

'Don't worry,' I say as I see the waiter coming back with a fresh bottle. 'Enjoy your wine and enjoy your meal, and we can enjoy whatever excursion Shannon has planned for us tomorrow. After that, she'll be dead, and we'll never get to experience this thrill again. There'll be no one else we need to kill after this. She's the last one who can hurt us.'

With that, Donovan and I vow to make the most of the rest of our evening, relaxed and content, while Shannon is upstairs in the hotel looking after our son, none the wiser about who we really are and the deadly threat we pose to her.

FIFTEEN

SHANNON

I stifle another yawn before the woman in the white uniform tells us that we are now allowed to board the ferry.

'Yay!' Barnaby cries as he moves forward, and Philippa sensibly has hold of his hand as she helps him step onto the boat that's taking us to the small island, just one and a half miles from the mainland.

Our destination is Owey Island, a mound of earth off the Donegal coast, an uninhabited place that is still accessible for tourists wishing to spend the day hiking and kayaking; and with lots of hills and caves to explore, there is plenty to do there. Rosalind and Donovan certainly seemed keen when I told them what the plan was after breakfast at the hotel, and Barnaby is more than a little excited too. I'm eager to get to the island myself. Even though I'm working, this should prove to be a fun experience for me as well. I've been here before, but it was a few years ago now, and the weather certainly wasn't as fine on that day as it is today.

'How long is this ferry ride?' Rosalind asks as we stand on deck and wait to set sail.

'Oh, it won't take long at all,' I say. 'Enjoy the view along the way.'

I know she will and, once the boat is in motion, I watch as Rosalind takes several photos of the sea and the land we are leaving behind, while Donovan leans on the rails and looks out across the water, and Barnaby keeps Philippa more than occupied running around on deck.

I plan on spending this boat journey having a sit down and a quiet moment to myself, not just because there's a busy day ahead but because I'm absolutely exhausted from a bad night's sleep. Rosalind and Donovan didn't come back to their room until almost midnight last night, meaning it was very late by the time I could leave Barnaby and go back to my own room. I felt it was bad that they stayed out so late when they knew we had a full schedule the following day, but didn't feel like I could really say anything. What was even more annoying was they didn't even apologise for doing so, seemingly totally oblivious to the fact that, while they had been in the restaurant having fun, I had been sitting with their son for several long hours. Barnaby had slept for most of that time, so it hadn't been too taxing, but it hadn't exactly been an evening off either, considering I was still the sole guardian for somebody else's child. What made it even harder for me was that I had been trying to process the things Barnaby had said to me before he went to sleep. Even as I had returned to my room just after midnight, leaving a very drunken Rosalind and Donovan to get into their bed, I still hadn't figured it all out.

I spent the whole night mulling it over, hence all my yawning today, but I still don't think I'm any nearer to knowing what Barnaby meant when he told me his parents were dangerous. I'm hoping that's just the ramblings of an overactive imagination. As for the fact that he says he is a year older than Donovan told me he was, that is weird, but maybe he's just trying to make himself seem more grown up. I know that's quite a common thing for kids to do, or at least I hear it is from people who have children of their own. Or what if Donovan slipped up when telling me his son's age? Maybe the father made a mistake. Plenty of men have been guilty of forgetting a birthday or confusing someone's age, so that could be the case here. Or Donovan might not be as close as he thinks he is with his child, and genuinely got his age wrong while thinking he was right.

But what if there's not an innocent explanation for those two things, and he was simply telling me the truth about both of them? I need answers, but I can hardly just ask Rosalind or Donovan, can I? That just leaves Philippa and, as I watch her playing with Barnaby on the deck, I decide to talk to her privately when the chance presents itself, which hopefully it will during the course of this busy day.

The journey over to Owey Island is simple and serene and the water we sail on is as clear as the sky above us. Once we reach the island, I tell everybody what we are doing first.

'We're going kayaking in the caves,' I say, which elicits excitement from the males in the group, but a little scepticism from Philippa, who says she's not a fan of going in the water so might sit this one out. I consider getting out of it myself, even though I'd love to be on the water, because it would be a perfect opportunity to talk to her about some of my concerns. But that's ruled out when Rosalind suggests that I share a kayak with her.

'You can come with me, Donovan will ride with Barnaby,' she says, aware that somebody has to go with the child to be safe.

'We could take our own kayaks,' I suggest, but Rosalind shakes her head.

'No, let's share one, just in case I struggle. I've never done this before.'

'Sounds like a plan,' says Donovan as we reach the hut where the kayaks can be hired out.

Once we have two, and once the four of us are wearing our

wetsuits and life jackets, we say goodbye to Philippa, who stays behind on shore but looks nervous about us going out.

'Be careful,' she tells us all, and I wonder if she is worried that something bad might happen to her employers and she'll be out of a job. But there's absolutely nothing to worry about – the water is very calm and the weather is perfect, so I don't envision any of us getting into difficulties, especially when there are two of us to a kayak, sharing the load; not that I need it. I've done plenty of kayaking in my time, and I tell the family about my trips with my father as a youngster as I set the pace and we leave the shore behind.

'This is awesome,' Barnaby cries as he uses his oars to cut through the water, though he's not driving the kayak on quite as much as his father is, sitting behind him.

As for my kayak, I seem to be doing most of the rowing, though I do try to encourage Rosalind to use her oars to more effect by giving her a few tips. But she's more of a hinderance than a help. I let her know that I'm happy to do most of it, otherwise we'll be spinning around in circles rather than moving forward at any great speed.

Our target is the group of sea caves just around the next curve of the island, and these caves are famous for the way the water inside them turns a wonderful turquoise colour at this time of year. I can't imagine how choppy the water here is in winter, or how bleak it is, but on a summer's day like this it looks like paradise. It'll only get better when we reach the caves.

It takes us a little while to get there, mainly because Donovan and I are slowed down by our companions, but as we enter the caves the sunlight dims, and our voices begin to echo off the walls around us.

'Hello!' Barnaby shouts as loud as he can, and we all hear his voice repeat back to us several times, which causes him great delight.

'Is this the kind of thing you had in mind?' I ask Rosalind as

I stop rowing. We sit bobbing on the water in our kayak in the centre of the gloomy cave.

'This is even better,' she says. 'Thank you for bringing us here.'

'No problem,' I reply as I watch Donovan steer his kayak towards one of the walls, before he and Barnaby touch the side of the cave.

'He's so grown up for a seven-year-old,' I say to Rosalind in reference to Barnaby, who is chattering away to his dad about how he learnt something about caves once at school.

'Yeah, he is,' is all that Rosalind says to that, not correcting me to say that he is eight, so she's either right herself or doubling down on the lie. I'll remember that when I speak to Philippa about this age thing later.

'How about we go over and check out the rocks too?' I suggest, and I'm just about to start rowing again when I feel the kayak lurch violently to the left. I don't know what just caused that disruption to our vessel. It must have been a rogue wave coming into the mouth of the cave. Before I can look around, the kayak lurches again, this time to the right, and suddenly I feel like I'm about to lose my balance and tip out.

I do my best to use one end of the oar to stabilise us, but then I hear Rosalind cry, 'Help!' And suddenly we tip over and I'm upside down under the water.

I quickly work to try and free my legs from the kayak so that I can swim to the surface, flip the kayak back over and help Rosalind get to the surface too. I feel her hand brush past mine before I see her face right in front of me in the murky water.

She looks scared and I assume she must be panicking, but we are wearing life jackets and we've only been in the water a few seconds, so I'm sure we'll be fine if we can just free ourselves from the kayak. But she's wriggling so damn much that it's increasingly difficult to get myself out. As the seconds go by, I begin to worry that we may be in trouble here.

I need to get to the surface so I can call to Donovan for help, so I grab Rosalind's hand and go to pull her up, aiming to propel us both out of the water.

But a strange thing happens when I take her hand.

While I'm trying to pull her up, *she seems to be trying to pull me down.*

SIXTEEN

SHANNON

I'm fighting as hard as I can to get back to the surface. Even though I'm a strong swimmer, I'm struggling – the woman keeping me under water is strong too.

What is Rosalind doing?

She's going to drown us both if she doesn't let go of me.

My fear is quickly turning into panic. I continue to thrash around in the water, failing to get a good look at Rosalind because of the bubbles everywhere. I can't believe that this is how it might end for me.

Here, in a cave, in an island off the coast.

So random. So unnecessary.

So planned?

Barnaby's warning about his parents being dangerous comes to me as I continue to struggle to hold my breath, my lungs burning with the desire to allow oxygen in, my brain fighting against opening my mouth – it knows I'll only be flooded with water.

Was this their plan? Take me somewhere quiet and drown me?

What have I got myself into, all for the sake of some money that I can't spend if I'm dead?

I'm almost at the point when I'm going to have to give up and breathe, even if it means certain drowning, when I feel an even stronger hand grab me, one that overpowers Rosalind and does something miraculous.

It pulls me up.

As my arm is yanked above my head, I kick my legs desperately and dare to believe that I might yet get to breathe in fresh air again. When I break through the surface of the water and see the roof of the cave above me, I'm flooded with endorphins because I'm going to live after all.

Gasping and choking, I suck in as much oxygen into my depleted lungs as I can, before turning to see what happened. When I do, I spot Donovan in the water alongside me; after seeing that I am okay, he lets go of me and goes to tend to his wife, who is also above the surface now and gasping for air just as much as I am.

He saved my life.

But why is he helping the woman who just tried to end it?

'What the hell were you doing?' I cry once I've got my breath back, aiming my anger at Rosalind, who is still very much in the process of getting her own breath back. She doesn't answer me, only coughing and spluttering, but that's not good enough. I want to know what she was doing when she almost drowned us both.

'You were holding me under the water!' I cry before I see Barnaby still sitting in his kayak, looking at the three of us in the water, a terrified look on his face. I feel bad for potentially frightening the boy, but my anger takes over any chance I have of calming down quickly.

'What? No, I wasn't!' Rosalind finally says in her defence, but it's a very weak one and I'm not buying it. I know what I felt.

'You were dragging me down! I couldn't breathe! I could have drowned!' I cry as Donovan and I tread water while Rosalind uses the overturned kayak for support. 'What the hell were you thinking?'

'Let's try and calm down. I know we've had a shock, but everyone's okay, so let's be grateful for that,' Donovan intervenes.

'Calm down? Your wife just tried to kill me!'

My words echo loudly around the cave, making them even more disturbing than they would be without the added effect.

'I didn't try to kill you! I was trying to get out of the water,' Rosalind insists.

'By pushing me down?'

'I wasn't pushing you down!'

It seems we're at an impasse, but we only stop shouting at each other when we hear another sound inside the cave.

Barnaby is crying.

The sound of his sobs, as well as the sight of him looking so distressed, disrupts the flow of my anger enough to stop shouting at Rosalind. I watch as Donovan rolls my kayak back over before helping his wife get back into it, using the rocks at the side of them to help.

Once Rosalind is safely back in the kayak, Donovan turns to me and offers his hand, clearly wanting to assist me too – but I don't take it.

'I'm not getting back in there with her,' I say, wanting to keep my distance between myself and that crazy woman who almost cost me my life.

'It's okay,' Donovan tries, but I shake my head and move over to the rocks. I rest against them with one arm, allowing myself the chance to regain a little energy.

Donovan realises I'm serious, so he swims over to me and then, with his back to his wife, he speaks quietly.

'My wife isn't a very strong swimmer and has been known

to panic in water before,' he says. 'I'm sorry. We should have mentioned it when we found out what you had planned for us today. It was silly and there was almost a serious accident, so it's my fault.'

I study his face to try and get a read if he is telling me the truth, but don't see any signs that he might be lying.

'She's panicked in water before?' I ask quietly, looking past him and at Rosalind, who is slumped forward in her kayak and still breathless. .

'Yeah, she had a childhood phobia of it. There was an incident in a pool when she was young back in Boston. She's mostly overcome it, for our children's sake more than anything, so that she's been able to take them swimming as they grew up, but she still does get scared in water from time to time. I guess when the kayak tipped over, she panicked, especially here, in this cave.'

Donovan looks incredibly honest, and the story is more than enough to give me pause for thought. As I look back at Rosalind, I don't see a woman with deadly intent in her heart. I see exactly what her husband has just hinted at to me: a woman who is confused and who probably shouldn't have put herself in this position based on her history with water.

'It just felt like she was pulling me down,' I say, and Donovan nods.

'She's done that to me before,' he says. 'We were on a family holiday in Florida once, swimming in the sea, and a big wave knocked her under. I went to help her, but she panicked and pulled me down. I don't know, it must be a reflex or something. She gets confused, doesn't know which way is up or down. I'm so, so sorry that it has happened to you. I feel terrible.'

I can see just how bad Donovan feels because he does look guilty and that, along with Rosalind looking so troubled and Barnaby looking so upset, makes me feel like I can't be mad anymore or I'll only be making this situation worse.

'How about I row back with my wife, and you go with Barnaby?' Donovan suggests now, giving me the option of not having to get back in the kayak with Rosalind.

That does sound okay, so I nod and he thanks me before swimming back to his wife. I swim to Barnaby and tell him that I'm getting in, and then the four of us are ready to get out of the cave.

It's a relief to see the blue sky when we do emerge out into the open again, and the more distance I put between myself and that cave, the more my breathing returns to normal and I convince myself that what happened in there was really just a misunderstanding and an accident. Of course Rosalind just panicked. Even for a strong swimmer, it must be pretty harrowing to suddenly find yourself underwater after your kayak tipped, and all in the dark surroundings of a cave. She got confused and distressed and I ended up the same, only adding to the hysteria. She wasn't intentionally trying to hurt me. Why would she do that in front of her son?

My mom and dad are dangerous.

I think about Barnaby's words though, and they've never felt truer after what just happened. Yet only Rosalind was a danger to me then. Donovan saved me, and the way he spoke to me afterwards showed how much concern he had for me. So why would Barnaby say both of them are dangerous when it might be that only one of them is?

I don't say a word as we row back to the point on the shore where Philippa is waiting for us, but I plan to say plenty to her when I get the chance.

That chance comes once we're back on land. After leaving the kayaks and taking a walk up one of the hills on the island, I manage to get a few moments with the nanny while Rosalind and Donovan walk ahead with their son.

'Hey, can I ask you something?' I say to Philippa, who seems unsure but nods as we keep walking. 'Does Barnaby tell a lot of lies?'

'I'm sorry?'

'I know he's a kid and some kids make things up all the time just to play games, which is fine, most of the time, anyway. But I was just wondering if Barnaby was like that. Does he make things up?'

'No, he doesn't,' Philippa says, surprisingly adamant. 'He's not like that.'

'Oh. Okay. It's just he said something to me last night.'

'What did he say?'

I glance ahead at the family again, making sure they are still out of earshot before continuing. 'He said that his parents are dangerous.'

Philippa doesn't say anything to that, nor does she really react, forcing me to check if she actually heard me.

'Did you hear me? He said they were dangerous,' I repeat. 'Why would he say that?'

'I don't know.'

'Are they?'

'What?'

'Dangerous.'

'No, of course not.'

Philippa seems sure of that, but I have to know why.

'How do you know? I mean, if Barnaby doesn't lie, why would he say such a thing?'

'You must have misunderstood him.'

'I didn't. He meant it.'

Philippa stops walking and looks ahead at the family as they carry on. I stop with her to hear what she has to say next.

'Do you really think I'd allow Barnaby to be around them if they were dangerous? Do you think I'd work with them and put myself in danger? Of course not. They can be harsh at times,

Rosalind especially, and they have so much money that they sometimes lose their sense of reality, but dangerous? No.'

Philippa carries on walking, and I have to scurry to catch up.

'Okay, then help me with one more thing. Donovan told me his son was seven, but Barnaby told me he was eight. Which is it?'

Philippa doesn't seem to take as much thought to answer this one.

'He's eight,' she says, going along with Barnaby's version.

'So why would Donovan lie to me about his age?' I ask.

'I have no idea. Maybe you misheard him.'

'No, I didn't,' I reply sternly, irritated that she suggest I have misunderstood something twice now when I haven't. 'He definitely said he was seven when I met them at the airport. It's just weird that he would lie, don't you think?'

Philippa sighs. It seems like she's getting annoyed with me. 'Look, you're getting paid to help them, just like I am. So just get on with it and make your money. Don't screw it up for yourself by overthinking and questioning the actions of a very rich couple who sometimes do very strange things. Do you know how many nannies there are out there who would kill to be in my position, getting paid what I get paid? I'm sure there are plenty of tour guides who wish they could be doing your job right now too. So just be grateful for it rather than ruining it.'

I stop walking as I process Philippa's words, but she keeps moving on, leaving me alone as she follows the family up the hill.

Maybe she is right. Maybe I should stop overthinking and just be glad I'm making a lot of money, like she is, working for this family. But now that I've got proof that Donovan definitely lied to me, I wonder what else he might have lied to me about. I also seem to have proof that Barnaby is not a liar himself; my life was just in danger with Rosalind, whether she intended it or not, which makes what he told me even more troubling.

If Barnaby is an honest little boy, and I have no reason to think he isn't, that makes his parents dangerous, just like he said. Perhaps Philippa has never seen anything to trouble her, so she isn't worried, but just because she hasn't seen anything, it doesn't mean it's false. Barnaby must know something about his parents that the nanny doesn't.

But what is it?

And what would happen to me if I found out?

SEVENTEEN

ROSALIND

I've had to wait all day to get the chance to talk to my husband in private. That's meant keeping my mouth shut when we rowed back in the kayaks, when we hiked up the hill and when we sat on the ferry back to the mainland. It also included the car journey back to our five-star hotel. That's a long time to have to wait to say something I'm desperate to say, but finally, after several hours, I have my chance. Philippa has taken Barnaby to get showered, and Shannon has gone back to her own room to freshen up, leaving me and my husband downstairs in the hotel bar.

Donovan looks like he's ready to order himself a glass of red wine and unwind.

But I have other ideas.

'What the hell were you thinking?' I say, glad there is no one else in the bar other than the bartender, but he's well out of earshot, polishing a few glasses across the room from us.

'Excuse me?' Donovan replies, looking confused.

'Saving Shannon like you did! I thought we wanted her dead,' I stress in hushed tones.

'What was I thinking? What were you thinking, trying to

kill her right in front of our son? And on an island where people had seen us get the ferry. Talk about stupid! How would we have gotten away with that?'

'It would have been a kayaking accident,' I say. 'Shannon tragically drowned when our kayak capsized, and we got into difficulty in the deep water in the cave. It could have worked.'

'It was far too risky! And Barnaby was there. He'd have been scarred for life if he'd seen a woman drown right in front of him, not to mention suspicious of the part his mother might have played.'

'He'd have been fine, he wouldn't have known what I did. Only we would have known, but it would have been over then.'

'No, it was stupid, and I can't believe you did it.'

'It was a chance to finish this sooner. Don't you want to go home?'

'Yes, of course I do, but I want my wife to come with me, not stay behind to languish in an Irish prison!'

The bartender looks in our direction – I guess our voices have become too loud, so I laugh to show that we are actually okay and not having an argument, before I remind Donovan to stay quiet.

'I was just acting on impulse,' I admit quietly. 'I saw an opportunity and I tried to take it.'

'Impulses are no good when it comes to getting away with what we intend to get away with,' Donovan lectures me. 'We need to stick to the plan, and that plan involves me being the one who sorts out Shannon, not you.'

I feel selfish, so I reach out for my husband's hand, but he pulls it back.

'It was stupid, and I can't believe I have to point that out to you,' Donovan snaps. 'I had to concoct a fictitious story about you having a phobia of water and almost drowning when you were younger, just so Shannon would calm down. Do you think that was fun for me?'

He shakes his head and tells me he's going to order a drink. As I watch him walk over to the bar, I'm wondering if he's so mad at me that he's only going to order one for himself, but he does return with two glasses of wine, so I guess we're okay. Once we have a sip, I decide to try and turn this into a positive thing.

'At least Shannon definitely trusts you now,' I say. 'The way you saved her and made sure she was okay. There's no way she's going to be wary around you now, and that's perfect.'

'I suppose you're going to pretend like this was all part of your masterplan,' Donovan replies with another shake of the head, and I laugh.

'Not quite, but you have to admit, it has done us a favour. This way, when we go to the beach tomorrow, she might be suspicious of me, but she won't be worrying about you. That's when you can strike.'

Donovan raises his glass and drinks to that, before reminding me that I have work to do yet.

'We need to talk to her about the beach thing,' he says. 'Maybe I should be the one to do it.'

'I'll do it,' I say quickly. 'I'm capable of that.'

'But she trusts me more, like you just said.'

'It's fine. I'll do it now. She's in Room 117, right?'

As Donovan confirms that is correct, I guzzle my wine. Using the boost of confidence it has given me, I go to leave the bar. 'Be right back,' I say breezily as I leave Donovan to enjoy his drink alone.

I take the lift to the right floor, then find Shannon's door before knocking on it twice. When it opens, I find her wearing a towel over her wet hair and another towel wrapped around her skinny torso. I guess she's just showered, and I bet she couldn't wait for it after spending several minutes thrashing around in that cave water earlier.

'Sorry to interrupt. I just wanted to apologise for what happened earlier,' I begin with.

Shannon seems surprised, both to see me at her door and to hear that I'm saying sorry.

'I panicked. I think my husband might have told you, but I've had a few bad experiences in water. When I went under, I didn't know which way was up. I just reached out and grabbed on to you, but I realise I might have been making things worse and I'm really sorry about that. I'm just glad my husband was there to help us both.'

I think of my drama teacher at school, the one who said I wasn't a very good actress. *If only she could see me acting now.*

'It's okay,' Shannon says once I've said my piece, which is big of her, I suppose, considering I almost drowned her.

'No, it's not. You must have been so afraid. I mean, I was afraid too, but I just made the whole thing scarier. I ruined the kayaking trip. It was great before that. Barnaby was having fun. We all were. I'm really sorry.'

'Seriously, it's fine,' Shannon says again. 'I'm just glad everyone's okay.'

'Thank you.'

I smile as earnestly as I can at the Irishwoman before I get to what I really came here to say.

'About tomorrow,' I begin with. 'It's actually an anniversary for me and Donovan, so I was thinking I might try and do something special for him.'

'Is it your wedding anniversary?'

'No, just the anniversary of one of our first dates, actually. He took me to a really secluded beach and we had a picnic, and it was amazing. I fell in love with him that day, and he says he fell in love with me then too.'

Shannon smiles, although she also looks a bit like she's wondering why I'm telling her all of this, so I get to the point.

'I was thinking of trying to replicate that date,' I say. 'I mean, going to a secluded beach and having a picnic, and I was wondering if you knew of a perfect place to do that?'

'A beach?'

'Yeah, preferably as private as possible, so we aren't sharing it with anybody. I'm thinking there must be a few secret beaches on this coast that a tour guide like you might know about.'

Shannon is thinking about it, but I decide to give her a little more motivation.

'Like I said, it's a special anniversary for us, so if you do find us a beach that we have totally to ourselves, I'm happy to pay you a bit extra on top of what we've already discussed.'

That financial incentive seems to give Shannon an extra boost.

'I'll have a think, but I'm sure I can come up with something,' she says confidently. 'Just leave it with me and I'll let you know.'

'Perfect, thank you,' I say as I back away from the door. 'I'll leave you to your evening. We're just going to get some room service and have a quiet one tonight. Are you staying in or going out?'

'Staying in.'

'Well, have a lovely evening,' I say generously. 'And once again, I am sorry for what happened earlier.'

I leave, walking away briskly. It takes a few seconds until I hear Shannon close her door behind me. But even before she does that, there's no way she could see what I'm doing as I leave her room and return to mine.

I am smiling widely.

Because this time tomorrow, Shannon will be dead.

EIGHTEEN

SHANNON

I was hoping to have a peaceful night, but I've ended up working after all. Rosalind's request that I find a private beach tomorrow for her and her husband to enjoy an anniversary picnic means I'm having to do some internet searches, instead of snuggling up on the bed and watching a little mindless television. I suppose I shouldn't grumble – I am being paid to give them a trip to remember, but it is late and, after what happened today, surely I deserve some time to switch off. At least Rosalind has apologised for the events in the cave. I suppose that's something, although quite whether an apology is enough to make up for almost drowning me is another thing. But I guess it took something for her to say what she did, especially if she was embarrassed or ashamed of her actions like she made out to be. *Unless she was pretending, and she wasn't really sorry at all.* I don't know; the more interactions I have with that woman, the harder I find her to read.

Pushing her from my mind for a moment, I look at the images of the beaches on my phone, the one the internet search engine has produced after I typed in 'remote beaches in Ireland'. That's a pretty basic search term, but it's given me some good results. Although when I click on the various photos and read more about the beaches in question, I fear they are not quite what Rosalind has in mind. She said she wants somewhere where nobody will go, totally unspoilt, so she and Donovan can have their picnic in peace without interruption from other beachgoers. That's a tall order, and potentially impossible – I can't control what other people do. If someone else decides to go to the same beach I take the American couple to at the same time, then that's not really my fault, is it?

But I have a feeling Rosalind would probably think it is.

What I need is a very small beach, a cove perhaps, rather than an actual long stretch of sand. Knowing how rugged the Irish coastline is, there are numerous little inlets, places that could be very private, although many of them are hard to get to. I hardly want Rosalind and Donovan to have to make their way down a cliff face to get some privacy. That would be far too dangerous and, after today's events, there's been enough danger for one trip.

There is one beach I can think of, a place I've been to before, but it's quite far from here, so it would be convenient if I could find somewhere closer, though that remains to be seen.

I keep searching, ignoring my rumbling stomach as I work. I was planning on going downstairs to see what the cheapest item on the restaurant menu was for my evening meal, but I've become waylaid by this task, and now I'm not sure when I'll get to it. I'm almost resigning myself to going hungry tonight when there is another knock on my hotel door.

I'm hoping it's not Rosalind returning to give me more work to do, or to try and guilt me into accepting another apology, but when I open it, I see that it's not her.

'Good evening, ma'am. I have your meal here. May I come in and serve it up?'

I frown at the sight of the porter in the pristine uniform, standing at my door beside a trolley with a hot plate on it.

'Sorry, I think you've got the wrong room. I haven't ordered room service.'

'Room 117?' he asks, and he glances at the number on my door to confirm that he is in the right place.

'Er, yeah. But I haven't ordered anything,' I repeat, starting to worry that I'm going to get charged for a very expensive meal that Rosalind and Donovan aren't going to allow me to expense.

'This meal is courtesy of the guests in Room 120,' the porter says. 'The Conways?'

'The Conways sent me this?' I double-check and, when I get confirmation, I guess there's only one thing to do.

'Please, come in,' I say as I step aside, and my meal is wheeled past me.

As the champagne cork is popped and a glass of fizzy bubbles is poured, I wonder why the couple would do such a thing for me. I'm licking my lips when the hot plate is lifted up and I see a succulent piece of steak beside a bed of roasted vegetables, along with a couple of bread rolls. With the champagne, this is going to be quite the meal.

'Thank you,' I say as the porter departs and I take a seat to tuck into my meal. But just before I do, I notice there is an envelope beside the plate, and I open it to find a handwritten note inside.

Thank you for saving my wife in the water earlier. And thank you for all your excellent work during this trip so far. You're doing a great job. Thank you and keep up the good work! Donovan.

Wow, so this wasn't from both of them – it's just from Donovan.

I wonder if Rosalind knows about this?

It's a lovely gesture from him, and I will make sure to thank him when I see him in the morning. I can't believe he would order this for me. I guess I'm not going to go hungry after all. After scoffing down one of the bread rolls, I cut into the steak and sample a slice of the perfectly cooked meat. This dinner is exquisite, and the champagne isn't bad either. I dread to think how much this costs to have delivered to a room, but I remind myself that money is no object for Donovan, so I'm sure it's barely made a dent in his sizeable bank balance.

I savour every forkful of my meal before I finish and lie back on the bed, a glass of champagne in hand and a very satisfied smile on my face. Donovan is such a great guy, I think, and maybe it's the feeling of a full stomach or the alcohol has gone to my head a little, but I allow myself to fantasise about what it would be like if I was his wife. I would be accustomed to this kind of dining every night, I imagine, as well as more than used to staying in fancy hotels like this one. How amazing must it be to have all the money in the world. Everything opens up to you, price is no object, you get what you want, not what you can afford. It's a dreamy way of living, but it doesn't take long for the material aspects of the lifestyle to fade, and I start to think about something more meaningful.

Like what it would actually be like to be with Donovan.

Intimately.

I close my eyes and see his chiselled face before me, as well as his athletic body. I remember how strong his arms were when he pulled me up from the water, and it's easy to recall how good he looked in that wetsuit. Forget the money, I'd be happy to be with Donovan even if he was dirt poor.

I think about him writing the note that accompanied my meal tonight, how his mind would have been on me and not his wife as he composed it, and that is a very exciting thought. It's almost as if he was putting me above her, if only for the time it would have taken him to write what he did. But still, that shows I am on his mind sometimes. Does he think about me in other ways too?

Like the ways I'm thinking of him now?

I wonder if Donovan is attracted to me, and even though I know nothing can ever happen between the pair of us, it is something I'd love to know the answer to. It's not like me to think in this way – I never thought I'd be the kind of person to have an affair, but I'm pondering it, all the same.

Has he secretly been checking me out when we've been together and I've been looking the other way? Did he admire me in my wetsuit as much as I admired him in his? I wonder if it was Rosalind who found me online or whether he did... Was he drawn to the photo on my employer's website?

I'm so lost in my daydream that I almost allow the glass to slip from my hand and spill champagne onto the bed, but I correct its balance at the last minute. Then I get up and tell myself to stop being silly. Deciding that the best way to forget about Donovan and what he has done for me tonight is to remove the trolley with the plate and champagne bottle on it, I wheel it out into the corridor for housekeeping to clear away when they pass. Then I go back into my room and start getting ready for bed, though as I do, one thought is strongest in my mind.

It was nice of Donovan to send me that meal tonight.

But I'd have much rather he turned up at my door himself.

Now that would have been even more appetising.

NINETEEN

SHANNON

After many hours of searching online, I gave up looking for the perfect beach for Rosalind and accepted that I already knew of a place. It's got everything she asked for – it's picturesque, it's remote and there is a very good chance she and Donovan could have the beach to themselves. It's quite off the beaten track.

There is just one small problem: the fact that it's on the other side of Ireland to where we are. I'm going to have to delicately explain that to Rosalind, and see if she doesn't mind going there tomorrow instead of today.

I'm aware that she wanted to go to the beach today, as it's her anniversary, but it's just too much of a drive to get them there in good time for her to have any kind of a picnic with her husband. The best I can do is drive us most of the way during the course of today, stopping off to see a few sights, and then after one more night in a hotel she can have the beach day tomorrow.

I'm just about to suggest that to Rosalind, although I'm quite nervous about it. I guess I'm worried she'll say tomorrow is no good and it has to be today or I've let her down. Or *maybe it's because I spent most of last night lying on my bed fantasising about her gorgeous husband.*

Thankfully, Rosalind cannot read my mind, or at least I assume that's one superpower she doesn't possess. She does, however, possess the power to cut somebody down with one withering look, which is why I brace myself to receive one of those as I give her the news.

'I've found a great beach, but it's a bit of a drive away,' I tell her. 'There are some closer ones, but they aren't as private. So we can either do a different beach today, or would you like to wait and go to the private beach tomorrow?'

As I feared, Rosalind's expression darkens, and I brace myself for a telling off about how I should have done better. I'm glad Donovan isn't here to witness what might be about to be said – I don't want him pitying me, or worse, feeling like I'm inept. But he's finishing breakfast with Barnaby and Philippa, so it's just me and his wife.

'This is disappointing,' Rosalind says quietly, looking right through me. 'I really hoped it would be today.'

'I know. I'm sorry, but I've tried to do what you asked and find the perfect beach, one where nobody will interrupt you. I think I have that, it's just quite far away. But we can do it tomorrow?'

'Tomorrow is not our anniversary.'

'You're right. I'm sorry. We'll go to a different beach.'

'No, it has to be somewhere private. If we have to wait for tomorrow, then so be it.'

Rosalind tells me to be ready at the car in ten minutes and then heads for the staircase, where her family quickly joins her to go and get their things out of their room and check out.

I guess that could have gone worse. Rosalind is clearly annoyed, but she didn't shout at me, so I suppose that's a win. I go to check myself out as well, but I see Philippa by herself and take the opportunity to have another private chat with her.

'Good morning!' I say breezily. 'How did you sleep?'

'Fine,' Philippa says, but she looks tired, so it must be a lie. I wonder how many days off this woman actually gets. One a week? Not even that? Surely no amount of money is worth working this hard and having no life. She mustn't have time for anything or anyone outside of this family.

'So, how long have you worked for the Conways?' I ask, genuinely curious.

'Almost five years now.'

'So they hired you when Barnaby was small?'

'Yeah.'

'Have you spent much time with their daughter? What was her name again?'

'Esme. Yes, for the first couple of years. But she's at private school now, so she's around a lot less.'

'That must be hard. For everybody, I imagine. I mean, how often do they get to see each other?'

'Why are you asking all these questions?' Philippa asks, her eyebrows furrowed sceptically, her mind trying to get a better read on me; I'm caught off-guard by the nanny's enquiry.

'Oh, no reason. Just chatting.'

'The Conways are quite private people. They don't need their affairs being discussed when they aren't present.'

'No, I wasn't trying to pry. I was just making conversation.'

'I know you're judging them. Thinking what kind of parents would send their eldest daughter away to boarding school and have their youngest raised by a nanny. You're not the first to make the assumption that they're bad parents. But they do provide for their children, far more than many other parents do. Many parents would love to give their children the opportunities Barnaby and Esme have, but they can't.'

'I wasn't saying they weren't good parents. I'm sorry. I think you've got the wrong idea.'

'No, I think you need to stick to your job. You're here as a tour guide. That's it.'

Philippa smiles at something past me, and I turn around to see Barnaby running down the stairs, followed by his parents and a porter carrying their luggage.

I wish I didn't have to leave it there with Philippa. I feel like that wasn't the best way to end our conversation, with her misreading me, but I can't say anything more about it now, so I have no choice. As we all head to the car, I decide to be on my guard around the nanny more now, as much as Rosalind, because she's clearly a little unpredictable too. The last thing I need is saying something to Philippa that ends up getting reported back to Rosalind, especially now we're getting towards the end of the trip. But as we get into the car and I start driving, I glance at the nanny in the back seat and wonder if she might have become sort of institutionalised by this family. I don't think they treat her particularly well, and they clearly work her far too hard, but she seems to defend them. It's like she's so blindly loyal to them, or so committed to whatever money they are paying her, that she fails to see how Rosalind is clearly not a nice woman. Working for someone like her for so many years has to have had some kind of effect.

But it's not my problem, I suppose. A couple more days and they'll all be flying back to America, while I'll be back in Dublin counting all my extra money.

Bring it on.

As I navigate us across the country, gradually bringing us closer to the beach we plan to visit tomorrow, I make sure to treat my passengers to several cool sights along the way. These include a glimpse of Carrauntoohil, the tallest peak in Ireland, as well as a walk in Killarney National Park. As we reach our next hotel, this one only twenty miles from the beach, I feel like it's been a successful day, and now I'm one day closer to getting paid.

We go inside to check in, but as Rosalind deals with the receptionist and Philippa watches Barnaby, I notice Donovan checking out a display in a glass case across the lobby. I go over to him; there's something I've wanted to say to him all day that I haven't had the chance to yet. As I join him, I see what he's looking at. There is an array of old Celtic weaponry on display here, ranging from swords and shields to arrows and spears, and Donovan seems intrigued by it all, so I take the opportunity to impress him with some of my knowledge.

'These arrows are just like the ones used in the Battle of Belahoe,' I say, and Donovan raises his eyebrows.

'Wow, you Irish sure knew how to put up a fight,' he chuckles.

'I've actually got one of those spears at home,' I say, pointing to a colourful Celtic spear behind the glass. 'It's a little smaller than that one, but does the same kind of thing.'

'You mean it impales English invaders?'

I laugh. 'Or ex-boyfriends. Whichever I need it for the most.'

Donovan laughs and then asks me a personal question. 'Do you have many ex-boyfriends?'

'Erm,' I stall, unsure how personal to get with this man. But he's been personal with me before, so I guess I can talk freely. 'I have an ex, but I'd rather not talk about him. So you could say that my love life is hardly a success story.'

'Why is that?' he asks, prying further. 'I mean, forgive me for saying it, but you're an attractive woman and clearly very funny and smart. I'd have thought the guys in Dublin would have been queuing up to get with you.'

I'm flattered by Donovan's description of me, as well as the assumption that there is a long line of men back in my city waiting to date me. But that is not quite the case, although I feel like I maybe shouldn't make that too obvious, in case it changes his mind.

'Thank you,' is all I say, acknowledging his compliment before I have another reason to be grateful to him. 'And thank you for the meal you sent to my room last night. I got your note. That was really kind.'

'No trouble at all,' Donovan says, turning away from the case and glancing back at his wife, who is still busy talking to the receptionist. 'Did you mention it to Rosalind?'

'No. Why? I wasn't sure if I should.'

'Good. She doesn't know I sent you a meal.'

'Oh, okay.'

That's interesting.

'It's not that she'd disapprove or anything,' Donovan quickly says. 'She's just a little different to me. No offence, but she'll see you as an employee just doing the job you're paid to do. But I'm not quite as cold as that. I know you're just a normal person like everybody else, trying to do your best.'

'Well, thank you again. It was a great dinner, and the champagne was lovely, although I probably shouldn't have had so much. I've had a bit of a headache today.'

'Sounds like you needed somebody to share that champagne with,' Donovan says, looking at me and smiling suggestively. 'Shame I was kept busy with my wife, or I'd have been happy to accompany that meal to your room.'

I try to figure out if what Donovan just said was a joke, or if he really was just hinting heavily that he wanted to visit me in my hotel room last night. But then he clarifies it for me.

'Sorry, I don't mean any disrespect. It's just, Rosalind and I have been having a few problems, and this trip has brought a few of them to the surface.'

'Oh, I'm sorry to hear that,' I say, surprised that all is not well in paradise.

'Don't be. You have nothing to be sorry about. Like I said in my note last night, you've been great. It's me. I've just got a lot on my mind right now.'

I don't really know what to say, but I can see that Donovan is a little troubled. I want to come up with something that will make him feel better. Before I can do that, he surprises me again.

'Rosalind has been having some early nights on this trip. She sleeps a lot more than I do, which means I tend to get bored in the evenings. Maybe you and I should meet up when she's asleep tonight?'

I'm stunned at the suggestion. *He wants to meet me while his wife is asleep?*

'What, for like a drink or something?' I say nervously. 'In the bar?'

'A drink, sure. But not in the bar. How about I order room service again, and we can share that bottle of champagne together. Sound good?'

It sounds like a lot of things.

Shocking. Risky. Dangerous. Tempting.

I would normally say no in such a situation, but I find myself seriously tempted. Maybe it's his good looks, or maybe it's because Rosalind has been so mean to me.

I say yes.

That doesn't mean I don't feel guilty when we go back to the reception desk, smiling at Rosalind, like we didn't just make a plan behind her back.

TWENTY

SHANNON

I entered my hotel room half an hour ago, but I haven't unpacked yet, nor have I even so much as sat down. Instead, I've been pacing up and down the stretch of carpet between the door and the window, going over what Donovan and I agreed to, thinking about what might end up happening if he does come into my room to share some champagne with me later.

Maybe it is just an innocent drink between two people on a trip together. He might just want to chat about Ireland and some of the things we've done during the tour. Or maybe I need to stop being so naïve and realise it is exactly what it feels like – a married man coming to get drunk with a woman who is not his wife in a private hotel room, where surely only one thing can end up happening.

I stop pacing and realise I can't let Donovan come in here later. It wouldn't be fair to Rosalind. It also wouldn't be fair on me. I shouldn't be put in such a position where I could end up feeling guilty. I'm just here to do a job, not get involved in somebody else's relationship and potentially make things worse for them. What if Donovan and I did take things too far and Rosalind found out? I can't even begin to imagine the fury that would be unleashed. Imagine if I was the catalyst for a divorce between two of the wealthiest people in Boston. It might make the news in America, or at least the social media gossipy type news. I don't want to be dragged into that. Then there's Barnaby to consider. I can't be the person to potentially break up his parents' marriage, nor could I feel good even if we got away with it; I'd just feel bad every time I looked at that boy and thought about what I'd done.

I should have nipped this in the bud right away and made it clear to Donovan that it wouldn't be a good idea to see him so privately, certainly not with alcohol involved. Then I suddenly get the fear that this was some kind of a test. What if Rosalind actually knows about this and she wants to see if I would dare try anything with her man? I could be being lured into a trap for their own entertainment, and if I do get caught in it, they might suddenly say that I'm not entitled to the rest of the money they owe me, making this entire trip a waste of time.

One thing is for sure.

I can't let Donovan in this room when he knocks on my door later.

I finally stop pacing and decide to take a shower, as if that might be able to wash away some of the guilt I'm already feeling, simply for not shooting down Donovan's suggestion earlier. As I wash, I can only imagine the guilt I'd be feeling if I slept with him – that would be much harder to scrub off.

This is a nice hotel, but I don't think the soap here is that powerful.

I'm not feeling much better even after my shower, and I begin to realise it's not just because I'm still anxious about Donovan coming here later. It's frustration emanating from every pore of my body as, not for the first time in my life, I seem to have attracted the wrong man.

On the face of it, attracting a guy like Donovan seems amazing. He's handsome, rich, kind and funny. What more could a girl ask for? But he's married, which ruins everything, and once again means there's a catch. Why am I always destined to be unlucky in love?

It's easy to blame myself but I never asked for any of this. I didn't ask for any of the men in my past to turn out to be such trouble, especially not the one man I got closest to, who ended up hurting me to the point where I've barely dated another guy since. I certainly didn't ask for Donovan to start hitting on me while his wife's back was turned.

It's their fault, not mine. I should just rise above them and do what's right, leaving them to do what's wrong.

So if that's what I'm thinking, why am I applying lipstick right now?

After getting out of the shower, I told myself I was just going to put my pyjamas on, leave my hair wet and scraggly and not even touch my make-up. That way I would be looking as unappealing as possible when Donovan called by later, hopefully quelling whatever lustful fire might have been burning inside of him. Yet here I am, wearing a low-cut blouse and tight jeans and, once I'm done with the lipstick, I'll apply some mascara too. Then I'll get to work on my hair.

Damn it, Shannon, you really don't help yourself sometimes.

It takes me a while to beautify myself but, once I'm done, I'm looking radiant and in far sexier shape than any of the other times Donovan has seen me. I expect him to be wowed when I open the door to him shortly, and I'll be disappointed if he isn't.

I tell myself that it's not my problem that he and Rosalind have marriage issues, and if they are doomed to break up eventually then whatever happens tonight won't be the catalyst for it. I also tell myself that whatever happens is going to stay in this room anyway, so there's no way Rosalind or anybody else in this hotel finds out about it. Then I tell myself that I should possibly call down to reception and order the champagne ahead of Donovan getting here, because that way I can have a pre-drink before his arrival and take the edge off the nerves I'm feeling.

I do just that, convincing myself that I can afford one expensive bottle of bubbly with what I'm making this week. As I wait for it to be delivered I add a couple of earrings to really complete my look. The man who delivers the champagne checks me out as he hands it over to me, no doubt thinking he is being discreet, but I catch him eyeing me up and down and possibly wondering which lucky guy is going to be sharing this bottle with me tonight. But he can't know who it is, nobody can, so I decline his offer to pour me a glass and thank him before quickly closing the door and popping the cork myself.

As I'd hoped, the taste of the fizzy bubbles goes some way to calming my anxiety, and I'm feeling much more confident after the first glass, though not quite confident enough to stop there. Sipping my second drink, I check the time and see that it is approaching nine. I wonder what time Rosalind falls asleep. Donovan said she usually goes to bed early, so I guess it could be anytime now. I'll just have to wait, so I kill some time by sitting on the edge of my bed and scrolling through multiple television channels, looking for something to distract me. But nothing works, and I'm back at the champagne bottle before I know it, pouring myself a third glass. I check the time. It's twenty to ten now.

It's getting a little late.

Is Donovan still coming?

Sure he is, he was certainly eager downstairs earlier, so I can't see what might have put him off. Unless Rosalind is still awake. He can't sneak out of their room if she is. What if she doesn't go to bed early tonight? Donovan won't be able to call by, and I'll just be left here all dressed up and drinking alone. My anxiety is quickly replaced by disappointment, and as the clock moves past ten, I'm starting to fear that I've got my hopes up for nothing. I'm certainly resigned to my fate by half ten and, as eleven o'clock comes around, I pour the last of the champagne down the sink before removing my earrings and looking at my pathetic reflection in the mirror, telling myself that I've been a fool and have got what I deserved for daring to seduce a married man.

And then I hear a knock at the door.

I freeze when I hear it and stay still until I hear a second knock, confirming that yes, there really is somebody at my door.

Approaching it cautiously, I wonder if I should put my earrings back on, but Donovan won't care about a little detail like that. He'll just be glad he's been able to get here, better late than never, and as I turn the door handle I'm glad too.

Then the smile fades from my face.

That's because it's not Donovan standing out in the corridor.

It's Rosalind.

When she sees me, she looks me up and down before asking me a very simple question.

'Were you expecting somebody else?'

TWENTY-ONE

ROSALIND

'No, I'm just surprised as it's late,' Shannon replies to my question, looking incredibly awkward. And that's not the only thing I notice about her appearance. I see the outfit she is wearing, as well as the fact her hair and make-up are immaculate, and it's a far cry from how she's looked for the majority of this trip. Her incredible grooming allows me to ask my next question.

'Have you been out this evening?'

'Me? Erm, no,' she replies, before surely realising that if she hasn't it makes no sense for her to be so dressed up. 'Well, I mean, I did go out for a little while. Just to the hotel restaurant.'

'Wow, you made all this effort for the hotel restaurant,' I say with a smirk. 'Was it worth it?'

'It was okay,' Shannon replies, and I'm enjoying watching her squirm, clearly unaware that I know exactly why she was dressing to impress tonight, and it had nothing to do with any restaurant, that's for sure.

'It's funny, because I was eating in the restaurant earlier and I didn't see you down there,' I say, stringing out her discomfort a little longer.

'Oh, we must have missed each other. I ate quite late,' Shannon replies, and I pretend that sounds like the truth to me before I finally show some mercy and move on.

'Can I come in?'

Shannon looks as if the last thing she wants to do is allow me into her room, but I add the word 'please' and she reluctantly steps aside.

I enter her room and immediately note the empty bottle of champagne, as well as the two glasses by the bed, though only one of them looks to have been used. I could ask about those things and see what Shannon has to say for herself, but I don't, preferring instead to ask a different question – and it's one that is far more direct.

No sooner has Shannon closed the hotel room door behind me than I fire it at her.

'Has my husband tried it on with you?'

I watch the colour drain from the face of my tour guide.

'I'm sorry, what?'

'Donovan. Has he tried anything with you? I'm talking about more than flirting, which I'm sure he's done plenty of, but that's hardly the biggest crime in the world. I'm talking about actually propositioning you or touching you or doing anything at all that makes it clear that he wants to sleep with you?'

There is no sign of the blood returning to Shannon's pale face, nor are there any signs of this woman beginning to tell the truth with me.

'No, not at all!' she replies, far too quickly to be believable.

'Are you sure about that?'

'Yes!'

That was another chance for Shannon to tell the truth, but she's skipped right past it and now the chance has gone.

'I see,' I say, taking a seat on the edge of her bed before lowering my head and shaking it. 'I'm sorry for having to ask. It's just, I've been worried. My husband is the adulterous type, and if he had tried anything with you, it wouldn't be the first time he's done something behind my back with another woman that he shouldn't have.'

I keep my head down and wait for Shannon's sympathy to start; it doesn't take long. She still keeps a little distance from me, standing rather than sitting next to me, but when I hear her speak again I get the sense that she is less worried about herself and more concerned about me.

'I'm sorry. I had no idea,' she tells me. 'I don't know what to say.'

'You don't have to say anything. It's not your problem, it's mine. I'm the one who married him. And I'm the one who's stuck with him. It's a relief to know he hasn't tried anything with you. I'd have expected him to have done something by now. I mean, all this time in the company of a woman as attractive as you. I know he would have thought about it, at least.'

'Nothing has happened,' Shannon firmly tells me.

'Thank you,' I say, before I pat the bed beside me, inviting her to sit down.

She does so more out of politeness than of any real desire, but once she is seated I can roll into the next part of my pre-planned speech.

'Do you think I'm a bad mother?' I ask, looking at the Irishwoman with what I hope is fear etched across my face.

'What? No, of course not!' Shannon replies even faster, sounding even more fake than her last answer.

'You don't have to lie. I know I'm not a great mother. Nobody's perfect at raising children, but I'm terrible at it, I really am...'

'Don't be so hard on yourself.'

'I'm not, I'm just being honest,' I go on, having to hold in a laugh at the idea that I would ever be honest in the presence of this woman. 'It's just so hard. Has Donovan told you that our children are adopted?'

Shannon hesitates for a moment and then nods.

'That's okay, I don't mind him telling you. There's no need for it to be a big secret. It's not easy, though it's not an excuse.'

'I'm sure you love your son and daughter just as much as if they were your own,' Shannon says, before it dawns on her what she's just said and how it could be misconstrued. She panics. 'I mean they are your own! I'm sorry, I didn't mean to make out like they weren't. I was just trying to—'

'You were just trying to make me feel better. I can see that, and I appreciate it. There's really no need for you to be so nice to me. Heaven knows I don't deserve your kindness, not with the way I've spoken to you for the majority of this trip. I've been rude and abrasive, and you must think I'm a right bitch.'

'No, not at all.'

I laugh and tell Shannon I know that's a lie, and she ends up laughing too when she realises she has been called out on it.

'Okay, there might have been a couple of moments when I thought you were a bit mean,' she confesses, and I smile to show I don't mind hearing that. 'But you're not a bad person, and you're certainly not a bad mother.'

'I guess I just worry about the future,' I go on. 'About what Esme and Barnaby will do when they find out I'm not their real mom. If they'll still love me the same or if they will want to find their biological mother and leave me behind. If all these years have been a waste and I'll end up alone.'

'That won't happen. Your children love you,' Shannon tells me.

'You can't predict the future. No one can. Anything can happen down the line and it might not be good.'

Shannon isn't sure what to say to that, so I go on.

'I guess it's why I lean on the nanny so much. I do feel bad for having Philippa do so many things, but I guess it's a defence mechanism. Having her around stops me from getting too close to Barnaby. I guess I'm afraid of being the best mother I can be to him, because deep down I know I might not be the mother he ultimately chooses when he's older. It's my way of trying to prevent a broken heart, I suppose.'

'You can't think like that,' Shannon replies. 'All you can do is try your best, and I'm sure that will be enough.'

I shrug my shoulders before suggesting something that might be a little controversial.

'I suppose I could just not tell my kids that they're adopted,' I say. 'I mean, if they never know, then they can't ever resent me or leave me or go searching for something else. Would that be so bad?'

Shannon seems conflicted by what answer to give, judging by the expression on her face and the time she takes to respond.

'You're right. I can't do that. They deserve to know one day,' I answer for her, filling the silence.

'I was going to say that I'm not sure what is best,' Shannon says now. 'It's difficult. For both the parents and the children.'

'It sure is. I do know one thing though, Shannon. You'll make an excellent mother yourself one day. You have compassion for others, even if they haven't always treated you well in the past, and that's a skill you'll need when you have kids.'

I stare at Shannon and my next question feels like an obvious one in that moment.

'Would you like kids one day?'

Shannon looks uncomfortable, so I carry on.

'Sorry, very personal question, and you might not even know the answer to it yet. Besides, you might be thinking about finding love first. Finding a good man, or woman, hell, that can sometimes be harder than actually having a baby.'

I shrug my shoulders, looking down at the wedding ring on my left hand, as a silence builds between us. But unlike last time, I'm not going to break it.

'I was in love once,' Shannon eventually says, speaking up after being quiet for a few moments. 'He was a great guy, or at least I thought he was. But he had his problems, and they became my problems and, in the end, it just all fell apart.'

'I'm sorry to hear that. What was his name?'

'Kieran.'

'Where is Kieran now?'

Shannon hesitates, but I smile at her to let her know it's okay to proceed.

'He's dead.'

'Oh my gosh, I'm so sorry.'

I put a hand on Shannon's shoulder and wonder if it does the trick of offering some comfort.

'He was an alcoholic,' she tells me. 'Then, when that wasn't enough, he started on the pills. He ended up overdosing, but we'd already broken up at that point. I left him when he hit me.'

'That's awful!'

'He did a lot of things he shouldn't have done. But he was a good man, or at least he was when I first met him. He was just very troubled, and as time went on he became trouble for me.'

'I feel terrible,' I say, keeping my hand on my tour guide's shoulder. 'Here I am moaning about my past, as if I'm the only person in the world with problems. I'm so selfish.'

'No, it's fine,' Shannon tells me. If that's the case, I could ask her another question.

'Has there not been anybody since Kieran?'

Shannon shakes her head.

'Why not? I mean, do you not think it would help to try and move on?'

'I tried moving on. But it's hard with baggage. Emotional scars. It's never fair to carry them into a new relationship, so I just stopped trying.'

'How long has it been since you tried?'

'Years.'

'Is it not time to perhaps try again?'

'I don't know,' Shannon admits, and she genuinely looks like she doesn't know, so I guess I should leave it there.

'Sorry for interrupting your evening,' I say as I stand up. 'And sorry for prying. I'll be going now.'

'No, it's fine,' Shannon says as she follows me to the door. Just before I open it, she says, 'Rosalind, wait.'

I stop and look back, but Shannon doesn't speak again.

'What is it?' I ask.

'Erm, it doesn't matter.'

I wonder what she was going to tell me, but she's clearly not in the mood to do so anymore, so I open the door and wish her a good night, then head back to my room.

When I enter it, I find Donovan lying on the bed, watching a video on his phone. He turns it off when he sees me.

'How did it go?' he wants to know.

'Just like we thought it would,' I tell him as I start to undress. 'She didn't admit that you'd both made plans for this evening, although—'

'What?'

'I think she might have been about to tell me just as I was leaving. But she stopped herself.'

'Interesting.'

'Not as interesting as what will happen to her tomorrow,' I say as I slide in under the duvet beside my husband. 'Are you ready?'

'More than ready. I can't wait to finish this.'

'Me neither.'

It feels good as we turn off the lights and settle down to sleep. That's because we both know that when we lay our heads down on our pillows again, we will have achieved our objective.

Shannon will be dead.

And by the sounds of it, after her difficult past, there won't be too many people who will miss her.

TWENTY-TWO

SHANNON

After a very bewildering evening in which Donovan stood me up and Rosalind came to my room to confess some of her deepest fears, I went to sleep confused about both of them. I was also a little confused at myself – I told Rosalind a bit of information about my past, and that's not something I tend to share with many people, let alone an unpredictable rich woman I only met a few days ago. It was little wonder I slept poorly, but there was one thing to feel good about when I woke up. I pulled back the curtains to see clear blue skies. Considering today is a beach day, it's the best thing I could have wished to see.

I get dressed quickly and head downstairs, though I'm not going for breakfast in the hotel restaurant. I'm going out into the car park to wait for a delivery driver who is on his way to drop off the package I ordered online yesterday. I see a white van approaching the hotel ten minutes later, and wave at the driver to get his attention, making it clear that the thing he has in the back of his van is for me.

'Beautiful morning,' he says to me as he hands over the heavy package, and I thank him before carrying it over to the car and putting it in the back. Then I open it to double-check it's okay and, thankfully, it is. It's a picnic hamper full of treats for Donovan and Rosalind to enjoy today, and I'm sure they will. I'm almost jealous that I won't get to enjoy it with them – there are some really nice things in here, from the truffles to the champagne, to the wrapped baguettes and the selection of cheeses, all kept cool by the ice pack inside the hamper alongside them. I expect this will be the last thing I get to do for this family as their trip gradually comes to a close, so I want to make sure I excel and that there are no doubts in the minds of the American couple when it comes to them paying me for my services shortly.

I know they still owe me $15,000, but it would be nice to get a 'tip' on top of that too.

There are doubts, however, about the legitimacy of this anniversary picnic that Rosalind requested with her husband. After what she told me last night, and what I know myself from Donovan's own actions, it seems they are hardly a couple who are loved up enough to do such a thing as share a picnic and reminisce about their love together. Rosalind told me that Donovan is a serial adulterer, a suggestion I find hard to disagree with considering he wanted to visit me in my room, although the fact he didn't turn up in the end suggests he's not quite as driven by his bodily yearnings as his wife would make out. But she's clearly not happy with him, and I guess he's not entirely happy with her if he entertains the company of other women on the side. As I look at this picnic hamper, I almost feel like it's a bit silly. But they asked for a day at a beach together, so I guess they get it.

Barnaby and Philippa are to spend the day elsewhere while I take the couple to dine on the sand in the sunshine. I'm not sure what the plan is for them, and then I begin to worry that I was expected to give them an itinerary of some sort, so I'm just about to suggest some ideas for them when I learn they will be fine today.

'We're going to have a swim in the hotel pool and then a nice lunch in the restaurant,' Philippa tells me when I see her and Barnaby passing through the reception area, holding bags full of towels and a change of clothes. 'We might also go out and have a walk around the grounds later. It does look like a nice day out there.'

'It is,' I confirm. 'Are you sure you don't want me to drive back here after I've dropped Rosalind and Donovan off at the beach? It's only thirty minutes or so. I'll be leaving them for a few hours, so I don't mind coming back if you'd like to go out anywhere?'

'Oh, there won't be any time for that,' the voice behind me says, and I turn around to see Rosalind has appeared in reception, her own bag with her, which suggests she is packed and ready to go too. 'In fact, you can say your goodbyes to Philippa and Barnaby now, if you like, because we won't be needing you after today.'

'I'm sorry?' I say, very confused.

'You can take us to the beach and wait to bring us back, but after that, you can go,' Rosalind says. 'We'll be flying home tomorrow, and we can take a taxi from here to the airport, so we don't need you after this. We will pay you, of course, but in terms of this trip, it ends today.'

'Oh, I see,' I say, surprised that my services are being dispensed with so abruptly. I did know they were going home tomorrow, but I thought they would require me to take them to their private plane.

'I am checked in here for another night,' I remind Rosalind, but she says it's not a problem and they will sort the bill. She suggests I go and pack my things and then check out early, so I can get home sooner if I wish.

'Everything is okay, isn't it?' I double-check, afraid that I've done something wrong, or that Rosalind is mad at me for something we said to each other last night and is now backtracking on our agreement. *I'm not at risk of not being paid, am I?*

'Everything is fine. Don't worry, you'll get your money as agreed,' Rosalind tells me with a smile, before saying she'd like to get going soon. That's my cue to do as she says and go and get my things from my room, so I can check out and we can set off to the beach.

I do just that, still a little bewildered by the speed of all of this, but ultimately satisfied as long as I get my money. If I end up getting back to Dublin earlier than I planned to, that's a bonus.

Once I have my luggage, I go back downstairs and see that Donovan has joined Rosalind. I expect him to be a little sheepish around me, considering he failed to show up at my door last night, but if he is feeling uncomfortable about it then it doesn't show.

'Morning, Shannon,' he says breezily. 'Shall we make a move? I'd hate to waste another second of this fine day.'

He strides out of the hotel with a rucksack over his shoulder, full of swagger in his smart T-shirt, cargo shorts and flip-flops, looking very much dressed for the beach and moving as if he doesn't have a care in the world. Maybe he doesn't, and last night really wasn't that big of a deal for him. I guess I'm not that big of a deal to him either if he didn't bother to come and see me. Although after Rosalind's appearance and her subsequent confessions I'm glad he didn't show up. This couple are troubled, there's no doubt about that, so it's better that I don't get in between them.

'What are we doing about the picnic?' Rosalind asks me before she follows her husband outside, and I wonder if she is thinking she has caught me out again, that I've forgotten to sort out her food and drink for the beach. But if that's the case, she would be wrong.

'It's all sorted. Don't worry about that,' I say casually as I stride past her and head for the car, feeling pleased with myself that, for once, I am one step ahead of this woman, not just literally but figuratively too.

Once the three of us are in the car, I wind the windows down, allowing a cooling breeze to blow through the vehicle as we head for the coast. There are days when I look around at my home country, mainly during rainy days, and wish I could live somewhere more exotic, but today is not one of them. This weather is incredible, and I know the beach will be too.

'Are you sure there won't be anyone else there?' Rosalind asks me from the back seat. 'Won't a lot of people be out enjoying this sunshine?'

'I promised you a private beach and that's what you'll get,' I say confidently as we drive on, and the further we go, the fewer cars we see out on the road with us, suggesting I am right and not many people are going the way we are. That looks even more correct when I turn off the main road and trundle along a smaller sandy track, before parking at the top of a cliff overlooking an impossibly calm sea.

'Wow,' Donovan says as he gets out and takes in the view. I guess that means he approves of my choice.

'How do we get down to the beach?' Rosalind asks, clearly focused on logistics rather than the natural beauty of this viewpoint.

'By being careful,' I say a little cryptically. I take out the picnic hamper that both Rosalind and Donovan eye hungrily. 'Follow me and watch your step as you go.'

I head for the edge of the cliff, treading over sand mixed in with clumps of grass and stones. The couple following behind me must wonder where I'm going, and I even hear Rosalind tell me to be careful as I reach the edge before I look back at her and smile – *then jump off.*

I hear Rosalind gasp. Donovan rushes to the edge and looks

over, and he sees me standing on another sandy verge only a couple of feet below him.

'Don't worry, I know what I'm doing,' I say, pointing out a very narrow path leading down the side of the cliff. 'That's the way we go. Take your time.'

I set off, lugging the hamper with me. I wouldn't let Donovan carry it even if he offered. That's because this is part of his treat, and he should enjoy it. Besides, there'll be plenty of time for me to rest once I've got them set up on the beach. I can go for a walk while they enjoy the picnic, maybe even do a bit of sunbathing myself before we have to leave.

We make our way down the side of the cliff, and while it takes some time and does carry a little risk if one of us was to slip and fall, those facts are also the reason why this beach is so quiet. Not many people know about the narrow path down to this section of beach, even fewer are willing to try and traverse it, which makes it the perfect hideaway for those who are a little adventurous.

'How did you find this place?' Donovan asks me as we near the foot of the cliff.

'My father used to bring me here when I was young,' I say. 'I've not been here for years, but it hasn't changed one bit.'

I reach the beach and it feels good not having to worry about falling off the path anymore. I look back and see Donovan and Rosalind are relieved to have made it down here too, but they quickly see that it was worth it when they look around at the environment they have to themselves now.

'This is truly breathtaking,' Rosalind says as she gazes across the golden sands that are flanked by tall walls of rock on three sides, the calm sea water on the fourth.

'Understatement of the year!' Donovan exclaims. 'This is paradise!'

He kicks off his flip-flops and starts running through the sand, kicking grains of it up into the air like an excited child seeing the beach for the first time. I laugh at his show of energy, and then I see that Rosalind is now doing the same thing, and I marvel at the couple as they frolic in front of me, suddenly looking happier than I've ever seen them before.

As they go to the water's edge, I look around for a good spot on the sand to set the picnic down. I lower the hamper before opening it and taking out the blanket inside. I lay it out neatly and am just about to pop the champagne for the couple when they return from the water and tell me to wait.

I see that their feet are wet, and the sand is sticking to their toes, but they aren't bothered about it, though they are bothered about me helping set up the picnic.

'Don't worry about doing that, you've already done more than enough,' Donovan says.

'Yeah, why don't you go for a walk and have a break?' Rosalind suggests. 'We'll be fine here. Thank you, this is perfect.'

'Okay, if you're sure?' I double-check, but they are, so I wish them a good picnic.

'Where will you go?' Donovan asks me before I leave.

'There are a few caves just around the curve of the coastline,' I say, pointing in the direction I'm talking about. 'I'll just go around there, out of your view. But I'll be nearby if you need me.'

'No problem, we'll come and find you when we're finished,' Donovan says. He picks up one of the baguettes and a bottle of water, holding them out for me.

'Take some lunch. And thank you for arranging this for us,' he says.

I gladly take the food and drink, mainly because I'd forgotten to bring my own supplies, and I leave the couple to it, silently congratulating myself on a job well done.

In a couple of hours, they will be finished with the picnic and our time together will be at an end. I'll get paid and go home and this whole experience will ultimately have been a success.

At least that's what I think as I head for the caves, the water lapping peacefully at the shore and the sun warming everything in this secluded, secretive spot.

Little did I know, but not all three of us were going to leave this beach alive.

TWENTY-THREE

SHANNON

I spend a few minutes with my shoes off, enjoying the feeling of the sand between my toes, before I put them back on and head into the entrance to the caves, where my father spent so much time as a boy with his parents. He brought me to the caves to make new memories with me, and he said that one day I could bring my own son or daughter and continue the family tradition of making memories here. But returning to this spot alone makes me feel a little melancholy, and not for the first time in my life I wonder if my father would be disappointed with me.

He'd have loved to have been a granddad, but never got the chance before he passed. *I denied him of that,* I remind myself. I shake the thought from my head and try to just enjoy being here in this picturesque place.

Stepping off the slippery sand and onto solid rock, I walk towards the open chasm in the side of the cliff. Years of erosion have formed these caves, although it's still surprising that not many people know about them. If this was Greece, I bet there would be lots of little tourist boats sailing by here every day for people to take photos, but this is Ireland, a place not always top of people's bucket lists. It's just one of many hidden treasures dotted around the rugged coastline that are much less explored than their more famous counterparts across Europe.

As I enter the first cave and stare up at the coarse ceiling above me, I wonder if Donovan and Rosalind are enjoying their picnic. I'm sure they're gorging themselves on food and champagne and feeling very happy beneath the hot sun, but I almost feel bad if I don't let them see this cave. Maybe I'll bring them here before we leave the beach, just so they can experience this. I doubt they'll ever come back here again, and maybe this will be my last time here too. It is well off the beaten track; while Dad did like the idea of me coming back with my own offspring one day, I don't think that's something that's in my future.

'Hey, Shannon. So these are the caves, huh?'

I almost jump out of my skin at the male voice behind me, and I manage to lose my footing on the rocks beneath my feet. But just before I tumble to the hard ground, a strong arm catches me and I stay upright.

It belongs to Donovan, and I'm lucky he caught me, although it was his fault I almost fell in the first place.

What is he doing here?

'Why aren't you on the beach?' I ask. 'Is everything okay with the picnic?'

'Everything is fine,' he says calmly, still holding onto my arm, even though I'm steady now. 'Rosalind is sitting on that blanket, basking in the sunshine, and I plan to be back with her very shortly to help her finish the lovely delicacies you provided for us today.'

'Did you want to see the caves?' I ask him, assuming that must be why he left the sun-kissed sand to come in here instead.

'Not quite. I wanted to see you.'

'Me?'

Donovan grins, but I don't return it. I'm feeling very uncomfortable, and not just because his hand is still on me. It's because it seems he's left his wife to see me, which is utterly inappropriate. Not only is she nearby, but she planned the picnic for their anniversary. He should be with her, not me.

'Yes, I wanted a private moment with you. Is that okay?'

'Is this about last night? Because if it is, I don't care that you didn't come to my room,' I say, trying to pre-empt what this is all about. 'In fact, I think it was better that you didn't. I don't want to do anything behind Rosalind's back and—'

'Shh, shh, shh,' Donovan says, using his free hand to put a finger on my lips to silence me. Him touching that part of my body sends a shiver through me that has nothing to do with the cool temperature inside the cave. 'It's not about last night, although I am sorry I didn't stop by like I said I would. We could have had some fun, although I'm going to have plenty now, don't worry about that.'

'What do you mean?' I ask, my voice cracking slightly as my nerves grow and Donovan's grip on my arm tightens.

I try to pull away, both to free my arm and to get his finger away from my lips – the one he used to shush me as if I am some naughty child, not a grown woman who has suddenly been cornered in a cave, where nobody would be able to hear my call for help if I screamed. Apart from Rosalind, of course. She might hear me. But would she come to my aid?

'Oh, Shannon, this is the part where I have to let you know the truth,' Donovan says now, his imposing presence making this cave seem smaller by the second.

'The truth?' I repeat, and then try to free my arm, but Donovan keeps hold of it.

'Yes, the truth, Shannon. About who we really are. And about why we're really here.'

'You're hurting my arm,' I say, trying to pull away, but Donovan keeps a grip on me.

'What's the matter? Worried you're trapped all alone with me in a remote location where nobody can help? Of course you are. Why else do you think my wife asked you to take us to a remote beach? It's so nobody can help you.'

I see a coldness in Donovan's eyes that I haven't seen before. As fear rises up inside me, I pull away again, harder this time, more desperately. To my surprise, Donovan lets go just as I do, and that causes me to fall backwards.

I groan as I land on the rocks and feel a sharp pain in my lower back, one that causes me to suck in air to try and ease it. But Donovan only laughs at that and, as he stands over me, he looks down on me with pity.

'Shannon, you really are a tragic tale, aren't you?' he says with a shake of his head. 'You're probably thinking you don't deserve this. But you would be wrong about that.'

I worry that Donovan is about to assault me. Is he more than just an adulterer? Is he physically dangerous to women? I wonder if that's why he didn't come to my hotel room last night. Would that have been too boring for him? Or too risky with potential witnesses in the rooms surrounding us. Does he prefer to get his victims somewhere like this, somewhere where nobody can see or hear what he intends to do? But that wouldn't make sense – like he just said, it was Rosalind who requested we come here, and surely she wouldn't have done that to help him, would she? But the way he said it, it was as if his wife is a conspirator in whatever is going on, which is almost as terrifying as what might happen next, if true.

'Stay away from me!' I cry as I shuffle backwards across the rocks, feeling some of the harsh edges scraping against my bare legs, not stopping because things might be worse if I do.

'What is it you think I want to do?' Donovan asks, clearly amused by my fear of him.

'I don't know, but you won't get away with it, I swear!'

'Oh, I won't? How do you know that?'

'Because I'll report you! I'll go straight to the police, and they'll catch you before you can fly back to America. You'll be arrested here, and you'll never get away with this, I promise.'

'You'll report me,' Donovan repeats, still looking amused. 'Tell me, Shannon, how do you plan to do that if you're dead?'

The horror of the situation dawns on me, but I'm too terrified to move.

'You're going to kill me?'

'Yes.'

'But why?'

'Because you're a threat, Shannon. It's as simple as that.'

'How am I a threat to you? I don't even know you!'

'But we know you. Yes, we know everything about you. About your past. About what you did.'

I'm still not getting it, but I do regain enough strength to get back to my feet, although there's nowhere for me to go. Donovan is blocking the way out of this cave. I'd have to get past him to get to safety, but he's confidently blocking my escape route and I don't fancy my chances of being able to get by him. That's why I keep my distance instead, slowly backing further into the cave.

'There must be a mistake. I'm not who you think I am.'

'And who do we think you are?' Donovan asks me, taking a few small steps towards me, closing the gap that has been growing between us.

'I'm a tour guide! I'm just doing this for money! It's my job. You reached out to me!'

'Yes, we did. We targeted you specifically. Everything that's happened during this trip has been building to this moment right here. The moment when I kill you. When I get to go back to my wife and tell her that there is nothing to worry about anymore.'

'I don't know what you're talking about!' I cry. 'What is your wife worried about?'

'You know what she's worried about. I believe she told you last night, when she came to your room.'

This is still not making any sense to me.

'What?'

'Think about it, Shannon,' Donovan says as he takes another step forward, so I take one more back to match his.

What did Rosalind talk about?

'You?' I ask. 'She was worried about you. She said you were an adulterer, and she wanted to know if anything had happened between us two. Is that what this is about? Does she think I'm a threat and wants you to hurt me?'

Donovan just rolls his eyes at that suggestion.

'Not quite. There was something else. Think about it, Shannon.'

What else did Rosalind say?

'She talked about your children,' I recall now. 'She's worried about telling them they're adopted.'

'Bingo.'

'What has that got to do with me?'

'Quite a lot, actually. Remember when we spoke in the pub, and I told you she was worried about the real parents of our children one day possibly coming back to try and claim them? Well, here we are, making sure that doesn't happen.'

I stare at Donovan – it feels like all the air is sucked out of this cave. He must see that I'm finally catching on to him because he smiles.

'We no longer have to worry about Esme's biological parents, because we took care of them,' he says, still smirking. 'We took care of Barnaby's father too. Now it's just his mother that needs to go. You understand now, don't you, Shannon?'

I understand perfectly. That's why I no longer take any steps back, nor do I even think about trying to run. All I can do is think about the little boy I've been in such close proximity to on this trip; the little boy who was a total stranger to me, but only because I didn't realise my real connection to him, the connection Donovan has just hinted at strongly.

This cannot be happening.

This cannot be real.

He wants to hurt me because of who Barnaby really is to me.

He must be the boy I gave up for adoption when he was born.

He must be my son.

TWENTY-FOUR

SHANNON

Nine years ago

I stare at the single blue line on the pregnancy test in my hand as tears roll down my cheeks. It's been less than a month since I ended my relationship with Kieran, the man I loved and tried to support through his alcohol addiction, right up until he turned violent and took out his anger on me. When I left him, I thought I was having a fresh start. A new beginning, on my own, a chance to figure out my future and what I wanted next. I had so many ideas about that.

So many dreams, so many things I thought I'd get to do.

There was one thing I certainly didn't want then, and it's the same thing I don't want now.

A baby.

Yet, according to this test, I'm pregnant.

I look up from the blue line to see my reflection staring back at me in my bathroom mirror. When I do, I see the lines of mascara running down my face, my make-up smeared from the tears I've already shed since the reality of this situation dawned on me. I thought that I'd just been feeling sick because I had some bug. I was hoping my period was late or it was just me getting my dates mixed up, as I've been known to do before. But there is a far simpler reason for what's been going on with my body lately.

There is a baby growing inside of it.

A baby that I am in no way equipped to raise myself.

I already know that I can't keep it. It's just not possible. I can't be a single mother. I have no money, or very little of it anyway, after Kieran depleted my funds so rapidly and uncaringly. With only one very modest income from my job as a tour guide to get by on, I have to do all I can to hold onto my cash, which means reducing outgoings as much as possible. Babies are expensive and while they take away time, they take away money just as quickly, if not quicker, and it's money I haven't got. I also have no support network, not with both my parents gone and no siblings. To be frank, I have no idea what to do with a baby. I'm only twenty-four – everyone else I know my age, from school friends to colleagues, is only bothered about which bar to go to on Friday night, rather than dealing with nappies and milk bottles.

I'm out of my depth.

I feel sick again, but not because of the changes going on inside my body this time. I might not consider myself equipped to deal with motherhood, but I also don't consider myself strong enough to deal with the aftermath of getting rid of this baby.

But what else can I do?

I would spend the next couple of months agonising over that very question, all the way up to my twelve-week scan, where I was told that my pregnancy was progressing perfectly. It was then I tearfully confessed to a nurse that I wasn't in a position to care for my baby, but I didn't want to end the pregnancy either. An option I had not considered was suggested to me by the kind nurse.

* * *

'Just try and stay calm, Shannon. We'll get through this together, okay?'

I squeeze the midwife's hand and see her grimace a little as we try to do exactly that and get through this together. But I'm the one in pain, because I'm the one giving birth, so it's easier for her to say.

I let out another guttural groan before squeezing her hand again and pushing as hard as I can, trying my best to get this over with as quickly as possible, for the sake of both my physical and mental health. Physically, my body is already exhausted after nine months of pregnancy, so going through labour is using what last reserves of energy I have. But mentally I feel even more drained. I've spent such a long time thinking about what is going to happen after the birth and, now it's here, it's all getting too much for me.

'I can't do it!' I cry as tears fill my eyes and I squeeze the midwife's hand, but she simply tells me that I can. But she doesn't know what I'm talking about.

I'm not referring to giving birth.

I'm referring to giving my baby up for adoption immediately after birth.

What was I thinking? I thought it was for the best. I figured the only thing to do was give my son a good start in life, and that meant somewhere else, away from me, with people who were equipped to raise him. Good people, people with a stable home and money in the bank and a balanced family unit that he could fit right into. People like the couple who had already been accepted to adopt the child I'm currently bringing into the world, a couple who I am not allowed to know the names of and a couple who, very soon, will take my baby and start their life with him in it – while I go back to my empty, lonely existence and try to process what I have done.

Is it too late to stop it? I don't know. I feel so confused, and so weak, not to mention scared. But then I start to feel euphoric, as if the pain has lifted along with all my worries, and things suddenly aren't so bad. It feels like a blessing from above but, in reality, it's just the medication kicking in and my pain being relieved enough to allow me to continue pushing so this baby can be born.

I can hear crying and then I get a glimpse of a little face, a baby boy, his eyes closed, his features all squished, but he is alive and well and it is over. I have done it.

But what happens now?

I don't know what I want at this moment in time, but it doesn't matter, because my baby is already being taken from the room I'm in.

'Is he okay?' I ask, afraid of what the answer might be.

'Yes, he's absolutely fine. Try and get some rest now,' a nurse tells me, seeming completely calm about the situation, which does put me at ease somewhat.

I could laugh at the suggestion to rest though – there's no way I can relax. Not with all the adrenaline pumping around my body, mixing in with the drugs that have already been administered, but somehow I am able to close my eyes and, when I do, sleep overcomes my fatigued mind.

I don't know how long I sleep for but, when I wake, the only person I see is a smiling nurse who tells me that everything went as it should have and I will be able to go home tomorrow. Then she leaves and all I can do is stare at the wall. Like the nurse just said, everything went to plan.

I had my baby. *Then he was adopted.*

I didn't get to hold him, that was agreed upon beforehand. It was my wish because I was afraid that I would bond with him in that moment and then never be able to let him go. But it was far easier to agree to that before I saw him – now I'm already regretting it.

It's hard to fathom that this was what I wanted, even if it is for the best.

I got my wish. I found a way to give my son a chance at life.

But now he's gone forever.

I'll never see him again.

* * *

'I made a mistake,' I say to the woman sitting across the desk from me. Her name is Gemma, and I have been waiting a while for this appointment with her. Now that I have it I am not wasting any more time, I make my feelings clear.

'A mistake?' she asks, looking up from the papers in front of her, at a woman who hasn't worn make-up in months. Nor have I eaten a healthy meal or had a full night's sleep, so I can only imagine what she's thinking about my mental state. But if it wasn't obvious by my appearance, it should be obvious by what I am asking her to do.

'Yes. I don't want my son to be adopted. I want him back,' I go on, urgency emanating from every pore of my desperate body. 'Please, you have to help me. You can get him back for me, right? You know where he went.'

'I'm terribly sorry, but the adoption order has already been made and it can't be reversed at this stage.'

'No! That's my son! He belongs to me!'

I promised myself that I wouldn't get overly emotional during this meeting, that surely won't help my case, but it's impossible to be reserved in these awful circumstances. It's even harder considering my hormones are still in the very long process of returning to normal after I gave birth six weeks ago. But along with the mood swings and periods of depression I've felt since experiencing childbirth, something else has happened too. As each day has gone by, I've started to feel more and more like I made a mistake giving my baby to another family, until I reached the point where I was absolutely certain, which is what prompted me to arrange this meeting. Unfortunately, it seems like I've left it too late.

'There was a window of time after the child's birth when you could have changed your mind. You were made aware of that at the beginning of this process, but that period of time has elapsed now.'

I don't remember that being explained to me before, though it wouldn't be the first time during these crazy few months that I have forgotten something important.

'How can this be happening? That's my baby!'

'This is a legal decision. You signed the adoption papers. I'm sorry, but it can't be changed now. There are rules in place to protect the parents who adopt, and to protect the child.'

'Please, help me! I can't live like this!' I beg. 'There has to be something you can do. *Anything*.'

'I'm sorry.'

'At least tell me who they are. What are their names? What are they like?'

'I cannot do that.'

'I just want to know that my baby is okay.'

'He is. We wouldn't have allowed him to go to an unsuitable home. He is safe and well, I can assure you of that.'

It feels horrendous to be told about my baby rather than getting to see him with my own eyes.

'How do you know? Have you seen him?'

'Shannon, I'm afraid I'm going to have to end this conversation here, as this is not the proper way of doing things. I must protect the identity of the family your child has gone to. There are avenues of support for you, which I would be happy to refer you on to, but as I've said, you cannot pursue this anymore.'

The offer of whatever mental health support might be available will surely be inadequate and unsatisfactory, because there's only one way I'll feel better about things.

'Where is he? Just tell me!' I cry, not allowing them to palm me off in this way.

I lunge forward at the stack of papers on Gemma's desk, wondering if my son's address is printed on one of them, or maybe the names of the parents. I just need something to go off, anything that can help me track him down.

'Stop this!' Gemma cries as papers fall from her desk, and she tries to control my flailing arms. But she can't contain me, and runs to her office door to call out for help in the corridor, while I frantically search through the papers, trying to find anything that might relate to the adoption of a baby boy born six weeks ago. As folders and files fall to the floor, I suddenly spot a photo of a young baby and grab it, trying to hide it in my pocket, as if it will magically be the thing I need to locate my son. It might not even be him, but if there's a chance it is, it might be all I have. But before I can safely hide the photo, I'm suddenly held back from the desk by a strong male colleague of Gemma's, and the photo is whisked away from me. I am then very sternly told that this is going to become a matter for the police if I don't leave it here.

Being arrested, getting a criminal record and potentially losing my job is about the only thing that could make things even worse, so I pull myself together for long enough to leave the adoption agency and return home.

No sooner have I walked through my front door than I collapse onto my bed, and I stay there for several long minutes, crying into my pillow and praying for all of this to be a bad dream. It's not though, and I know that I will have to carry this with me for the rest of my life.

I gave away my firstborn and can't bear these feelings, so to make sure it won't happen again, I will shut myself down to men. I'll bury my past so deep that it can't hurt me anymore. If I can't find my son, I'll just have to act like he doesn't exist – it's the only way I'll be able to carry on.

I suppose it will get easier with time. This is the worst of it, but as the years go by, maybe I will slowly forget. While I do that, my baby's new parents will be getting on with their own lives, raising the child I conceived and probably not even sparing me a thought ever again.

That'll be how this plays out, right?

We all move on and forget about each other.

Life goes on, everyone always says.

I guess time will tell.

TWENTY-FIVE

SHANNON

Present day

I'm staring at one half of the couple I once wanted to find so badly, one half of the couple who got to raise my baby after I made the grave mistake of making him available to be taken. From begging adoption officials to searching through paperwork on a desk to scouring the internet and spending countless nights lying in my bed, wondering where my son might be, I now have my answer.

My baby's adoptive father is standing right in front of me.

And he wants me dead.

But that's not even at the forefront of my mind. The only thing I can think about is that I've spent the past few days in the presence of my son and didn't know it.

Barnaby is my baby.

Oh my God, he's mine?

I've sat in the same car as him. Asked him questions and listened to his answers. Seen him laugh and cry. Watched him gaze in wonder at a spectacular view. Observed him rubbing his eyes when he gets sleepy at the end of the day.

All this time, I had no idea who he was, and he had no idea who I was either. But now I know the truth, although he still doesn't.

If Donovan has his way, my son will never know who I am.

Not unless I can get out of here and tell him.

'How?' is all I can say at this point.

'How did we find you?' Donovan asks. 'Or perhaps you'd like to know how I plan to kill you to ensure that you can never, ever find Barnaby as he gets older, nor can he ever find you.'

'You think you can just kill me, and he'll never have the right to try and find his real mother one day? Is that it?' I ask, my fear now being counterbalanced by a grim determination to make it out of this cave, whatever happens, especially now I really have something to fight for that's more than myself.

'You gave up the right to be his mother the day you decided to give him away,' Donovan snaps back. 'We've raised him. We're his parents. It's unfair that you can just skip his childhood then get to have a relationship with him when he's older.'

'That's not what would happen,' I try, desperate to make this man see that.

'Yes, it is, because it's what almost happened before!'

I pause to hear what happened to Donovan to make him think that resorting to these extreme measures is the best course of action.

'Our daughter was twelve when we received a letter from the adoption agency, telling us that her birth parents were interested in making contact with her again,' he begins, his solid frame blocking most of the sunlight filtering into this dark cave. 'That's twelve years of us caring for her, and let me tell you what that entails. It's all the sleepless nights, the diapers, the tantrums, the anxiety every time she got sick. But it wasn't all bad. There was the good stuff too. The milestones. The holidays. The hugs. The laughter. They are all our memories, the highs and the lows of parenthood, and they belong to my family, no one else's. We experienced all of that together and, suddenly, everything changed. I was furious, but Rosalind, she was just afraid. Afraid that if we let this couple make contact, then Esme would gradually get closer to them and, one day, when she was an adult, she might love them more than she loved us. Imagine it. I spend her whole life looking after her only to watch another man walk her down the aisle on her wedding day, while Rosalind has to risk having her heart broken if her baby girl chooses to confide in her other mother instead of her. I wasn't going to allow it. So we wrote back to the adoption agency and said no, we didn't wish to have any contact with them.'

'And?'

'The couple didn't take no for an answer. More letters came, so we sought legal advice, and we were told we had every right to shield our child from this until she was an adult. But then, if she was aware of her adoption, she had the right to find her parents herself. I simply decided then that we would never tell her the truth, so she wouldn't even know to look. Rosalind reluctantly agreed. But it wasn't enough. Once we had that paranoia about the future, we couldn't shake it. It started to dominate our lives. That is, until we decided to do something about it.'

I'm afraid to hear exactly what Donovan did about it, but he's going to tell me, whether I like it or not.

'I decided to tell the adoption agency in New York that we were willing to meet the parents after all, so a meeting date was set. But Rosalind and I didn't attend, although we did sit in our car outside the meeting venue, looking to see who turned up at the right time. When we saw a couple, we figured it was them, so we followed them after the failed meeting. We followed them all the way to the airport and, after a bit of detective work by my wife, who struck up a conversation with them to find out where they were flying to, we learned they lived in Dallas. Rosalind learned their names too, so once we had those, along with their city and their appearance, it only took a little digging around online to learn more about them. I found out where the man worked and flew to Dallas, where I kept watch outside his office so I could follow him home. That's all it took to get their address.'

'You stalked them?'

'They were the ones pestering us to meet, remember!'

I don't bother arguing that point – I can see that Donovan has already justified all of this in his mind, whatever this is.

'The adoption agency called and asked why we had failed to attend the meeting, and I just said we'd changed our minds. The couple tried to rearrange, but we declined. Little did they know we already had what we needed. We knew who they were, all we had to figure out then was how we were going to get rid of them.'

I'm aghast at the thought of an innocent couple coming to harm simply for trying to reunite with their baby, but Donovan just seems to be revelling in recalling it all.

'So what? You hired somebody to kill them?' I ask, presuming that's something a rich and vile person would do.

'Hired somebody? No, that would have been too risky. We did it ourselves.'

Donovan is showing no signs of telling me that this is all one big joke as he goes on.

'Rosalind and I decided that starting a fire would be the easiest way for us to get rid of them. We each flew to Houston, then travelled by car to Dallas, not wanting to make it too obvious that we had been in that particular city, in case we were ever looked into by the police one day. Then we staked out the house, wanting to ensure that nobody else was in there besides the couple. Once we were confident, we started a fire at the front and the rear of the property, blocking the escape routes. We left, and later heard about what happened on the news.'

'You burnt them alive,' I say, horrified at the cruelty of it.

'We did what we had to do to protect our family.'

'You're sick!'

'Really? We are? Not the ones who willingly let somebody else walk away with their baby?'

'You have no idea what it's like to come to that decision. They must have had their reasons, just like I had mine!'

'I don't care. All I want is for my family to be protected and, with them gone, that took care of Esme.'

As I stare at Donovan, I see that the craziest part of all is that he genuinely believes he had no other choice. But how could he get away with this?

'Didn't the police know it was arson?' I ask.

'Of course they did. But they didn't know who had done it, and once we were back on the east coast we were a very long way from the crime scene. Why would anybody come looking for us? They never suspected us of a thing.'

It seems Donovan and Rosalind really have got away with murder.

'We knew we might encounter similar problems with Barnaby, which is why we decided to do something about his parents too,' the killer in front of me goes on. 'It was much trickier, as neither of his parents had reached out to try and meet him, so we had no leads to go off. There was also the not so small matter of him being born in Ireland, so we assumed we were in a different country to his parents too. It was going to take a lot more work to find you and his father.'

I get a chill at the thought of this couple actively trying to track me down from America while I went about my life in Ireland, totally oblivious to the danger lurking out there. But I get an even bigger chill when I realise something else.

'Did you hurt Kieran?' I ask, suddenly afraid that his death wasn't purely down to his addiction after all.

'What do you think?' Donovan says with a smirk.

I think about my ex-boyfriend, the man who had so many

flaws, the one who hurt me, which forced me to leave him, and that decision played a huge part in my decision to give away the child we had conceived together. But as bad as some of the things he did were, he didn't deserve to die so young, and he certainly didn't deserve to be murdered.

'You came to Ireland and made it look like he overdosed?' I ask as Donovan takes another step towards me.

'I did what I had to do to get him out of the picture,' he replies as I step back, getting further away from the exit as I do. 'And now I'm doing what I have to do to get rid of you, the final piece of this jigsaw.'

'I don't understand. How did you find us? Me and Kieran? How did you know we were Barnaby's parents?'

'I hired somebody to look into it for me. There's not much I can't afford, so I paid a man to track you both down. Then, once I had that information, I formulated a plan. Kieran went first. Given how much of a waster he was, it was easy work. I figured not many people would miss a guy like him. But I wasn't in a huge rush with you, mainly because you hadn't ever tried to find Barnaby, barring a little bit of fuss in the early days.'

'You knew about me regretting my decision?' I ask, and Donovan nods.

'We were told by the adoption agency in Dublin, yes,' he says. 'We'd gone through the adoption process for Barnaby while we were living in Ireland, but by the point we got him, we'd already set everything up to move back to America. Then things died down once we knew the adoption agency couldn't reveal our identities to you.'

I think back over that period of time that was so difficult for me. While I was crying myself to sleep every night in my bed, this man was flying my son to Boston as if he was returning from a holiday with some one-of-a-kind duty free.

'There was no imminent threat with you like there was with Esme's parents,' Donovan goes on. 'That allowed me to take my time and come up with this plan right here. I discovered you were a tour guide, so it made sense for us to hire you, privately of course, so nobody actually knows we're together. Then all Rosalind and I had to do was get you somewhere like this. A remote beach where nobody can see what we do to you and, with the sea only a few metres away, we have the perfect place to hide your body forever.'

'You're insane if you think this will work,' I say as forcefully as I can.

'Are we? I mean, all we have to do is kill you, and then we can fly back home. You'll eventually be reported missing, but nobody will know about your connection to us, and we'll be thousands of miles away back in Boston. We'll keep tabs on the Irish news, of course, but I expect this one will go down as a mystery, just another young woman going missing, and nobody knows what happened to her.'

Donovan steps forward again, and I suddenly feel rocks at my back. I turn around and see that I have inadvertently backed up into a corner of the cave. That can't be good with him still moving towards me.

This is really happening.

I'm going to die in this cave, and it will be just like Donovan says. Nobody will ever know what happened to me, just like nobody really knows what happened to Kieran, or Esme's parents in Dallas. The only people who will know will go back to Boston and carry on raising their kids, kids who will have no idea that they are adopted, or that they had other parents out there, ones who have been murdered by the two people they think they're safe with.

I can't let this happen.

I am Barnaby's only chance at the truth, and Esme's for that matter too.

I have to make it out of here alive.

So that's why I start running.

To Donovan's surprise, I don't run towards him to try and get out of the cave.

I just run further inside it, and even when he calls for me to stop, I keep going.

I keep going until I'm in total darkness. Now I'm so far inside the cave, not even Rosalind would be able to hear my screams.

TWENTY-SIX
ROSALIND

I check my watch before looking back down the beach to see if there is any sign of my husband yet. But Donovan isn't coming back to me, and I'm beginning to wonder what is taking him so long. It's not like I'm uncomfortable where I am, sitting on a blanket on this beautiful beach, looking out at the rolling waves while I nibble on picnic food. It's just that I would have thought I'd have company by now after he had got rid of Shannon, and the pair of us would be free to celebrate the end of our worries about our children's birth parents.

I'm sure everything is fine. It's not as if he hasn't done this kind of thing before. Donovan is a ruthless killer, which could put me off him, but it makes me admire him more when I know he's doing this for the sake of our family. That's why I know he's taking care of business just around the curve of this coastline and, any second now, he's going to reappear with a big grin on his face, and tell me that he has done what we came here to do.

I cannot wait for that to happen. It will be a huge weight off my shoulders when Shannon is dead – she is the final piece of the puzzle in ensuring our children never know that they were adopted. Barring either of the kids ever doing a DNA test –

something we can make sure doesn't happen, as we'll give our kids zero reason to ever doubt their origins – they will go their entire lives without being aware of the truth. That peace of mind is crucial for my mental stability; I've spent far too many nights lying in bed and worrying about what might happen if the truth ever came out. How my vibrant home would suddenly feel so empty if Esme and Barnaby decided they wanted to live elsewhere before they naturally became adults and branched out on their own. How I'd have to face my family members and friends and answer questions about how this all happened, putting on a brave face as my kids are spending time with their biological parents. How every birthday and big occasion in their adulthoods would have to be shared between four of us instead of two, me forcing a fake friendship with their moms while Donovan has to have a beer with the other dads. It would have been hell for us, so we've made sure it never becomes a reality.

It's a reality that I know is all too possible. I know that because, growing up, one of my mother's friends, Nancy, faced the very same thing. Having adopted a daughter and raised her into her teenage years, she sat the daughter down and told her that she was adopted. Nancy believed she was doing the right thing – and I suppose she was – but it didn't go the way she hoped. The daughter immediately withdrew from her adoptive mother and began seeking her birthmother. Eventually she found her. The last time my mother told me about Nancy, she hadn't seen her daughter in years.

I look down the beach one more time in the direction my husband went, but there is still no sign of him. I check inside the picnic hamper, wondering if Shannon was thoughtful enough to pack some sunscreen for us today. The temperature is rising and I'm sitting out here totally exposed to the elements, so I'm worried I'm going to burn if I stay out here unprotected much longer. But there is no sunscreen and Shannon has failed to meet my high expectations once again. Then again, I didn't really hire her for her job skills. That poor woman has no awareness of what we brought her here for, although she should know by now.

She'll certainly know when my husband has his hands around her neck and is squeezing the life out of her.

I don't feel bad for Shannon, but I do feel a little bad for leaving Donovan to do the final part of this by himself. However, I did offer to help him, though he told me he would take care of it and that I was to occupy myself with the picnic and the sunshine until he returned. So that's what I'll try to do.

I pour myself another glass of champagne, careful to leave enough in the bottle so there is plenty for the two of us to toast when my husband gets back to me. When he does, we'll finish this fizz, as well as the food, and then carry the hamper back to the car, where we'll drive back to the hotel. We'll rejoin Philippa and Barnaby, and tell them that we dropped Shannon off at the train station as planned, as the tour is over. Then we will pack up our own things and head back to the airport, where Donovan will already have messaged our pilot to get our private plane ready for take-off. We'll be back in Boston before we know it, far away from where Shannon's body lies at the bottom of the sea.

The champagne is still cool to drink, thanks to the ice pack Shannon considerately put in the hamper for us, but the more of it I drink, the less I enjoy it. It's not much fun drinking alone at the best of times, but even more so when I'm starting to get very anxious that something has gone wrong with my husband.

Putting the champagne down, I stand up and look down the beach, as if changing my vantage point is going to help me see Donovan better. I still see nothing but sand and a few rocks where the beach curves around. He's around that curve with Shannon, but I don't know what is happening between the two of them, and I guess I won't unless I go and investigate. The more I think about it, that might not actually be a bad idea. If I do go, I might at least get a look at her dead body before it's washed out to sea, as confirmation that my nightmare is finally over. I wonder if Donovan would be annoyed if I interrupted his work. Surely not – it would just be something extra we could bond over.

I've made my mind up.

I'm going to go and see what is taking my husband so long.

And if need be, *I'll help him finish the job quicker*.

TWENTY-SEVEN

SHANNON

It seems to be getting darker the further back I go into the cave, which is some feat – it was already pitch-black a minute ago. I can't even see my hands in front of my face, though my hands are currently outstretched in front of me, feeling out for any rocks so that I don't run into them headfirst. While it might seem like I'm foolishly scrabbling around in the dark without a hope, I'm actually working from memory. Having been here before with my father, and crucially with headtorches, I can remember a little bit about the network of tunnels in here, although that was many years ago and, without light, it's harder now.

But I do have a big motivation that I didn't have back then – *I'm fighting for my life here.*

I know Donovan is coming after me because I can hear him calling out my name as he follows me deeper into the inky blackness, and the only thing scarier than disappearing into the dark is knowing that there is someone lurking behind me who wants to hurt me if they get their hands on me. I've given myself a chance by going this way rather than trying to leave the cave, because if I'd done that, I'd have easily been caught and almost certainly be dead already.

I briefly think about using the torchlight on my phone to illuminate a pathway for me, but that would just tip off my pursuer as to my location, so I don't do that. Because of the lack of light, I end up banging my knee against a solid chunk of rock and the pain has me finally seeing something for a second.

Stars.

The groan I let out only serves to help Donovan narrow down my location, and he has no such qualms about using the torchlight on his phone to guide the way, which is proven when I see a huge bright beam to my right. Knowing exactly where he is helps me, but Donovan can see me too, so I quickly run down one of the tunnels and round a corner, desperate to get out of sight of that light again. I manage it and am soon back in darkness, but the downside of that is again I have no idea where to go.

I suddenly feel a solid wall in front of me and fear I have run into a dead end. Now I'll be easy prey for my attacker. But as my hands run along the rough edges of the cave wall, I suddenly feel a gap. When I figure out it is big enough for me to crawl into, I waste no time capitalising on my potential hiding place.

I immediately feel safer once I'm no longer wandering around in the dark on foot, but lying in a more concealed position, where surely Donovan won't be able to find me, even if he does end up in this corner of the cave. I hear his footsteps and hold my breath as he passes right by where I am, calling out my name, which echoes down the various tunnels and sends another shiver down my spine.

The torchlight flashes off the walls but doesn't come low enough to pick me up down here. As I listen to him move away, I'm wondering if I'll be able to sneak out of my hiding place and go back the way we came and escape this cave while he's still lost down here. I'm aware there's no way I'll be able to find my way out again unless I use the light of my phone to guide me, and I can't do that until I'm certain Donovan is far enough away so as not to see it.

'You know you can't get away from me, right?' Donovan calls out, though he must be mad if he thinks I'm going to give him a response. 'You have to die, Shannon. There's no other way!'

I figure out that his voice is to the right of my hiding place, and it sounds like it's gradually getting further away, so it seems I'm safe hiding here for now. That's good, because my knee is still throbbing from where I banged it, and I imagine it's bruised and bloodied, as well as a little swollen, though that is the least of my worries.

Suddenly, it's Donovan's turn to let out a groan, and I assume he's just inadvertently injured himself too, which can only help my cause. With a bit of luck, he might have sprained an ankle, and I could potentially outrun him. But, as I listen, I learn something much worse has happened to him.

'No! Come on!' he cries, though I have no idea what he is referring to. He continues to struggle and, from the sounds he's making, I get the impression that he might have managed to get himself stuck somewhere.

There's no doubt that this cave system is full of tight spaces, and I wonder if Donovan has accidentally got himself wedged into a place he can't get out of. I'm praying that is the case, but I know his cries might also be a ploy to lure me out of my hiding place. I stay where I am just in case it's a trap. But the more that time goes by, the more I realise Donovan really is struggling, and that becomes even more apparent when I hear his phone clatter onto the ground and he doesn't pick it back up again.

'Damn it!' he cries.

I can see the light from his torch pointing up at the roof and it doesn't move again, suggesting he can't pick up his device.

'Shannon! Help me!' he tries, which would be a preposterous thing for me to do but, again, only makes me think he is in serious trouble now.

After another couple of minutes of biding my time, I tentatively crawl out of my hiding place, though I am fully prepared to scurry back into it if need be. I don't need to because, once I am out, I see exactly the predicament Donovan has got himself into.

As I suspected, he is stuck. As I cautiously step towards the light on his phone, I see just how bad it is.

'Help me,' he says when he sees me coming closer; in place of the evil look that was in his eyes earlier I see only fear now. He really is scared, and for good reason. The lower half of his body is wedged in between two walls of the cave. While his top half is free for him to twist his torso and move his arms, he can't free his hips and legs.

The bottom half of the wall must have been narrower than the top.

He really is stuck.

So what am I going to do about it?

'Help me, please!' Donovan tries again after I've stopped approaching him.

I take out my own phone now and turn on the torchlight, shining it right at him to confirm that he is totally stuck. I check the injury to my knee, seeing blood, which I feared, but it's not as bad as it could be. It's certainly not bad enough to stop me making it out of here on foot.

After that, I simply pick up Donovan's phone and turn to leave.

'Wait, where are you going?' he cries. 'You can't leave me down here! You have to help me!'

I have to do no such thing and, to prove it, I rush away from him as quickly as I can, using the two phones to guide me. But I'm not just taking his phone to help light the way. I'm taking it because I don't want the police or anybody else tracking his signal and locating him down here. That's because I've not quite made my mind up about what I'm going to do about Donovan when I leave this cave.

I could get out there and, once I'm safe, send help for him to be rescued.

Or I could leave him down here to die.

The further I go to get out of the cave, and the more that Donovan calls after me and begs for me to go back, my decision becomes clearer. *He was trying to kill me.* It becomes even clearer when I think of what this man did to innocent people, including my ex-boyfriend, who is dead because of him. But most of all, I think about Barnaby, my son, who almost lost the chance to grow up and find his mother one day if he so wished.

Screw that desperate man screaming at me to help him as I get myself out of this cave.

I'm leaving him down here.

I'm leaving him to die.

TWENTY-EIGHT

SHANNON

It's a relief to see daylight ahead of me, meaning I no longer have to use the torchlight on the phones to find my way out. As I stumble towards the mouth of the cave, I see the water ahead of me and the brilliant blue sky. Only a few moments ago they were sights I never thought I'd get to savour again, when I was lost in the bowels of the cave and was pursued by a man who wanted to kill me. But it's that devious man who is still trapped in the dark while I am breaking out into the light. After checking over my shoulder one more time to make sure Donovan hasn't managed to get out too, I am assured that he is still very much trapped back there.

It sends a chill through my body to think of anybody trapped in the pitch-black like he is, but that chill soon fades when I step out into the warm sunlight, and I refuse to feel guilty or worried about a person who was trying to kill me and keep me from my son. My only concern now is my child and finding my way to him, so I can tell him the truth about who I really am, and be reunited with him.

I know that conversation won't be easy, not just because Barnaby is so young and might struggle to understand, but because of how emotional I will be trying to get my point across. I've spent such a long time pushing the trauma of giving my child away deep down that, to have it all dredged up now so suddenly, my emotions are all over the place. That's even before I consider the fact that a man tried to kill me and I'm lucky to be alive at all. My plan now is to keep calm and make it back to the car and drive away from this beach as quickly as possible, before finding Barnaby at the hotel and telling him the truth. After that, the police can get involved and deal with Donovan and Rosalind and, so far, I've not done anything that would get me into trouble. I didn't trap Donovan down in that cave, he got himself trapped, so I'm not fearing being arrested for anything myself. What I am fearing is encountering Rosalind on my way back to the car, because if I do see her, she's obviously going to want to know where her husband is. I guess my appearance will signal to her that something has gone terribly wrong with their plot, and she'll know her partner might be in danger if I'm still alive, so it will be hard to get past her then. I'm hoping I won't have to – if I can stick close to the rocks and work my way around the edge of the beach without moving out into the open, then I might be able to make it past Rosalind and that picnic hamper without her knowing.

I tentatively peer around a pile of rocks to where I last saw that woman sitting on the sand, and I expect to see her still there now on that blanket, sunbathing and sipping champagne. But while I do see the blanket and a bottle of champagne, I don't see her.

Where the hell is Rosalind?

I scour the beach for any sign of her but find none. She doesn't seem to be here, but where else would she be? She surely wouldn't leave without waiting for Donovan to kill me. She'd surely want to make sure that I was the one who ended up dead and not her husband. But I cannot see her. Not on the beach, not on the cliff above it and not in the sea that rolls into it.

'Shannon?'

While I can't see Rosalind, I have just heard her voice.

And it is right behind me.

Turning around cautiously, I see the American woman, but she seems far more surprised to see me. In fact, she looks like she's seen a ghost – given that I should be dead by now, she might just be thinking that she has.

'What are you doing? Where's Donovan?' she asks me, clearly afraid what my answer might be. But what can I say to her? That I've foiled her and her husband's deadly plan, and now intend to go and claim her son, while she runs into that cave to see if she can free her partner from a perilous position?

'I don't know,' I say, opting to lie.

'What do you mean you don't know?'

'I haven't seen him,' I say, doubling down. 'I've just been for a walk.'

'You haven't seen him?'

Rosalind looks very confused and looks all around herself to see if she can spot Donovan.

'No, I thought he was with you having a picnic. Is everything okay?'

Rosalind does not look like everything is okay, but I already know that. Part of me would like nothing more than to tell her the truth – that I've outsmarted the pair of them, and the game is up. But that would be too risky to do, so I keep quiet and keep playing dumb.

'You really haven't seen him?' Rosalind tries, no longer looking around the quiet beach but straight at me, and that's when I fear that she doesn't believe me. She's trying to get a read on me, and she might know something is wrong.

'Nope,' I say, but my attempt to reply casually comes across as false, and Rosalind frowns.

'I mean, he must be around here somewhere,' I say quickly. 'Could he have gone back to the car? I was just heading there myself. Shall I go and have a look for him up there?'

I take a step to leave.

'Stop,' Rosalind says firmly. Even though every cell in my body is screaming at me to run, I do as she says.

'What's wrong?' I try lamely.

'You know what's wrong. What have you done with my husband?'

'What? I haven't done anything. I just told you, I haven't seen him.'

'I know you're lying. I'm a liar myself, Shannon, a damn good one, and part of being a good liar is being able to spot when someone else isn't telling the truth. You're lying to me right now, aren't you? So tell me, Shannon, what's happened? Where is my husband?'

I know she's seen right through me, so I could just turn and run, abandoning all hopes of making out like I'm still blissfully unaware of what is going on, trying to get back to the car before her. I very much intend to beat her to the car and will start running in a few seconds' time. But first, I want to look into the eyes of the woman who has spent a lot of this trip telling my son to be quiet, or not to do things, or just generally being mean to the boy she is supposed to love so much.

She doesn't deserve him.

And now I know the truth, she isn't going to get him back.

'Your husband is in that cave,' I say calmly, pointing to the opening in the cliff to our right, and Rosalind turns, looking into the inky black beyond. 'He tried to kill me, just like you knew he planned to, but I got away from him. He's in there now, trapped between two rocks, and he'll die in there unless he gets help. But I'm not going to give him that help. I'm on my way to see my son, the son you two thought you could prevent from ever knowing the truth. I don't know what you plan to do with that news, Rosalind, but one thing is for sure. If you try and stop me, I will hurt you, and then there will be nobody to help your husband make it out of that cave alive.'

With all of that off my chest, I stand firm and wait to see what Rosalind's next move is. I'm half expecting her to charge at me, but she doesn't. She just looks back to the cave, clearly thinking about how the man she loves is trapped in there and must be so afraid of never seeing daylight again.

'He needs you,' I say. 'Go and help him. The game's up, Rosalind, but neither of you has to get hurt if you just leave me alone now. Don't make this any worse than it already is.'

I am praying that she takes my advice and runs into that cave, and when she takes a step towards it, I think I might be about to get my wish. But then she turns and looks at me and, when she does, I see the look of pure venom in her eyes.

She's angry and rightly so.

I'm winning right now.

But she wants to turn the tables.

'You bitch,' she says, and then almost laughs. 'You really think you can get away with this. You have no idea who you're messing with.'

'I know exactly who you are,' I reply defiantly, trying to match her strength with my own. 'Your husband told me all about what you and him have done to innocent people. But you aren't doing it to me. This is where you lose and I win.'

I decide to turn and make a run for it, hoping that in a foot race I can beat Rosalind to the car and get away from her, leaving her stranded here with no hope of help. But she is quickly in pursuit. As the pair of us sprint across the hot sand, I know the odds are in her favour because my knee is throbbing and slowing me down.

Trying to claw back an advantage, I bend down and scoop up a handful of sand before hurling it backwards into Rosalind's face, but the grains just hit her chest rather than her eyes and she keeps coming for me at the same speed. I almost wish I hadn't bothered to try that – it slowed me down and she's gained ground. Things only get worse when I stumble on the sand and fall, my damn knee weakening further at just the wrong moment.

Rosalind is almost upon me, but I rise up to meet her, though she pushes me straight back down. Now the two of us are rolling across the sand, our hands scratching at each other's faces as we both desperately fight to gain control.

Rosalind strikes me across the cheek when she is briefly on top of me, but I quickly push her off and hit her back, before I try my sand-throwing trick once more – and it works. The sand I throw at her hits her right in the face, and she cries out as she closes her eyes and tries to protect them from the harsh granules that are grazing against her corneas.

That gives me the time I need to get back to my feet and start running again, and I make sure I don't do anything as disastrous as fall over. Rosalind is soon back to her feet and in pursuit, but there is more of a gap between us now. I make it to the path first, ascending the cliff and feeling the burn in my legs as I run up the steep slope, huffing and puffing like some fitness freak who incorporates hill runs into their daily regime. But I am no fitness freak and the only reason I am managing to make it up this path at such a pace is because I am fuelled by adrenaline – and a desperate desire to make it to Barnaby and tell him that I'm his real mother.

But the woman chasing me is just as desperate to keep Barnaby thinking she is his real mother. I can hear her behind me, panting just as hard as I am, but not giving in to her lung-busting breathing or the lactic acid build-up in her legs.

I make it up the trail in what could be a record time and see the car parked a few feet away. I know it's going to be almost impossible for me to slow down, get inside it and start the engine before Rosalind can catch up with me. That's why I make the decision to turn back and face the incoming storm. As Rosalind reaches the top of the path, I greet her with one very strong push back the way she came. But I make sure to direct my push so that she won't simply fall onto the sandy path she has just run up, nor the ledge that I jumped down onto when I first arrived at this beach and was showing off to the wealthy couple.

I make sure to direct my push so that Rosalind goes backwards over the edge of the cliff, and suffers the fall all the way down to the beach below.

I see Rosalind's eyes go wide and hear her let out a terrified scream as gravity takes control of her body. She disappears from view as she goes over the cliff. But I race to the edge and peer down to try and see her again and, when I do, I spot her lying on a pile of rocks below me, her body contorted and crumpled, her lifeless eyes staring up at the sky above, or perhaps at me looking down at her from the clifftop.

But either way, it's over now.

She is dead, her husband is trapped and now there's nothing stopping me from getting to my son.

But something has changed – I'm no longer entirely innocent in all of this.

I just murdered somebody.

That might make me think twice about speaking to the police about what really happened at this beach today.

TWENTY-NINE

SHANNON

I don't spend too long looking at Rosalind's still body, not just because the sight of it makes me feel sick. I am desperate to get to Barnaby and see him, now that I know he is my son. That's why I leave the edge of the cliff and run to the car before starting the engine and speeding away.

As I drive and the sea recedes in my rear-view mirror, I think about how it could easily have been Donovan and Rosalind driving away from here and leaving my body behind. That was their intention. He would have killed me, taken the car key and left, and nobody might ever have known what happened to me. But I am still here, surviving, while Rosalind's corpse lies in the sand and Donovan still struggles to free himself from the cave.

I don't have to worry about her anymore, but what about him? Could he get out? No, he was really stuck. Not only that, but he was in the dark and I took his phone, so even if he gets free he won't have a torchlight to guide him out.

He's not a threat anymore, and neither is his wife.

But the police could be.

If they ever found out that I pushed Rosalind off the cliff then I would be in trouble, just like I would be if they found out that I left Donovan trapped in the cave. I could try and explain this crazy story to them, but would they believe me? I can't take the risk. If I am arrested then who will look after Barnaby? Probably somebody in Donovan's or Rosalind's family back in America, and I can't have that. I can't be languishing in a prison cell while my son is raised by somebody else across the Atlantic.

My plan now is to drive back to the hotel and find Barnaby. I'm sure that won't be a problem, but it will be a problem that he'll be with his nanny. Philippa is currently taking care of him, so how am I going to explain to her what just happened? I can't, she'd surely just call the police. Or worse – what if she is in on Rosalind and Donovan's plan and knew what they really came to Ireland to do? I can't let her know that something has gone awry, just in case she's a threat. I suspect that she isn't, but I thought that about the couple not so long ago, and look how that turned out.

I expect to encounter Philippa at the hotel, so I need a cover story, one that is believable enough for me to get some alone time with Barnaby, then drive the pair of us away from the hotel. Once I've done that, I'll have time to consider what to do next. The main thing is that I get time with my son.

The further I get from the beach, the better I feel about what I'm leaving behind, though I know it will still come to me in the darkest hours of the night. As the hotel comes into view, I focus on the future – and the priority now is being reunited with my baby.

I feel incredibly on edge as I park up, almost as petrified as I felt back in that cave when I realised my life was in danger. What if Barnaby rejects me when I tell him that I'm really his mother? What if he says he wants Rosalind, unaware that she is already dead? And what if I end up with nothing and ultimately in prison, just a criminal resigned to spending the rest of my life behind bars?

I can't face a reality that harsh, so I tell myself that I have to find a way to make this work. I head into the hotel and start looking for my child. But I can't find Barnaby or Philippa anywhere. They're not at the pool or the restaurant or the gardens outside. They must be in their room, which is a problem, because how am I supposed to talk to Barnaby privately if Philippa is right there with him?

'Hey, Shannon!'

A blur races past me and I realise it was Barnaby, running through the reception area of the hotel. He is giggling as he disappears behind a door to my left, and I'm just about to go after him when I see Philippa giving chase.

'Did you see where he went?' she asks, looking concerned. It's probably because she doesn't want Barnaby's parents to think she has lost their son. Little does she know that she is standing right in front of Barnaby's biological mother. Or does she?

'He went that way,' I say, pointing to my right, which is the opposite direction to where Barnaby went.

'Thanks,' Philippa says before heading off, seemingly more eager to catch up with him than to ask me why I'm back from the beach so early.

Once the nanny has left on the wrong trail, I go the right way and enter the room that I saw Barnaby run into. When I do, I see what looks like an unoccupied conference room. There is a long table running through the centre of the room, surrounded by chairs on all sides, as well as a podium at the front where I guess businesspeople make presentations during corporate events. It doesn't look like anybody is in the room now, although I know Barnaby must be hiding in here somewhere.

I check under the table and pull a few chairs out but he's not under there, which means there's only one other place he can be. Moving quickly, because it might not take long for Philippa to figure out that I sent her the wrong way, I rush towards the podium and find Barnaby sitting behind it, still giggling and very amused that he found such a good hiding place. But I'm not here to play games, and I have to make that clear quickly.

'I need to talk to you about something,' I say as Barnaby laughs. He seems very giddy, and I wonder if he's had some sugar recently.

'You go and hide now,' he says to me, eager to keep the game alive, but there's no time for that.

'Barnaby, listen. This is important,' I try again, but Barnaby just closes his eyes and starts counting, as if giving me time to go and find my own hiding place.

I nervously look back to the door but there's no sign of Philippa yet, although it surely won't be long until she retraces her steps and thinks to check in here. She'll probably be getting frantic that she still can't find him. I would be the same in her position, but I can't worry about her when I have so many worries of my own.

'Barnaby, please. Just be quiet for a second and let me speak,' I try again, and this time Barnaby opens his eyes. While he does stop counting, he isn't ready for the game to finish yet.

'Okay, I'll go and hide instead!' he cries as he leaps up and starts running away.

'No, wait!' I cry as I reach out and grab his arm. I manage to stop him leaving, though he looks confused as to why I would do that. I guess he's going to be even more confused when I tell him who I am.

'You have to come with me,' I say.

'Why?'

'Because...'

I don't know how I'm supposed to say this.

'I'm...' I try again.

'What?'

'The thing is, you have two mommies, not just one.'

Barnaby looks very puzzled by that.

'I'm really sorry. I don't know if I'm even doing this right,' I say. 'What I'm trying to say is that when you were born, you had a different mommy to Rosalind. She has looked after you, but that's because she adopted you. Adopted means when a person raises a child as their own.'

'I don't understand.'

I can't blame him. I wouldn't understand either if somebody told me such a thing when I was his age.

'That's okay. It's a little complicated, but we can talk it all through and you'll understand soon. The main thing to know is that I am not just your tour guide. I am your mammy, the one who gave birth to you. I just made a mistake when you were born. A very big mistake,' I say, trying not to allow my emotions to overwhelm me. I can't have any sobbing getting in the way of making my point. 'I thought I couldn't cope and that it would be best if somebody else looked after you. I just wanted you to have a good life. So you were taken away, but I have thought about you every day since, and I am so sorry for what happened. I should have been the one to look after you, nobody else. Not Rosalind or Donovan. Me.'

Barnaby is very quiet now, and I'm not sure if that's a good or bad thing. Either he's processing what I've just said to him or he's getting very upset about it. Either way, I hope he's got the message.

'Where are Mommy and Daddy?' he asks me, suggesting he hasn't fully understood, although it's understandable that he would be wanting them. They're all he has ever known.

'They're not here. We need to go,' I say now, and I take Barnaby's hand to try and lead him away. But he doesn't want to leave with me.

'Am I in trouble?' he asks quietly.

'Trouble? No, not at all. I promise.'

'I don't want to get shouted at again.'

'You won't. I swear. You're not in trouble, but we really have to go now.'

Barnaby is still reluctant, so I decide to employ a tactic that many parents will have used when trying to get their kid to do something they don't want to do.

'Shall we play a game?' I ask, and Barnaby thinks about it before nodding.

'Okay, the game is still hide and seek, and we're playing against Philippa,' I tell him. 'We have to try and get to the car before she catches us. That is our base where we'll be safe. Okay?'

Barnaby nods and seems keen on this game.

'Let's go,' I say, and we head for the door, holding hands and working as a team. When we reach the door, I peer cautiously out of it but don't see Philippa, so I keep us on the move. As we pass through reception, there is still no sign of the nanny.

We make it out of the hotel and into the car park – only bad luck will see me get caught here. But there is still no sign of Philippa, and I quickly unlock the car and tell Barnaby to get in. Once we're inside, I tell him the game isn't ending here.

'Do you want to go on a road trip?' I ask him.

'To where?'

'Dublin. You can see where I live. Would you like that?'

Barnaby nods.

'Okay, let's go,' I say as I start the engine. The fact that Barnaby is no longer asking for his mommy or daddy might mean he is far happier spending time with me than them. But Philippa is still a problem. As I reverse out of our parking spot, I catch a glimpse of her coming out of the hotel.

She must have seen the car. I know she has when I see her waving at me and trying to get me to stop. But I just keep going, afraid to park up again – doing so might mean I lose my only chance at getting to know my son better.

There is so much we have to catch up on.

And I have to do it all quickly, in case the police come looking for us.

THIRTY

SHANNON

For somebody who loves to travel, I've never been so happy to see my home.

It's a relief to be in Dublin again, and even more of a relief that, as of yet, I have not been pursued by any police officers about the things that have happened since I left this city a few days ago. The fact that I haven't been pursued tells me that Philippa mustn't have reported me taking Barnaby from the hotel without her permission, which I am grateful for, but at the same time also anxious about why. From her point of view, I have just abducted a child who was under her care, so what must she be thinking? She'll be wondering where we are and also where Rosalind and Donovan are. I get confirmation of that when, after ditching the hire car on a random street a mile or so from my flat, I check Donovan's phone that is still in my possession. When I do, I see that Philippa has been trying to reach him. There are two missed calls from her as well as a message that I can read on the locked screen.

Where are you? Is everything okay?

I guess the fact that Donovan hasn't replied will give her the answer, and I presume she sent the same message to Rosalind, who also won't have been able to reply. But what is Philippa doing now? Going to the police, surely, and I've spent the entire drive home worrying about what will happen if and when they come to my door. It's why I've decided that I need to do the right thing and go to them first – tell them what happened before they have to ask me, and hopefully they'll see that I had no other choice. It will also give me the chance to tell them that there was more to Kieran's death – that it wasn't the accidental overdose it was believed to be. But first, I want to get Barnaby somewhere safe, and that is inside my flat. Once I've done that, I can explain to him what is going to happen next.

'Is this where you live?' Barnaby asks for the third time since we left the car, as we walk through the busy Dublin streets.

'No, it's just around the corner from here,' I say, pointing ahead, and the little boy nods and continues skipping along beside me.

As he does, I get a vision of a different life, one in which I never gave my son up for adoption, and now I have just picked him up from school and we are walking home together. He'd be telling me all about his day, what he learnt in some of his lessons, whether or not he has any homework to complete tonight. I might also be hearing about which friends he played with at lunchtime, or which one of his teachers is his current favourite, as well as which ones he doesn't like, and maybe his overall opinion on school in general. He might enjoy it or he might be hating it like it I did when I was his age, feeling restrained by the classroom and wishing I could break free and do something else instead. That is the pleasant, perfect version of my life, but that is not the version that exists today. The circumstances that have led to the pair of us walking through the streets of Dublin couldn't be more extreme.

'Is this where you live?' Barnaby asks for a fourth and final time. We have now made it to my flat, and I confirm that this is my home. I want to ask him how it compares to the home he lived in with Rosalind and Donovan, but there is no point. Of course it'll be much smaller and cheaper, without a big garden or hired staff, and there are definitely no toys to play with here. But as I unlock the door and we go inside, I wonder if I can make Barnaby feel something that he hasn't ever felt before in that big house of his in Boston.

Real love.

'Cool!' Barnaby cries after we have entered my flat. He has quickly spotted the Celtic spear hanging on my wall. 'What is that?'

'It's a weapon that armies used to fight with,' I tell him, which only makes it seem even cooler to a little boy like him. He asks if he can play with it.

'Maybe later,' I say sensibly, hoping he'll have forgotten about it by then and I won't have to try supervising a young child running around with a very sharp object. 'We need to talk first. Would you like a drink?'

Barnaby shakes his head, so I offer some food, but he's not hungry either, so I invite him to take a seat on my sofa. He does that and I sit beside him, internally comparing this situation to all the nights I have spent by myself on this same sofa, thinking about what my life would have been like if I had a child to share my evenings with. It seems I've finally got my wish, but as the old saying goes, be careful what you wish for.

'I have to do something now,' I start explaining to Barnaby. 'I have to phone some people and tell them that we are here. Then they are going to come and visit us and ask me some questions.'

'What kind of questions?' Barnaby asks, his little head turning as he looks around my flat while we talk.

'Questions about me and you and how we ended up here.'

'Will they ask if you're my mommy?'

I pause before nodding.

'What about my other mommy?'

'Yes, they'll ask about her too. And your daddy, although you have two of those as well.'

'Do I?'

I nod. 'Yes, and I can tell you all about your other daddy, but I'll have to be quick. I really need to call these people so they can come here and speak to me.'

'Okay,' Barnaby says, and I don't waste any time.

'Your other daddy's name was Kieran,' I say, and Barnaby repeats the name back to me as if practising it. 'Me and him were together for a while, but we split up. I was pregnant with you by then, and didn't know what to do. I was young. Scared. Confused. So I made a decision that I thought was best. That's why, when you were born, your American mammy and daddy took you.'

I have no idea how much of what I'm telling Barnaby is going to be understood by the little boy, but I say it all anyway – I have to try. If he doesn't understand me now, hopefully he will one day.

'Where is Kieran now?' Barnaby asks me.

I don't know how to tell him that the real dad I just told him about is dead.

'He's not here,' I say. 'He's in heaven.'

Barnaby nods, showing understanding, and I wonder who he knows that died for him to get the concept of heaven.

'Are you going to come back to America with me?' Barnaby asks.

'No,' I say. 'I'm going to stay here. But you might be able to stay here with me if you like. Would you want to?'

Barnaby shrugs.

'I need to tell you something about your other mammy and daddy now. Unfortunately, they have done some bad things and

I had to stop them. You're a bit too young for me to explain it all to you properly, but I just want you to know that I love you very much and, as long as you are with me, you will be safe. I promise.'

'What if I'm not with you?'

'Hopefully, you will be.'

'Am I in trouble?' Barnaby nervously asks me now, scratching his arm, which looks more like a nervous gesture than because he genuinely has an itch.

'No, of course not.'

'Are you?'

That's not so simple to answer.

'I might be.'

'Then don't call them.'

'Who?'

'The people you said you need to call. Don't call them. Let's just stay here.'

'I would love to, but I have to speak to somebody about what has happened.'

It's sweet that Barnaby clearly doesn't want me to get in trouble, and I wish the world was as simple as it probably is in his head.

'I don't like my mommy and daddy. They're mean to me and never play with me. You're nicer.'

I already knew that, but it's a sad thing to hear coming from such an innocent child. Then I remember what he said to me before. He tried to warn me about them.

Does that mean he knew what they were capable of?

'When you told me that they were dangerous, how did you know that?' I ask Barnaby nervously.

'I heard them talking one night. They thought I was in bed, but I'd sneaked downstairs. They were talking about some people they hurt in a fire. They said they were glad they did it. I was scared so I went back to bed, and they didn't hear me.'

Barnaby heard about the poor couple who died in Dallas. Rosalind and Donovan must have been reminiscing over it one evening, probably with a bottle of wine, as if they were catching up on the day's events in a relaxing manner and not actually talking about murder. But it was murder, and poor Barnaby knew something was wrong when he overheard them, which is what he was trying to warn me about.

'Will I see them again?' Barnaby asks me.

'Erm...'

'Are they in heaven now too?'

Tears fill my eyes as I try to stay strong for the pair of us, but I don't know what to do. Today has been so overwhelming. I fear it's only going to get worse when I phone the police.

But I have to do it, right?

Barnaby asks me for a drink and I go to get it for him. Then he asks if we can have the television on, so I do that for him too. Before I know it, another hour has gone by, and I spent it all just watching him and wishing there was a way that we could stay like this forever.

Maybe there is.

Maybe I don't call the police.

Maybe I see if I can somehow get away with what happened at the beach.

If I can, maybe I won't lose the little boy I have only just been reunited with.

THIRTY-ONE

SHANNON

I've had a sleepless night, but not just because I've been thinking about Donovan trapped in that cave, or Rosalind lying on those rocks, or Philippa possibly talking to the police. It's because I've been lying beside Barnaby in my bed and watching him sleep, studying every little detail on his face and committing it to memory, in case the police kick my door down and take me away and I never get to see him ever again. As dawn breaks and sunlight filters around the edges of my bedroom curtains, my front door is still intact, and I'm not in handcuffs yet.

I don't know what is going on, but I'm still a free woman, and that means I can carry on being a mother to Barnaby while I am. In the process, that will give me a little more time to think about my next move.

I leave my son sleeping and go into the kitchen to make him breakfast – nothing major, just some toast and fruit juice. When I take it in to him he is very excited about the prospect of breakfast in bed. I presume that's because he usually spends this first part of the day with the nanny while his parents go about their business. But here he gets a lot of attention from somebody who actually wants to give it to him, rather than someone who is just paid to do it, and there's a big difference there.

As he eats, I check Donovan's phone again and see that there is a new message on there. This one is from a contact saved as 'Pilot'.

Good morning, Boss. Just confirming that everything is cleared for our departure this morning. See you and your family shortly.

I realise that this must be the pilot of Donovan's private plane – it sounds like Donovan had a flight scheduled to depart this morning. He's obviously not going to be there to board the plane, nor are any of the other passengers, and what will happen then?

I think about texting back, pretending to be Donovan, saying that there is a change of plan and I don't need to fly today. But then I have second thoughts. Posing as somebody else might only make things worse for me in the long run. It would be another thing the police could use against me as they are compiling my crimes, so I decide to turn the phone off. I should have done that yesterday. What if the signal on it can be tracked?

So much paranoia, and it's only half past seven in the morning.

After breakfast, during which Barnaby eats a lot and I barely touch mine, the two of us spend the morning chatting about all sorts of things. He asks me about my parents, who are of course his grandparents, and I tell him a few heart-warming stories about them that only bring more tears to my eyes. I just wish things had been different and they could have met my little boy. I could have given my father his wish and made him a grandad, but I didn't, just like I never got to see my mother playing with a grandchild either. I explained to Barnaby that they had both gone to heaven with the angels before he was born, and he seemed to understand that. What he probably wouldn't have understood if I had tried to explain was that if they had still been alive when I was pregnant with him, maybe I wouldn't have made the decision to give him away. That extra support that my parents could have offered would have been priceless, but it was not an option for me. Though that's a conversation for another day, when Barnaby is much older, provided I get the chance to have that conversation in time.

Barnaby also asks about my hobbies after he tells me what he likes, and I am having fun as I learn more about him, while letting him know more about his mammy too. The elephant in the room is the fact that I know this cannot continue this way forever. There is no world in which I can just pretend like everything that led up to this moment didn't happen. How would I explain having a child with me to my friends or even my neighbours when they see me and Barnaby together? People would want to know who he is, how we know each other and what resulted in us being together, and I can't just lie and make up some weird story. Not only would that not work but it would only confuse Barnaby, a little boy who needs the truth to be able to put together the pieces of his very fragile life. I do have the $5,000 that Rosalind transferred to me as a deposit before she and her family came here, but that's not very much money to go on the run with. I can hardly get all the things I need to start a new life with those limited funds, and I'll soon burn through that cash, feeding and clothing the child now under my care.

There's only one thing I can reasonably do.

I have to go to the police. But I decide it can wait until tomorrow, so that Barnaby and I can have a little more time together.

Late the next morning, after Barnaby and I have finished playing a game of hide and seek in my flat – which doesn't take long because of the lack of good hiding places – I mention making a phone call again.

'It's the police, isn't it?' Barnaby says, guessing.

My silence gives him his answer.

'Why don't I phone them?' he suggests. 'I could say I lost my mommy and daddy and you found me and have been looking after me and are my real mommy.'

That sounds great, but it also sounds like the naïve ramblings of an innocent child who doesn't really understand how the world works. While I would love nothing more than for Barnaby to get me out of this mess with a simple phone call, explaining that he is perfectly happy with me and that he wants to stay here forever, that just wouldn't work in reality. I'll be questioned by the police without Barnaby present, and they will want to know exactly where his legal parents are. Whether or not I direct them to the beach, I'll be in trouble.

There's no choice here.

I'm the one who has to make the phone call, and I'm the one who has to take responsibility for this.

'You sit here and watch the TV and I'll be right back, okay?' I say to Barnaby as I turn the television on, giving him the remote control so he can flick through the channels and choose what he wants to watch.

He does that so I leave the room, take out my phone and, after several deep breaths, I go to make the phone call that is going to change my life forever. By the end of the day, I could be in a cell, while my image is flashed all across the news channels in connection with two dead bodies that have been found at a picturesque beach. But what else can I do? Somebody will find Rosalind's body eventually, and even if they don't, Philippa must be talking to the police and alerting them to the fact that a child is missing.

The call connects and I'm just about to speak when I hear something from the room I just left.

It's a female voice, and she says something that turns my blood cold.

'An American family, believed to be in the country on vacation, have been reported missing, and efforts are underway to locate them as quickly as possible out of fear that they might have come to harm.'

'Hello? Which emergency service would you like?' says the voice at the other end of the line, but I end the call and rush back to the television, where I find Barnaby watching the news report. But he's not just watching a reporter talking about him and his family being missing – he is looking at a photo of the three of them on screen.

I see the image that the media are using of Rosalind, Donovan and Barnaby, highlighting to the viewers exactly what this missing family looks like, and of course they've chosen a photo that makes it seem like this was one perfect, happy family. Donovan is beaming with his arm around his smiling wife, while she has her arms on Barnaby's shoulder. Funnily enough, he's not smiling himself. But to anybody who doesn't know this couple, and is seeing and hearing about them for the first time, they would assume they are normal people who have never done anything wrong in their lives. That couldn't be further from the truth, but how often is the truth expressly given in the national news?

'I'm on TV!' Barnaby cries as he gets closer to the screen, staring at his image with excited and wide eyes, like anybody his age would if they saw themselves on television. But I'm not excited – the fact that this is making headlines already means I'm too late, and the police are aware of something being very wrong in relation to this family. I've now lost the power to try and get ahead of this, to get my story out there first, which might have made it more believable. As it is, whatever happens next, I will look more like a woman with something to hide than the innocent victim I actually am.

'Oh no,' I say as Barnaby touches his own face on screen. 'What have I done?'

I don't know what to do, but before I can think about it any longer, I hear a knock at my front door.

It feels like my heart instantly stops beating in my chest as I turn to look at the door, wondering who it could be on the other side of it. I'm not expecting anybody, but even so, I have a feeling I know who it is.

It has to be the police. Philippa will have reported what happened, and the police have tracked me down and come to question me about the family currently dominating the Irish headlines.

'Barnaby. I need you to listen to me,' I say as I hear a second knock.

Barnaby is still enamoured by the TV, especially when the reporter says his name, but I grab hold of him and demand his attention. 'Barnaby. Look at me! I love you and want you to know that whatever happens, I always will. Okay?'

Barnaby looks afraid, though he can't be as afraid as I am of opening that door, of being pushed against the wall as I am arrested. I can't ignore the knocking forever, and I doubt the police would let me anyway. They'll kick this door down any second now, so I might as well save them the trouble and open it before that happens. I leave Barnaby by the TV and go to get this over with.

Opening the door, I brace myself for a swarm of officers rushing towards me with handcuffs.

But what I see instead is a surprise.

It's not the police at my door.

It's the nanny.

THIRTY-TWO

SHANNON

'Hello, Shannon,' Philippa says calmly as she looks at me, then at Barnaby sitting on the carpet behind me. 'Can I come in? I think we need to talk.'

I stare at the nanny on my doorstep before looking past her to see if she is accompanied by police officers. She seems to be by herself, so it could be worse. It's still a shock to see her, although she seems very calm as she waits for me to let her in.

'What are you doing here?' I ask as the news report about her missing employers continues to play on the TV behind me.

'What do you think?' Philippa replies. 'Can I come inside or not? I will say that there are a lot of people out here looking for that little boy behind you, so the sooner you can close this front door again, the better.'

I know she is right, so I let Philippa in and then shut my front door quickly, concealing Barnaby from view of the outside world, for a little longer at least.

'Hello, Barnaby,' Philippa says as she approaches my son, and he looks happy to see her, standing up and giving her a hug, before telling her that he has been on TV.

'Wow, that's exciting, isn't it?' Philippa says, allowing him to have his moment before she looks to me with a serious expression on her face, proving how it's really anything but.

'Are you okay?' Philippa asks, making a quick visual check on the child, but he lets her know that he is, and she seems satisfied. Once she has seen that I've not been mistreating Barnaby, Philippa tells him that she will play with him soon but has to talk to me first.

'Come here,' she says as she walks past me and goes into my bedroom, which is the only private place we can talk in here.

I leave Barnaby staring goggle-eyed at the TV and follow Philippa into my room.

'Close the door behind you,' she instructs me, and I do as she says.

'Philippa, let me explain. I—'

'Stop talking and listen to me. What happened with Rosalind and Donovan?'

That's a scary question to answer, so I'd rather not.

'Where are they?' Philippa goes on. 'What did you do to them?'

'They tried to kill me! They got me to that remote beach to hurt me, then they were going to put my body out to sea and go home and nobody would ever have known what happened to me!'

'Kill you? Why would they want to do that?'

'Because—'

The next part is almost just as hard to say.

'Because I'm Barnaby's real mother.'

Philippa looks stunned by my revelation.

'You know he's adopted, right?' I say, and Philippa nods, trying to follow along with me. 'Well, I'm his birthmother. They tracked me down and they planned to kill me. They didn't want me and Barnaby ever finding each other when he got older. I'm not the only one they did this to. They murdered Barnaby's father too, and Esme's parents in America. They killed them and they were going to kill me. But I got away.'

'You got away? How?'

'It's a long story. The main thing is that I made it off that beach and, when I did, I just wanted to see my son and take him somewhere safe, so I brought him here. I'm sorry I took him from the hotel without telling you what was happening. I was just in shock and afraid and didn't know who to trust. I'm sorry if I worried you, but Barnaby's okay, you can see that. He's fine. He's safe here.'

Philippa listens to all I have to say but doesn't let me get away with not giving a little more detail.

'What happened to Rosalind and Donovan?' she repeats.

'They were going to hurt me. I had to do whatever I could to get away from them. I—'

'Shannon, what happened?'

'She's dead,' I admit. 'She fell off a cliff as she was trying to stop me driving away.'

Philippa goes very pale, but not as pale as Rosalind's lifeless face on those rocks.

'And Donovan?' she asks.

'He chased me into a cave, but he got stuck. I left him. I don't know, maybe he's still alive, but if he's stuck then...' I let my sentence trail off – it's obvious what will happen to him if he can't get out, if it hasn't happened already.

'Oh my God,' Philippa says as she turns away from me and begins pacing.

What is she thinking? Does she think I'm evil? Is she preparing to go to the police with this information now? But she must have already spoken to the police, mustn't she?

'They're already on the news,' I say. 'That was you, right? You reported them missing?'

Philippa stops pacing and shakes her head. 'No, I haven't spoken to the police.'

'You didn't? Why not?'

'Because I didn't know what was going on.'

I find that hard to believe, not just because she must have worried about what had happened to her employers, and the child who was in her care, but because every police officer and journalist in Ireland seems to be on the case now.

'But if you didn't report this, then why is their photo on the news?' I ask sceptically. 'Why is everyone looking for them?'

'It's the pilot of their private plane. He reported them missing when they failed to show up for their flight back to Boston.'

That suddenly makes sense, but the news report I just saw seemed to be missing something.

'Why didn't he report you as missing too?' I ask Philippa. 'The report I just saw only talked about the family members.'

'He did. I've been mentioned in a few other reports. But I guess the majority of the media is just focusing on the rich family. The nanny isn't as interesting as them. Nobody cares about the hired help.'

That's probably right, as wrong as it should be.

'It was all self-defence,' I plead now, as if Philippa is a judge or member of the jury and has a say in my fate. 'Honestly, you have to believe me. They were going to kill me, and I had no choice. I fought for my life, and I fought so that Barnaby could know the truth.'

'Does he?' Philippa asks.

'That I'm his real mother? Yes,' I confirm.

'What did he say?' she asks me.

'He's shocked, obviously. I'm not sure he fully understands. He also doesn't seem very upset about me looking after him rather than Donovan and Rosalind. He doesn't seem to be missing them at all.'

'Why would he? They treated him terribly,' Philippa states matter-of-factly, and she doesn't seem quite as upset about her employer's demise as I thought she might be. 'They treated me terribly too.'

I saw glimpses of both of those things while I was in their company, and I can see that Philippa, like Barnaby, feels freer rather than upset without them around. Even if it is a blessing for them, there's still the small matter of everybody in Ireland looking for that couple, and only the pair of us knowing where they are.

'What do we do now?' I ask, hoping this woman is on my side. 'How do we explain this to the police? How do we protect Barnaby?'

'You haven't said a word of this to anybody else?' Philippa asks me, and I confirm not.

'Good. We need time to make a plan, but for now I think the best thing is to lie low. Barnaby cannot leave this flat. He'll be recognised. I shouldn't go out either. People will be looking for me. The pilot will have given the police my description, and I've already seen references to me in the news.'

'What about me? Am I in the news?' I ask nervously.

'No, at least not yet, anyway,' Philippa replies.

'Why not?'

'The pilot never saw you or met you. Nobody knows Rosalind and Donovan hired you as their tour guide, nobody but me, anyway, and I won't tell anybody. Sure, you'll have been spotted with them and there might be a few reports of people describing you, but the police must not have your name yet or they'd already be here.'

'How did you find me?'

'What?'

'How did you get my address? You saw me driving away with Barnaby, but you didn't know where I lived. So how did you find me?'

I wait for Philippa's answer, suddenly sceptical as to whether or not she is actually on my side after all.

'It wasn't that difficult. I just searched for Shannon O'Sheas in Dublin and found a council notice online, referring to a dispute between you and a neighbour. It listed both your addresses.'

I think back to the time I registered a noise complaint about my neighbour with the council; I didn't know those kinds of things could end up documented online.

'I could have found you in other ways too,' Philippa adds. 'And if I can find you easily, the police won't have any problems. That's why we need to decide what to do. It really won't be long until they find some CCTV footage from over the past few days when you were with them and, when that ends up on the news, somebody will come forward and say they recognise you.'

I know Philippa is right, but I have no idea what the solution to the problem is.

'I was going to call the police just before you got here,' I say. 'I was going to tell them the truth. Maybe if you help me, back my story up, say how horrible that couple were, they will have more chance of believing me.'

'You want me to help you? To lie?'

'Not lie, just say what you know.'

'What I know is that Rosalind and Donovan could be mean. I don't know for sure that they tried to kill you. I'm just taking your word for that.'

'I'm telling the truth!'

'Fine, but you have to understand that it's risky for me to support a woman I barely know. What if we both end up in prison? Who looks after Barnaby then?'

Philippa is right. We have to put that little boy first, and we can't both be at risk of getting in trouble.

'What shall we do?' I ask. 'I'm all out of ideas.'

'We should probably go somewhere else,' Philippa decides. 'Find another place to stay in case the police do come. That'll give us time to think things through.'

'But where can we go?'

'I don't know.'

'Where are we going?' says a little voice behind us.

Both of us have been too busy to notice that Barnaby had peeped through the door and has just overheard the last part of our conversation.

'Oh, hey!' Philippa says, forcing a smile on her face. 'Are you okay?'

'I'm hungry,' Barnaby says quietly, and I realise then that a few hours have passed since I made him breakfast. The problem is, I don't think I have any more food in the flat.

'I could go to the shops and get something for us all,' I suggest. 'It would give me a chance to see what it's like out there.'

'Be careful,' Philippa warns me. 'There'll be TV crews around. Cameras. Journalists.'

I don't like the thought of having to pass by a load of people who are all looking for the couple I left on that beach, or the little boy who I currently have in my home, but my son is hungry and it's my duty to keep him fed.

'I would send you, but people are looking for you,' I say to Philippa, which is true. If she goes wandering around the streets, it won't be long until somebody recognises her from the news reports, and I can't risk that. But that means I have to trust leaving her alone with Barnaby, although having seen how she looked after him when Rosalind and Donovan were with us, I have no doubts she can manage it.

'I'll be back as quickly as I can,' I say, grabbing a baseball cap from my wardrobe to pull over my head, hopefully disguising me a little just in case anybody has started looking for me.

'Be careful,' Philippa says again, under her breath so Barnaby can't hear her warning, and I nod at her to show I have understood. I leave the pair of them in my living room watching

TV, though thankfully not any more news reports, and head out onto the street, nervously looking left and right as I go in case anybody is watching me. But the only people I see are pedestrians hurrying about their business, so all seems fine. That's the case until I make it to one of the main roads that cut through this bustling city. That's where I get my first glimpse of what Philippa was warning me about.

I see TV vans. Camera crews. Reporters with microphones. All of them are clearly using this road as one of their bases from which to produce their reports and also be an active part of the community, stopping pedestrians for soundbites as well as keeping a close eye on the unfolding investigation. Unfortunately for me, they have picked a good spot to do just that, because members of the media are not the only people I see here. *I also see a lot of police officers wandering around amongst them.*

It's a busy, problematic scene, and my first instinct is to turn and walk back to my flat as quickly as possible. But that won't satisfy my son's appetite, and part of being a good parent is making sacrifices, so if I have to walk past all these people to get my child some food then so be it.

I keep my head down and the visor of my baseball cap low as I walk right by the media and the police and, thankfully, nobody stops me, and I make it to the supermarket without incident.

I quickly throw a few things into my basket, just bread and sandwich fillers, as well as some big bags of crisps, some chocolate and some sugary drinks. It's hardly the healthiest selection of items for a growing boy, but I don't have time to do a more selective shop, and at least I know he'll eat these kinds of things.

I pay for my goods before bracing myself to leave the supermarket. When I get back out onto the street, it's even busier than it was ten minutes ago. This part of Dublin really has become a hub for the rapidly escalating investigation into where that missing family might be, probably due to the proximity to the city's radio station studios nearby, and it seems the interest is only going to grow until there are answers.

I hurry past all the people again, hearing gossiping pedestrians as well as reporters talking to cameras, but my only focus is getting back to my street. As I reach it, I think everything might just be okay after all.

I'm seconds away from my front door when I see the police cars.

They're parked outside my home and there are several officers getting out of them, moving with intent, possibly about to give all the journalists in this city something to spice up their next reports.

No, this can't be happening. How have they found me? How do they know about my involvement with that family?

I stop walking as it dawns on me in horrifying detail that I can't go home now or I'll be arrested. But what can I do? Turn around and walk the other way? That might not be an option either. Not with the secrets I'm hiding.

I have to stop the police getting closer. I can't let them enter my home. If they do, they'll know what I've done. But I can't stop them. They'll just detain me and go inside anyway.

I'm screwed and have no choice.

I have to run.

But how can I if it means leaving Barnaby behind?

I'm grappling with that when I feel a strong hand on my shoulder, and I know it's already too late. I get confirmation when I hear the voice of a man standing right behind me.

'Tell us where they are, Shannon. Or else this isn't going to end well for you...'

THIRTY-THREE

SHANNON

It feels like the whole of Dublin is closing in on me as I nervously turn around to see who has stopped me in the street, asking me where the Conways are. It feels like I can breathe again when I see that it is not a police officer or a reporter asking me the question, but Patrick, my boss, and he has a big grin on his face.

'All right, Shannon? You look a little pale. I thought you'd be all refreshed after your time off work.'

I am still waiting for my heart rate to go down before I can even think about answering him. Patrick simply laughs, clearly amused at the prank he has just played and totally oblivious to the fright he just gave me. But I'm not laughing – while I haven't been accosted by a police officer, there still seems to be a swarm of them outside my flat. I can't believe they have found me already.

'So how has it been?' Patrick asks as I look back to the police, who still haven't seen me yet.

'Huh?'

'Your time off. Your holiday. Have you enjoyed it?'

'Oh, right. Err, yeah. It's been good.'

Are the police going into my flat? Or wait – *are they going next door?*

'You could sound a little more convincing,' Patrick says, still laughing. 'Don't tell me. You missed being around me at the office. I'm flattered.'

Patrick winks, but I don't laugh at his sarcastic joke. My mind is still frazzled, and my stomach is doing somersaults.

I really thought the game was up and I had been caught.

I really thought I'd blown my second chance at getting to be a mother.

Another police car arrives on my street. What is going on? If they are looking for me, surely they could see me here. And surely they would have already brought out Philippa and Barnaby by now? But there's no sign of them.

Then I see my next-door neighbour being marched out of his flat.

And he's in handcuffs.

'Shannon?'

Patrick's voice snaps me out of my trance. I look away for a second – at my neighbour being bundled into the back of a police car – and then turn to my boss.

'Sorry, you just surprised me,' I say, getting my head back in the game. 'What are you doing sneaking up on me? Shouldn't you be at work?'

'I was just out grabbing lunch and saw you. Anyway, since when did the employee check up on the employer?' Patrick fires back with a smug grin. 'So, what have you been up to?'

'Oh, not much. Just hanging out,' I say as casually as I can, hoping he believes it as I watch the police car with my neighbour in it being driven away. Several reporters have clearly got a sniff that something is going on, because some of them have trickled onto this street from the surrounding ones. I see a few camera flashes as well as a reporter stick a microphone in the face of a possible detective, though he ignores it and gets into another car before leaving the scene too.

'Really? You took all this time off work just to hang out?' Patrick asks me. 'I thought you would have had something exciting planned.'

'Nope, not really,' I say, praying that he just leaves it there. I really need to go and figure out what the hell just happened.

The police were so close to uncovering the truth, yet they went next door and just arrested an innocent man.

What is going on?

'Do you want to come back to work early?' Patrick asks me now, still distracting me from the more urgent task at hand.

'What?'

'Well, I was just thinking, if you're not doing much with your time off, do you want to come back to work?'

'Erm,' I stall as I watch a few more police cars leave the scene, though a couple have stayed back. The officers who travelled in them are still searching the property next to mine. That's a problem – I'm going to have to walk right by them to get back into my flat.

'Hello? Earth to Shannon? Is anybody there?'

Patrick laughs as he tries to get my attention again.

'I'm sorry. I've got to go,' I say as I leave him and head for my flat, keeping my head down again.

'Hey? Is everything okay?' Patrick calls after me, but I ignore him and hope he won't think too much about our weird interaction as he goes about the rest of his day. Hopefully he's got his own problems to worry about rather than ponder what might be troubling me. Right now, what is troubling me is why the police are on my street.

I hold my breath as I pass the officers next to my flat, but they don't pay me much attention, which is a relief. This gives me a sudden burst of confidence and, just before I enter my own home, I do something that might be very stupid.

'What's going on?' I ask them.

One of the officers looks up at me and, as his eyes meet mine, I can tell he doesn't know who I am. Nobody must be looking for me yet, thank God.

'Don't worry, miss. Just go inside your home. Everything is fine.'

That doesn't give me much, but the fact he told me everything is fine suggests I'm safe at least, so I smile and quickly enter my flat before closing and locking the door.

'You're back! What's going on out there?' Philippa asks as she rushes towards me.

'I have no idea. They arrested my neighbour,' I reply, before Barnaby rushes towards me too.

'Did you hear all the police cars?' he cries, and I nod. Looking out of the window, I see that the two officers are still guarding my neighbour's flat.

'I got you some treats,' I say to Barnaby as I hand him the shopping bag, and he eagerly looks inside before tucking in. I step aside with Philippa, and she asks me what I saw out there. I tell her, but now she is just as puzzled as I am.

'I don't know what's going on,' I admit. 'I mean, what are the chances of me having Barnaby here, the boy everybody is looking for, and the police go next door to arrest my neighbour instead?'

'It could just be a coincidence. You don't know what he had been doing,' Philippa says, but I don't believe much in coincidences. Then again, this is a neighbourhood where crime is fairly common.

'I don't know what is going on,' I say, simply being honest.

I spend the next few hours nervously looking out of the window of my flat, but I'm still no nearer to knowing, until Barnaby suddenly shouts out between mouthfuls of chocolate.

'I'm on TV again!' the little boy cries, and Philippa and I rush over to join him on the sofa to see what he means. When we do, we see that he is right. The same photo of him with Rosalind and Donovan is on screen again. As I turn the volume up, I hear the reporter mentioning their names. But then he says something else.

'A man was arrested earlier in connection with the family's disappearance at an address in the west of Dublin. No details have been released yet, but the lead detective is due to give a statement shortly and, so far, sources suggest the arrest came about after a tip-off from an anonymous member of the public.'

'A tip-off?' I say before looking at Philippa. 'So it wasn't a coincidence.'

She can't argue with me there. We want to go back to watching the rest of the news report, to see if any more information is forthcoming, but it's difficult with Barnaby as he might see something that upsets him. Philippa distracts him with a game while I lower the volume on the TV and try to get an understanding of what is going on now.

All we see from the latest report is some scrambled camera footage of my neighbour being led from his home in handcuffs and put into the back of a car, and I guess it's the best the media could get considering it all happened so quickly. What the camera footage has failed to pick up, thankfully, is me standing only a few yards away from where the arrest took place, watching on in shock and horror, trying to figure out how the police could be so close to discovering the real truth, yet so far.

Obviously, my neighbour has nothing to do with this. The only thing I've ever known him to do wrong is play music too loudly, which I made complaints about to the council, and that's how Philippa found me. But playing loud music has not got him this kind of attention from the police. Something else is going on here, and I have a horrible feeling that this is all part of some twisted game in which my poor neighbour is being used as a pawn.

'Somebody knows what I've done,' I say. 'Somebody is playing games with me.'

'What?' Philippa asks, but I ignore her and go over to the window to check the street again. When I do, I see the last police car leaving as the sun sets and, for now, all is quiet. But will it stay that way?

'Let's get Barnaby into bed and then we'll talk about what to do next,' I say, and Philippa agrees. We turn off the TV and take Barnaby into my bedroom, where he gets comfortable under my duvet.

'Try and get some sleep,' I tell him.

'What's going to happen?' he asks me innocently, clearly no longer just excited about the fact he is on the news but worried about it now too.

'Everything will be fine,' I assure him, making a promise that I cannot possibly keep. 'Just go to sleep. I love you.'

I wonder if Barnaby will say it back, but he doesn't, though that's okay. It's still very early in our relationship. But I hope I get to hear him say it one day – that remains to be seen.

I close the bedroom door and take a seat beside Philippa on the sofa, and I see that she has been quietly checking the TV channels for any more news.

'The detective made a statement,' she tells me. 'Somebody told the police that they thought they saw a boy matching Barnaby's description going into the flat, so they raided it and arrested the homeowner.'

'Somebody saw Barnaby!' I cry, before remembering that I have to keep my voice down because he is trying to sleep. 'They must have seen me bring him back here. They got the wrong address though.'

'Lucky.'

That's the understatement of the year.

'They'll realise they got it wrong when my neighbour has nothing to hide,' I say. 'They must be finishing questioning him soon, and then what will they do? Come and check the other flats on the street?'

'Maybe not. I don't know.'

'I do. It's only a matter of time until they come and ask me if I've seen anything. I need to go and talk to the police, right now.'

I get up and head for the door, grabbing my jacket and asking Philippa if she is okay to stay here and look after Barnaby for me.

'Yes, but are you sure this is the right thing to do? We need to get our story straight. What are you going to say?'

'I'll tell them that Rosalind and Donovan were cruel, heartless people who tried to kill me because of Barnaby. You can back me up by saying you lived in fear of them. They threatened you too. We'll say we've been frightened for our safety because of the money and power that couple have, but now we have Barnaby safe, we realised the right thing to do was to come forward and tell the truth.'

Philippa thinks about it before nodding.

'As long as you don't implicate me in whatever happened at that beach,' she says. 'I am not involved in that.'

That sounds fair enough to me, so I assure Philippa that she won't get any heat from the police for that.

'Okay, I'm going to go,' I say, zipping up my jacket and catching a glimpse of my very pale reflection in the mirror by my front door. 'Wish me luck.'

'Good luck,' Philippa says, looking very worried for me.

She has every right to be.

Just before I leave, I peep around my bedroom door and take a look at Barnaby, who is sleeping on my pillow. My heart is already so full of love for the little boy I have just been reunited with, and I want nothing more than to climb into that bed and snuggle with him, but I have to do this. This way, there is a chance we get to live happily ever after.

'Here goes,' I say as I unlock my door and turn the handle.

Then I prepare to step outside and face my fate.

But it's not the police who I see first.

It's a ghost, or at least it looks like one, until I see that this person is actually very much alive.

It's Donovan.

THIRTY-FOUR

SHANNON

I try to shut my door, but Donovan shoots out a hand and prevents me from doing so. As he pushes the door back at me, it forces me to retreat further into my flat. The shock of seeing him again, coupled with his strength, suddenly makes me feel very vulnerable. He enters my home and closes the door behind himself, and I feel as trapped as he must have done when I left him in that cave.

'How?' is all I can say, as I move backwards until I am in front of the bedroom door, which is my way of shielding Barnaby from this man, although he won't know my son is sleeping in there yet.

'How did I get out of that cave?' Donovan asks, finishing my question for me. 'With great difficulty. But I knew I had to do it. I knew you weren't going to send for help.'

'You tried to kill me,' I remind him. 'Didn't you expect me to try and defend myself?'

'Defending yourself? Is that what you were doing when you pushed my wife off that cliff?'

His question tells me that he must have found Rosalind's body when he left the cave and, if so, it's no wonder there is a look of pure anger in his eyes. If he's seen what I did to her, there's no saying what he wants to do to me in return.

'Donovan?'

Philippa's voice behind me surprises him as well as me.

'What are you doing here?' he asks his nanny, clearly expecting me to be alone, or at least the only other adult here.

'Shannon told me what happened,' Philippa says now, and I see her check that I have the bedroom door covered so that there is a line of defence between this crazed man and the young boy in bed.

'Did she?' Donovan says, scoffing. 'I wonder if she told the truth. I bet she's made out like I'm the dangerous one and she's the innocent one.'

'I am innocent!' I cry. 'You and your crazy wife tried to kill me, but I stopped her, and I'll do the same to you if you take one step closer!'

I see something that could help me stop Donovan and reach out for it, taking it off the wall and holding it steady, pointing in the direction of the American man.

'What do you think you're going to do with that?' Donovan asks, chuckling as he looks at the Celtic spear in my hands.

'I'll drive it right through your body if you take one step closer to me, and you'll end up just like your wife,' I reply viciously, forcing myself to seem more confident than I actually feel. But that does little to put Donovan off whatever mission he has come here to execute.

'You think I fought my way out of that cave, passed my wife's dead body and made it all the way to Dublin without the police spotting me, just to let you win now?' Donovan asks with a smirk. 'That's not going to happen. What is going to happen is you are going to give me my son back. Where is he?'

'He's not here!' Philippa says, helping me, but sadly Donovan does not believe her. He observes each of our positions, me in front of the bedroom door and her just behind me, and it doesn't take long for him to figure out why we're standing where we are.

'Move out of the way,' Donovan says as he steps towards the bedroom door, but I thrust the spear towards him to keep him back.

'I mean it. Leave us alone or you will get hurt!'

'You're not going to hurt me,' Donovan replies calmly. 'You might have pushed my wife, but you're no match for me. I was able to track you down. I've had your address for a while, ever since we found out you were the person we wanted. I was able to get here, even though every police officer in Ireland is looking for me. I was even able to play a game with you, having your neighbour arrested and giving you something else to worry about.'

'That was you?' I ask, thinking of my neighbour being taken away in handcuffs.

'Yep, I was the anonymous caller. I thought it would be fun to make you sweat. And you did sweat, didn't you? You thought the police were here for you, that you were going to be arrested. But not yet, though they will be here soon. They'll be here any second. That's because I just made a panicked phone call to them and told them I was being held captive in this flat along with my son.'

'You did what?' I cry, mortified at what I've just heard.

'That's right. I've told the police where I am, and they'll be on their way here right now to arrest you and free us. So if I was you, I'd put down that weapon of yours, because it won't be a good look for you if they come in here and find you with it, although it will certainly help my story. The fact that I can direct the police to my wife's dead body will help me too, because I'm sure you'd struggle if you were questioned about her death.'

The thought of being questioned in a claustrophobic interview room is a frightening one, just as frightening as the thought of dozens of police cars racing to my address as we speak. But if they are coming here, maybe they will believe me and help me get out of this. Or maybe, just maybe, Donovan is bluffing, and the police aren't coming at all.

'I don't believe you,' I say defiantly. 'I don't think the police are coming. I think you're here on your own and you're desperate for revenge. You wouldn't risk the police getting in the way of that.'

Donovan smiles now, almost impressed with my powers of deduction.

'You're right, Shannon. I haven't told the police that I'm here. Why would I do that? I want to kill you first, and then I want to take my son and get back on my jet to America. You can come with me if you like, Philippa. There's still a job for you if you want it. But as for you, Shannon, I'm afraid this is where it ends.'

Donovan reaches out quickly, grabs the end of the spear with both hands and holds onto it tightly. I try to wriggle it free from his grasp again, to pull it away from him, but he keeps a firm grip on it. Without having full control of it, it'll be much harder for me to use it as a weapon.

'Let go of the spear,' Donovan says, almost sounding bored of me and this interaction.

'No, you let go,' I try, before turning to Philippa to see if she is going to help me. But she is just watching on very nervously, as if she hasn't yet decided which way this is going to go, so she almost doesn't want to pick sides in case she picks the losing one.

'Philippa, help me!' I cry, desperate for her to provide backup, but she doesn't move. As Donovan pulls on the spear, it starts to feel like I am going to lose my grip on it. But I can't let him gain control. He might kill me with this spear himself, and then he'll have Barnaby. That's why, rather than trying to pull the spear back, I decide to use Donovan's momentum against him. As he pulls to take the weapon from me, I surge forward with it, surprising him with the sudden weight shift, and watch as the tip of the spear goes straight into his abdomen.

Donovan lets out a cough before I see blood form around his lips. As he looks down to inspect the damage, I keep hold of the spear, afraid to let go, even though the end of it is now impaled inside the man in front of me.

Donovan tries to speak but only coughs up more blood. Things are not looking good for him. But they're not looking good for me either – if the police come now, how do I explain this? Then I hear the bedroom door opening behind me and suddenly fear that, before them, I'm first going to have to explain this to my son.

'Stay in your room!' I cry and, thankfully, Philippa finally springs into action and rushes inside the bedroom, closing the door behind herself so that Barnaby can't see this gruesome scene.

I feel the spear move as Donovan tries to free himself from the end of it, but it only causes him great pain to do so, and he quickly gives up when he realises it would be making things worse for him at this point.

'I was just...' Donovan starts, trying to speak in between heavy breaths and a few more blood-splattered coughs. 'I was just... trying to... keep my family together. You can... understand... that, right?'

I look at the now feeble man, who looks like he is clinging onto the last moments of life. Suddenly, I feel a little sorry for him. That's because I can understand what he was doing.

'I'm just trying to do the same thing,' I reply quietly.

I hear sirens now in the distance. The police are on their way. Donovan must have called them after all. But it looks like they'll be too late for him by the time they get in here.

It also looks like, despite this being over, I am going to have a hell of a lot of explaining to do.

THIRTY-FIVE

SHANNON

As I feared it would be, sitting in a small interview room in the bowels of a police station – being questioned by a detective who was recording my every word for future reference – was daunting. It was made even more difficult by the fact that I'd barely had time to process things since I had been taken into custody.

The police entered my flat moments after I first heard their sirens and, when they did, they found Donovan slumped against the wall by my front door while I stood over him. They also found Philippa and Barnaby cowering in the bedroom and, very quickly, it was obvious to them that something terrible had happened.

While I don't regret attacking Donovan with the spear – because it was him or me – I do regret not having the chance to talk to Philippa and get our stories straight before we were separated and taken for questioning. I also regret being unable to talk to Barnaby, to make sure he was okay, as well as assure him that I would be okay too and that we would be back together again before long. As it was, I didn't get time to do any of those things, but I can't really blame the police for that. Having entered what was quite clearly a crime scene involving two missing people, they were hardly going to give me time before the handcuffs came out.

Once the questioning began, I decided that honesty was the only policy, so I told the detective everything that had happened in minute detail, from the Conways originally contacting me about a guided tour around Ireland – and I had the emails to prove that. I then explained how the trip went, which was fairly normal, right up until it became clear they had an ulterior motive and my life was in danger. I spoke about what happened at the beach with Rosalind, and about what happened in my flat with Donovan. While it was scary to tell a detective that I had killed two people, I had no choice but to own up to it and hope that they believed me when I said I had no other choice. But while they might have been stunned to hear me account for these events, which were shocking Ireland as more and more reports leaked out into the media, there was a shock in store for me too.

'Only one person is deceased,' I was told, which sounded very strange to me.

'Excuse me?'

'Only Rosalind died. Donovan survived his injuries and is currently in a critical but stable condition.'

It had felt like the walls of the interview room were closing in on me in that moment. Donovan was still alive? *Would that man ever die?*

I'd started to panic before the detective tried to put me at ease.

'Don't worry. He is recovering in a prison hospital, and he'll stay there under careful watch until we can get his version of events. But he can't harm you or anybody else.'

I couldn't believe he had survived, but it did at least allow me to not have to carry another death on my conscience, even if he would have more than deserved it. The problem was, with him still alive, it gave him the opportunity to refute everything I had told the detective, so technically he could still harm me, just in a very different way. That's why I was then worried about which one of us the police would ultimately believe.

Fortunately, I had my trump card, and that came in the form of Philippa, the nanny who had been in my flat to witness the exchange with Donovan, who also knew the exact reason why he had been trying to hurt me. I needed her to come through for me and tell the police that my side was the real version of events and not Donovan's. Thankfully, after an excruciating and nail-biting wait while the detective questioned her, she did just that. She told the detective why Rosalind and Donovan had been trying to hurt me, and how everything that had happened had all been about one thing – keeping an innocent little boy safe from harm.

I know that the detective would have spoken to Barnaby too, although it would have had to be in a more delicate, patient fashion than he demonstrated with the adults involved in this whole sorry tale. My heart was breaking every time I thought of Barnaby, all the stress and upheaval he had been through in such a short time, and then having to deal with the police after all that. But my little boy is brave, and he must have told the truth because, eventually, once all the stories had been analysed, I was told that I was free to go. Donovan would remain under watch while he recovered from his injuries, and then he would be charged with conspiracy to murder. If he continued to profess his innocence, a trial would take place, one in which I would be expected to be the key witness. I hated the idea of having to stand up in court and recount my story, but if that's what it would take to get the wealthy man the punishment he deserved, then so be it. I would do anything to see him locked up for life. But that would be for another day. My first priority would be my number one priority for the rest of my life.

My son.

· · ·

It's been one week since Donovan showed up at my flat, like some evil spirit rising from the dead, and since then I've been impatiently waiting to see my little boy again. In all that time, Barnaby has been looked after at a children's clinic, where he has been assessed both physically and mentally. Not just to see if there were any signs of him having suffered during his ordeal recently, but if there were any signs of trauma before that, back when he was living in Boston with Rosalind and Donovan.

Thankfully, I've been told by the detective keeping me informed that he is doing well, and the doctors are happy to release him soon. But before then, I am due to visit him. As I enter the clinic with a shopping bag full of toys and junk food for the patient, I cannot wait to see my little boy and start the process of cheering him up. More than that, I want to start the process of actually having a mother–son relationship, and there is so much to sort out. He will be coming to live with me in the future, and there's the matter of getting him into a local school so that his education doesn't suffer. It might not quite be the expensive education he would have had in Boston, had he continued to live with the Conways, but what he will lose out on there will be more than made up for by the love he will feel living with me rather than them.

'I'm here to see Barnaby,' I say to one of the nurses on the reception desk. 'Shannon O'Shea. I'll be on the visitors list.'

I wait for the nurse to check that list and then show me to the room where my son is. But instead, she frowns.

'I'm sorry, but I'm afraid Barnaby doesn't want to see you.'

'Excuse me?'

I figure I must have heard the nurse wrong.

'He doesn't want you to visit him today,' the nurse goes on, not saying anything that makes me feel better.

'What? What's going on? I'm on the visitor list, right? This has been arranged. I was told it would be okay for me to see him today.'

'Yes, you are on the list, but we won't let anybody in if the children do not want to see them, and I'm afraid Barnaby does not want to see you.'

'Why not?'

The nurses hesitates.

'Hey! I asked you a question! Why doesn't he want to see me?'

'He says that you're a liar,' the nurse replies sheepishly, barely able to look me in the eye as she speaks.

'A liar? What have I lied about?'

'I'm sorry. I can't say anything more. I think you should talk to somebody else about this.'

'Somebody else? Who?'

'Hello, Shannon,' a male voice says behind me.

I spin around and see the detective who questioned me last week has joined us. But what's he doing here?

'What's going on?' I demand to know. 'Why can't I see my son?'

The detective glances past me at the nurse, who seems to understand what he wants her to do and leaves her station, giving us some privacy. But I don't like that. Something doesn't feel right about this. What is going on here?

'Please tell me what is happening!' I beg, starting to panic. I thought this nightmare was over, yet it still seems to be ongoing. Then the detective answers me, though when he does it would have almost been more merciful of him not to.

'We've got the DNA results back from the maternity test you took after we questioned you,' the detective tells me. 'And it's not a match.'

'What do you mean it's not a match?' I ask, incredulous.

'What I am telling you, Shannon,' the detective says, with a very grave look on his face, 'is that Barnaby is not your son after all.'

I must have misheard him.

'Excuse me?' I say, before laughing – that's all I can do in this surreal moment. This has to be a joke, so laughing is the appropriate response in this situation, right?

'You are not Barnaby's mother,' the detective repeats sternly, proving that this is no joke. But it has to be. Surely. What else can it be?

'Barnaby is my son!' I cry, the laughter having faded, panic rising up inside of me in its place. 'Donovan told me he was and it fits. I gave my baby boy up for adoption around the same time when Barnaby would have been born. That's why Rosalind and Donovan wanted me dead! Because I'm his real mother!'

'It seems they were wrong,' the detective replies with a shake of the head. 'He isn't your son. I assure you of that.'

I feel like I'm having a panic attack as I try to process this disturbing, shocking information. My palms are sweaty and the lights in the clinic seem to be getting brighter, to the point where I feel like I am about to be blinded. Just before I pass out and everything goes dark, I have only one question for the detective in front of me.

'If I'm not Barnaby's mother, who is?'

THIRTY-SIX

BARNABY'S MOTHER

'Come on, Barnaby, pick up your bag, we don't want to miss our flight.'

I wait for my son to collect his small rucksack, which is mostly filled with colouring books and crayons, before he takes my hand and I walk with him to the gate from which our flight back to America is due to take off.

It feels comforting, as it always does, to feel his little hand in mine. I never take it for granted, although I could be forgiven for doing so now that I will be getting to experience it even more than usual. That's because I'm now the sole custodian of Barnaby, meaning he will be with me all the time, and there will be nobody else to get in the way. Finally, I got what I always wanted, although I've certainly had to bide my time to get here. But I had all the time in the world to give for my son, and it's been worth every second so far.

I join the queue at the gate alongside Barnaby and take out our passports so they are ready to be handed to the airline official for final checking before boarding. But we've already been through customs and security to get to this point, so I don't envisage any problems now, just like I don't envision any problems from the Irish police once we have left here, because they wouldn't be allowing us to leave their country unless they were satisfied with how things had turned out.

As the queue shuffles forward, I look through the large windows in this part of the terminal and see the plane that is going to fly us to America. It's very different to the one that we left there in, but I am more than happy to go home on a commercial 747 rather than a private jet, owned by a very wealthy and very dangerous couple. But that's not the only difference. While Barnaby and I arrived here with company, we go back by ourselves, free from the shackles of the tyrannous pair who ruled over each of us. One half of that pair is dead, while the other languishes in an Irish jail while awaiting trial, hoping to hear back from whatever contacts he has at the US embassy or within the American government – I'm sure he'll be hoping his wealth can help him out there. But he may find that all his powerful 'friends' back home suddenly don't want anything to do with him, and I hope that is the case. Whenever he does go on trial, mine and Barnaby's contribution as witnesses will be done via video link from back in America.

We won't come back to Ireland again and see Donovan.

That means we won't risk having to see Shannon again either.

As we reach the front of the queue, I hand our two passports over to be checked by a very presentable woman, wearing the uniform of the airline we are flying with today. I don't feel bad for the tour guide we are leaving behind to pick up the pieces of what has been a very baffling time. It's not that I hate Shannon – I don't – it's just that, like Rosalind and Donovan before her, she was just another person who falsely thought they could lay claim to what was truly mine.

Barnaby was never that couple's son, nor was he Shannon's, despite the crossed wires between those three people that led to death and destruction. Barnaby has been and always will be my baby boy, the boy I gave up for adoption when he was born, but managed to track down to living with the Conways, at which time I applied for the role of their nanny and thankfully got it. That has allowed me to be around Barnaby every single day since, getting to experience my son growing, but without anybody else knowing who I really was and my true connection to the child. It also allowed Rosalind and Donovan to treat me dreadfully and get away with it, because once I had the job of Barnaby's carer, I was not going to give it up for anything.

My initial plan had been simply to spend time with Barnaby and be his nanny for as long as I could. I knew that wouldn't last forever, but by that time, I would have something that would help me in the future. I would have a relationship with him that I could use to hopefully make things much easier when the day came for me to tell him the truth.

I planned to wait until Barnaby was legally an adult before telling him that truth.

He was adopted.

And I was really his mother.

The reason I had chosen not to tell Barnaby the truth sooner was because, despite my misgivings about Rosalind and Donovan, they provided a great lifestyle for my son. A huge house, a fantastic education, a safe upbringing, far away from the crime-ridden parts of Boston where I had grown up. I knew he was unhappy at times, having parents like them, but it was still far better than the alternative life I could have given him if I had played my hand too soon. I had to bide my time and save money. The more I got, the better our life could be when the truth finally came out. I wanted to ensure that I could give Barnaby what he needed in adulthood, whether that be help with college fees or funds towards a house of his own, perhaps, so I chose to keep saving the money that the Conways were depositing into my bank account every month. It was far more money than I would have got elsewhere, and with a roof over our heads and food on the table, there was no need to rock the boat and risk it all until it was absolutely the right time.

However, I hadn't counted on Rosalind and Donovan turning out to be much more than just a pair of rich, rude people. I had no idea that they had a sinister plot to rid the world of their adopted children's birth parents, and I certainly had no idea that they had already eliminated three of them, or so they thought. They got the couple in Dallas right in terms of Esme's birth parents, but they got false information about Barnaby's birth parents. They tried to take out the wrong people there, being successful in part, before they failed with who they thought was the fourth and final piece of the puzzle. I genuinely thought the trip to Ireland was a family holiday and Shannon was just a tour guide, but everyone turned out to be much more than first met the eye, and I guess I am no exception.

I'm lucky that Rosalind and Donovan were given incorrect information that led them to believe Shannon was Barnaby's mother and not me, because without it my life would have been in danger instead.

Once the Irish police realised Shannon had no real claim to Barnaby, I was given permission to leave the country with him, and I'll be the one looking after him full-time when we get back to America. That's because I have a DNA test proving I am his real mother.

It's a test I took years ago, secretly, of course, by taking some of Barnaby's hairs after a day of caring for him at the Conway home. Once it was confirmed, I stayed close to my son, but after everything that happened in Ireland, I felt it was the right time to reveal the test, to show that I was the one who should lay claim to him.

The detective was shocked at the revelation, as well as suspicious. If I was Barnaby's real mother, maybe I had engineered this whole plot to my own advantage. But I simply explained the truth – that I had used my position as a nanny to get close to Barnaby, which made me guilty of a few lies, but not of all the serious crimes that occurred after that. Thankfully, I was eventually believed. Then I just had one more potential hurdle to overcome.

Would anybody in the wider Conway family try and claim the boy they had come to know?

Perhaps unsurprisingly for a rich and unpleasant family, none of the relatives of Rosalind or Donovan did come forward to make a case for custody of the boy – not once they found out what had happened in Ireland, and how Barnaby would always be connected to the death of Rosalind and the incarceration of Donovan. It was as if enough shame had been brought on the prestigious family name and they didn't want to be tarnished any further by becoming embroiled in a legal battle. They also have enough on their plate dealing with Esme, the daughter who Rosalind and Donovan adopted, but given what that couple did to Esme's birth parents, it might not be long until she ends up being removed from their care too. I have considered trying to adopt her at some point in the future – she is Barnaby's sister, I suppose – but I will have to give that some more thought. For now, I am focused on him. As I receive our passports back and stride forward towards the plane, I look down at Barnaby and smile, because this is how it was meant to be all along.

Me and my son and nobody in between us.

I was studying abroad when I found out I was pregnant with him. Originally a Californian student at USC, I was attending Dublin University for four semesters while gaining my degree in travel tourism, and had a one-night stand with a cute Irish guy on my course. It was very out of character for me to do such a thing, coming from a strict church background like I did, but I blamed it on the Guinness and the Irish air and thought nothing more of it. That was until I discovered I was pregnant, and I panicked. I feared returning home to my parents and them finding out what I had done, breaking the sacred rule of no sex before marriage. That was why I stayed in Dublin until I gave birth and, once delivered, I made it clear the baby boy was to go to a good home – I didn't have the resources to look after him myself.

I returned to America after my year in Ireland, but I was never the same again. While no one knew what had happened to me while I was overseas, supposedly doing nothing but studying, I couldn't move on and thought about my baby every single day. Eventually, after a couple of years had passed, I vowed to track my child down and do whatever it took to get close to him again. That led to borrowing money off family members, and working in various jobs, saving what I could, until I was able to pay a substantial amount of money to a man who could hack into the records of the adoption agency I used in Dublin. He gave me the names of the couple who had claimed my son.

That was how I came to meet Rosalind and Donovan Conway.

As Barnaby and I board the plane, I tell him to get what he wants out of his rucksack before it goes up into the overhead compartments ahead of take-off. Barnaby quickly removes a colouring pad and set of crayons, before allowing me to put his bag away for him, and then we take our seats and strap ourselves in.

I'm not anxious about the flight ahead, nor am I nervous about what the future holds. I'm sure, after all I've been through, that I'll be able to make it work. I'm confident about that because of how Barnaby acted towards me when he found out the news of who I really am. After he got upset that Shannon had apparently lied to him about being his mom, I not only told him the truth but showed him the DNA test results, backing up my claim that I was his real mother instead. It took a while, but due to the great relationship we have built over the years since I've been his nanny, Barnaby has quickly warmed to the idea of me looking after him permanently now, though there are still a few issues to iron out, like how he addresses me.

'Can we order a drink after we've taken off, Philippa?' Barnaby asks me.

'Of course we can,' I say, smiling at him as he starts to use his crayons. 'But remember what I've said. I'm not just Philippa anymore. You can call me Mom.'

EPILOGUE

Shannon O'Shea.

That's what I should write here, in this part of the online application form where it asks for my name.

But I'm not going to do that.

Instead, I write Seraphina O'Shea. That is the name I go by now, after legally changing the first part of it so that, in essence, I have a brand-new identity. I felt it okay to keep my original surname though, given how common it is in this part of the world. My father used to say that an O'Shea will never be lonely in Ireland, and he's certainly not wrong there.

I have all the new documents to go along with that new identity, from a passport to a birth certificate, although I had to tell a few lies to obtain those. While changing my first name is perfectly legal to do, lying in official documents about my previous name is not. When I ordered my new passport, I was obliged to say if I had ever gone under another name, but I chose to tick 'No' for that one. For my birth certificate, I had to purchase a fake one, because, of course, I wasn't born with the name Seraphina, but as of now, for all intents and purposes, Shannon O'Shea never existed.

Why have I gone to all this trouble to change my name and conceal my former identity?

One part of the answer is that there is a man currently serving time in a local jail cell who is surely interested in having his revenge on me, if he can. Donovan, one of Dublin's newest inmates, must hate my guts, and while he might struggle to get to me himself from behind bars, he has the means to pay somebody else to do it for him. I have to reduce the chances of him being able to do so.

The second part as to why I've changed my identity lies in the application form in front of me.

This application is in response to a job vacancy at a place in Dublin that holds particular significance for me. It's a place I haven't been to for several years, but a place I have thought about every day during that time. I hope to soon be working there if my application is successful.

I write my new name at the top of the form, then proceed to answer all the other questions that come after it, which include my address, my previous work history and my reasons for wanting to obtain this vacant position.

My address is simple enough – it's the new flat I'm renting on the opposite side of the city to where I lived before. Using the $5,000 that Rosalind gave me before all the drama with her family and their nanny, I had the funds required to put down a deposit on a slightly bigger place, and the money left over to pay the associated bills for the next few months. As for my previous work history, this is where I have returned to lying again, not mentioning the truth: that I spent all of my working life as a tour guide in Dublin, but instead claiming that I have worked as an administration manager at a local school. Of course, I've done no such thing, but it's easy to make up a list of all of my fictitious experiences, and it's just as easy to provide the contact details of my previous manager so they can be checked as part of my employee reference.

I write down Oonagh's name and number, easily recalling the digits of my best friend who I have already told I will need to do me this favour. I expect Oonagh will receive a call from the person looking at my application and, when she does, she knows that she is to pretend that she was my former boss and can wholeheartedly recommend me for this new position. As far as my best friend knows, I have just decided to have a complete career change and no longer wish to be a tour guide. I need a way of entering another industry, despite the fact I lack the relevant experience.

That just leaves my reasons for wanting to apply for this job, and that is where I have lied to Oonagh. I don't want a career change because I fancy a new challenge – *I need a career change because it's the only avenue open to me if I am to stand any chance of ever finding out where my real son is.*

I thought my son was Barnaby, but it turned out I was wrong, just as wrong as Donovan and Rosalind. But that whole experience, as shocking and dangerous as it was, taught me one thing very clearly.

I have to find my child and, if it's not Barnaby, I have to keep looking.

In this last part of the application, I have written that my reason for applying for this job is because I am interested in applying my extensive administration skills to a profession that does a lot of good in the community. An adoption agency, I say, sounds like a wonderful place to work, and I would love to be just one cog in the machine of making sure that parents who desperately want children are able to be blessed with them. But that's not my real reason – I can't write that.

If I did, there's no way I'd ever get this job.

As I complete the application and prepare to press send, I think about my real motivation for applying for this role. It has everything to do with the fact that, if I am successful, I will have full access to the adoption agency database – the very same agency where I gave up my own son so many years ago. That means that, given the opportunity, I will be able to trawl through the records and hopefully find out who adopted him.

If I can get that information, I might be able to get the most important thing of all.

His current location.

I don't hesitate for one second as I press send, allowing my virtual application to land in the inbox of the recruiting officer at the adoption agency where I once screamed and shouted and begged for access to the baby I had given up. Soon, I hope to be back in that place and, when I go there, nobody will ever know that I was there before. Along with my new name is the fact that I look very different to how I did back then. I've lost weight, recently dyed my hair and am also helped by the fact that almost a decade has passed, meaning not only will I naturally look different, but anybody who worked at the agency back then and might have seen me will potentially have moved on by now.

All I need is one chance.

I need to get this job.

If I do, I will be able to find my son.

I have no choice but to wait impatiently to see if my application will lead to an interview, one in which I'm confident I will thrive, because who else can have the same passion and desperation to land this role as me? I think about Philippa and how she is with her son now, getting to spend her days with him – playing, laughing and making precious memories.

I don't hate that woman for what she did. She only did what I am doing now and, as far as I'm concerned, lying to be closer to the child that you love and miss is no crime.

I simply envy her. She has what I want. She has access to her son.

Fingers crossed, I'll get that one day soon.

It's my only wish.

I'll do whatever it takes to make it come true.

A LETTER FROM DANIEL

Dear reader,

I want to say a huge thank you for choosing to read *The Family Trip*. I hope you enjoyed following Shannon's story! If you did enjoy it and would like to keep up to date with all my latest Bookouture releases, please sign up to my Bookouture newsletter at the following link. Your email address will never be shared and you can unsubscribe at any time.

www.bookouture.com/daniel-hurst

I hope you liked this book and, if you did, I would be very grateful if you could write an honest review. I'd love to hear what you think! You can read my free short story, 'The Killer Wife', by signing up to my Bookouture mailing list.

You can also visit my website where you can download a free psychological thriller called *Just One Second* and join my personal weekly newsletter, where you can hear all about my future writing as well as my adventures with my wife, Harriet, and daughter, Penny!

Thank you,

Daniel

KEEP IN TOUCH WITH DANIEL

Get in touch with me directly at my email address
daniel@danielhurstbooks.com. I reply to every message!

www.danielhurstbooks.com

 facebook.com/danielhurstbooks

 instagram.com/danielhurstbooks

PUBLISHING TEAM

Turning a manuscript into a book requires the efforts of many people. The publishing team at Bookouture would like to acknowledge everyone who contributed to this publication.

Audio
Alba Proko
Melissa Tran
Sinead O'Connor

Commercial
Lauren Morrissette
Hannah Richmond
Imogen Allport

Cover design
Lisa Horton

Data and analysis
Mark Alder
Mohamed Bussuri

Editorial
Natasha Harding
Lizzie Brien

Made in the USA
Monee, IL
25 June 2024

60638288R00152